ETIQUETTE & ESPIONAGE

ETIQUETTE & ESPIONAGE

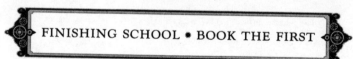

FINISHING SCHOOL ✦ BOOK THE FIRST

GAIL CARRIGER

Little, Brown and Company

New York Boston

Copyright © 2013 by Tofa Borregaard
Excerpt from *Curties & Conspiracies* copyright © 2013 by Tofa Borregaard

Little, Brown and Company

Hachette Book Group
1290 Avenue of the Americas, New York, NY 10104
Visit our website at www.lb-teens.com

Little, Brown and Company is a division of Hachette Book Group, Inc.
The Little, Brown name and logo are trademarks of Hachette Book Group, Inc.

The publisher is not responsible for websites (or their content) that are not owned by the publisher.

First Paperback Edition: October 2013
First published in hardcover in February 2013 by Little, Brown and Company

Library of Congress Cataloging-in-Publication Data

Carriger, Gail.
  Etiquette & espionage / by Gail Carriger.—1st ed.
    p. cm.—(Finishing school ; bk. the 1st)
  Summary: In an alternate England of 1851, spirited fourteen-year-old Sophronia is enrolled in a finishing school where, she is surprised to learn, lessons include not only the fine arts of dance, dress, and etiquette, but also diversion, deceit, and espionage.
  ISBN 978-0-316-19008-4 (hc) / ISBN 978-0-316-19010-7 (pb)
  [1. Boardingschools—Fiction. 2. Schools—Fiction. 3. Etiquette—Fiction. 4. Espionage—Fiction. 5. Robots—Fiction. 6. Great Britain—History—Victoria, 1837–1901—Fiction. 7. Science fiction.] I. Title.
  PZ7.C23455Eti 2013
  [Fic]—dc23   2012005498

Printing 16, 2021

Book design by Alison Impey

LSC-H

Printed in the United States of America

With eternal thanks to all those who finished me,
at each stage, and in the best of all possible ways:
Kathy, Carol, Harriet, James, Anne,
Joe, Timi, Judith, and Tom.
There is no job harder than teaching,
and to be truly great at it? Heroic.
And for Willow, representing for the next generation.

THE START OF BEING FINISHED

Sophronia intended to pull the dumbwaiter up from the kitchen to outside the front parlor on the ground floor, where Mrs. Barnaclegoose was taking tea. Mrs. Barnaclegoose had arrived with a stranger in tow. *Meddling old battle-ax.* With the hallways patrolled by siblings and household mechanicals, eavesdropping was out of the question. The only way of overhearing her mother, Mrs. Barnaclegoose, and the stranger was from inside the dumbwaiter. Mrs. Barnaclegoose had decided opinions on reforming other women's daughters. Sophronia did not want to be reformed. So she had pressed the dumbwaiter into the service of espionage.

The dumbwaiter disagreed with the whole idea of stopping at the ground floor, and instead kept on going—up all four stories. Sophronia examined the windlass machine at the top. Several lengths of india-rubber strapping made up part of the drive mechanism. *Perhaps, once the strapping was removed, the dumbwaiter might shake loose?*

The dumbwaiter had no ceiling; it was simply a bit of platform with a support cable on the inside and a pulling cable on the outside. Sophronia reached up and liberated the strapping. Nothing happened, so she took more.

It was while she wrapped the india rubber protectively around her boots—her mother had been complaining about the state of Sophronia's shoes of late—that the dumbwaiter started shaking.

Sophronia squirmed over to the pulling cable, but before she had a chance to grab it, the dumbwaiter began to descend—fast. Very fast. Too fast. The loading door on the third floor sped past, and then the one on the second. *Perhaps removing the rubber was not such a brilliant plan.*

As the top of the next loading door appeared, Sophronia dove forward, tumbling through it and into the family's front parlor. The top skirt of her dress caught on the lip of the door and made an ominous ripping sound.

Unfortunately, Sophronia's grand escape coincided with one of the maids loading a half-eaten trifle into the dumbwaiter.

Sophronia hit the pudding on her dismount. The maid screamed. The trifle arched up into the air, scattering custard, cake, and strawberries all over the blue brocade and cream furnishings of the well-appointed parlor.

The bowl landed, in glorious perfection, atop the head of Mrs. Barnaclegoose, who was not the kind of woman to appreciate the finer points of being crowned by trifle. Nevertheless, it made for quite the spectacle as the bowl upended the last of its contents over that good lady's bonnet. Until that moment, the bonnet had been rather smart—red with black velvet ribbons and crimson ostrich feathers. The addition of a trifle, it must be admitted, made it less smart. Sophronia, with great restraint, held back a triumphant giggle. *That'll teach her to meddle.*

Mrs. Barnaclegoose was a large woman of progressive inclinations—which is to say she supported vampire and were-wolf social reform, played a good deal of whist, kept a ghost in her country cottage, and even wore the occasional French gown. She accepted that dirigibles would be the next great means of transportation and that soon people might fly through the aether. She was not, however, so progressive as to accept flying food. She squealed in horror.

One of Sophronia's older sisters, Petunia, was playing at hostess. White with mortification, Petunia rushed to the aid of the older woman, assisting her in the removal of the trifle bowl. Mother was nowhere to be seen. This made Sophronia more nervous than the fact that she had just assaulted an aristocrat with a trifle.

Mrs. Barnaclegoose stood, with as much dignity as possible under the circumstances, and looked down at Sophronia, sprawled on the plush rug. Most of Sophronia's top skirt had ripped off. Sophronia was mortified to realize she was in public with her underskirt on display!

"Your mother is occupied in an important private audience. I was going to await her leisure. But for this, I shall disturb her. It is 1851, and I believed we lived in a civilized world! Yet you are as bad as a rampaging werewolf, young miss, and someone must take action." Mrs. Barnaclegoose made it sound as though

Sophronia alone were responsible for the disreputable state of the entire British Empire. Without allowing Sophronia a rebuttal, the lady waddled from the room, a plop of custard trailing down her fluffy skirts.

Sophronia flopped over onto her back with a sigh. She should check herself for injuries, or see to finding the rest of her dress, but flopping was more dramatic. She closed her eyes and contemplated the possible recriminations soon to emanate from her upset mother.

Her musings were interrupted. "Sophronia Angelina Temminnick!"

Uh-oh. She cracked a cautious eyelid. "Yes, Petunia?"

"How could you? Poor Mrs. Barnaclegoose!" *Stepping in as understudy mother today, we have elder sister. Fantastic.*

"As if I could plan such a thing." Sophronia was annoyed by the childish petulance in her own voice. She was unable to control it when around her sisters.

"I daresay you would if you could. What were you *doing* inside the dumbwaiter? And why are you lying there in your petticoats with india rubber wrapped around your feet?"

Sophronia hedged. "Uh, um, well, you see . . ."

Petunia looked inside the open cavity of the dumbwaiter, where the remains of Sophronia's skirt dangled merrily. "Oh, for goodness' sake, Sophronia. You've been climbing again! What are you, a ten-year-old apple boy?"

"Actually, I'm right in the middle of a recovery period. So if you wouldn't mind shoving off until I'm finished, I'd appreciate it."

Petunia, who, at sixteen, considered herself *all grown up*, was having none of it. "Look at this mess you've created. Poor Eliza."

Eliza, the now trifle-less maid, was trying to put some order to the chaos that had resulted from finding an unexpected Sophronia departing the dumbwaiter.

Sophronia crawled over to help with the strawberries and cake that now covered the room. "Sorry, Eliza. I didn't mean it."

"You never do, miss."

Petunia was not to be distracted. "Sophronia!"

"Well, sister, to be perfectly correct, I did nothing."

"Tell that to the poor woman's lovely bonnet."

"The trifle did it."

Petunia's perfect rosebud pout twisted into a grimace that might have been an attempt to hide a smile. "Really, Sophronia, you're fourteen years old and simply unfit for public consumption. I refuse to have you at my coming-out ball. You'll do something dreadful, like spill the punch on the only nice-looking boy there."

"I would never!"

"Oh, yes, you would."

"No, I wouldn't. We don't happen to be acquainted with any nice-looking boys."

Petunia ignored that jibe. "Must you be so tiresome? It's always something." She looked smug. "Although I believe Mumsy has finally determined what to do with you."

"She has? Do? Do what? What's going on?"

"Mumsy is indenturing you to vampires for a proper education. You're old enough now for them to actually want you. Soon you'll be putting your hair up—what else are we to do with you? You are even starting to get décolletage."

Sophronia blushed with embarrassment at the very mention

of such a thing, but managed a sputtered protest of, "She never!"

"Oh, yes! Who do you think she's talking to *right now*? Why do you think it's such a secret meeting? *Vampires* are like that."

Mumsy had, of course, made the threat when any of the Temminnick children were being particularly wayward. But never could Sophronia believe such a thing actually possible. "But it's tea! Vampires can't be here. They can't go out in daylight. Everyone knows that."

Petunia, in her Petunia-ish way, dismissed this defense with a careless flap of one hand. "You think they would send a *real* vampire for the likes of you? Oh, no, that's a drone Mumsy is talking with. I wager they're drawing up the papers of servitude right now."

"But I don't *want* to be a vampire drone." Sophronia winced. "They'll suck my blood and make me wear only the very latest fashions."

Petunia nodded in an I-know-more-than-you manner that was highly aggravating. "Yes. Yes, they will."

Frowbritcher, the butler, appeared in the doorway. He paused on the threshold while his rollers transferred to the parlor tracks. He was the very latest in domestic mechanicals, about the size and shape of a daphne bush. He trundled over and looked down his beaky nasal protuberance at Sophronia. His eyes were jet-colored circles of perpetual disapproval.

"Miss Sophronia, your mother wishes to see you immediately." His voice, emanating from a music-box device deep inside his metal body, was tinny and grainy.

Sophronia sighed. "Is she sending me to the vampires?"

Petunia wrinkled her nose. "I suppose there is a possibility they won't take you. I mean to say, Sophronia, the way you dress!"

The butler only repeated, without any inflection whatsoever, "Immediately, miss."

"Should I make for the stable?" Sophronia asked.

"Oh, do *grow up*!" said Petunia in disgust.

"So I can be a puffed-up poodle-faker like you?" *As though growing up were something one could do contagiously, caught through associating with officious older sisters.* Sophronia trailed after Frowbritcher, nervously brushing her custard-covered hands against her apron. She hoped the pinafore would hide the disreputable—well, absent—state of her skirt.

The butler rolled down the hall, leading her to her father's library. An elaborate tea service was arranged there, including lace tablecloths, sponge cake, and the family's very best china. This was far more effort than was ever spent on Mrs. Barnaclegoose.

Across from Sophronia's mother, sipping tea, sat an elegant lady wearing a sour expression and a large hat. She looked like exactly the kind of woman one would expect to be a vampire drone.

"Here is Miss Sophronia, madam," said Frowbritcher from the doorway, not bothering to transfer tracks. He glided off, probably to marshal forces to clean the parlor.

"Sophronia! What did you do to poor Mrs. Barnaclegoose? She left here in a dreadful huff and—oh, simply *look* at you! Mademoiselle, please excuse my daughter's appearance. I'd tell you it was an aberration, but, sadly, it's all too common. Such a troublesome child."

The stranger gave Sophronia a prim look that made her feel about six years old. She was painfully conscious of her custardy state. No one would ever describe Sophronia as elegant, whereas this woman was every inch a lady. Sophronia had never before considered how powerful that could be. The strange woman was also offensively beautiful, with pale skin and dark hair streaked with gray. It was impossible to discern her age, for, despite the gray, her face was young. She was perfectly dressed in a sort of spiky lace traveling gown with a massive skirt and velvet trim that was much more elegant than anything Sophronia had ever seen in her life. Her mother was more a follower of trends than a purveyor of fine taste. This woman was truly stylish.

Despite her beauty, she looks, thought Sophronia, *a little like a crow.* She stared down at her feet and tried to come up with an excuse for her behavior, other than spying on people. "Well, I simply wanted to see how it worked, and then there was this—"

Her mother interrupted. "How it worked? What kind of question is that for a young lady to ask? How often have I warned you against fraternizing with technology?"

Sophronia wondered if that was a rhetorical question and began counting up the number of times just in case it wasn't. Her mother turned back to their guest.

"Do you see what I mean, mademoiselle? She's a cracking great bother."

"What? *Mumsy!*" Sophronia was offended. Never before had her mother used such language in polite company.

"Silence, Sophronia."

"But—"

"Do you see, Mademoiselle Geraldine? Do you see what I must endure? And on a daily basis. *A bother.* Has been from the beginning. And the other girls were such little blessings. Well, I suppose we were due. I tell you this in complete confidence— I'm at my wit's end with this one. I really am. When she isn't reading, she's taking something apart or flirting with the footman or climbing things—trees, furniture, even other people."

"That was years ago!" objected Sophronia. *Will she never let that go? I was eight!*

"Hush, child." Mrs. Temminnick didn't even look in her daughter's direction. "Have you ever heard of the like with a *girl*? Now, I know she's a little brazen for finishing school, but I was hoping you might make an exception, just this once."

Finishing school? Then I'm not being sent to the vampires? Relief flooded through Sophronia, instantly followed by a new horror. *Finishing school!* There would be *lessons.* On how to curtsy. On how to dress. On how to eat with one's finger in the air. Sophronia shuddered. Perhaps a vampire hive was a better option.

Mrs. Temminnick pressed on. "We are certainly willing to provide compensation for your considering Sophronia. Mrs. Barnaclegoose told me, in confidence, that you are masterly with troublesome cases. You have an excellent record. Why, only last week one of your girls married a viscount."

Sophronia was rattled. "Really, Mumsy!" *Marriage? Already?*

As yet, the crow had said nothing. This was a common occurrence around Sophronia's mother. The stranger merely sipped her tea, the bulk of her attention on Sophronia. Her eyes were hard, assessing, and her movements very precise and sharp.

Mrs. Temminnick continued. "And, of course, there is dear Petunia's coming-out ball to consider. We were hoping Sophronia might be presentable for the event. This December? Well, as presentable as possible, given her...defects."

Sophronia winced. She was well aware she hadn't her sisters' looks. For some reason the Fates had seen fit to design her rather more in her father's image than her mother's. But there was no need to discuss such a thing openly with a stranger!

"That could be arranged." When the woman finally spoke, it was with such a strong French accent that her words were difficult to understand. "Miss Temminnick, why is there india rubber wrapped around your boots?"

Sophronia looked down. "Mumsy was complaining I kept scuffing them."

"Interesting solution. Does it work?"

"Haven't had a chance to test them properly." She paused. "Yet."

The stranger looked neither shocked nor impressed by this statement.

Frowbritcher reappeared. He made a motion with one claw-like mechanical arm, beckoning. Sophronia's mother stood and went to confer with the butler. Frowbritcher had a sinister habit of turning up with secrets. It was highly disconcerting in a mechanical.

After a whispered interchange, Mrs. Temminnick went red about the face and then whirled back around.

Oh, dear, thought Sophronia, *what have I done now?*

"Please excuse me for a moment. There appears to be some

difficulty with our new dumbwaiter." She gave her daughter a pointed look. "Hold your tongue and behave, young lady!"

"Yes, Mumsy."

Mrs. Temminnick left the room, closing the door firmly behind her.

"Where did you get the rubber?" The crow dismissed Sophronia's mother with comparative ease, still intrigued by the shoe modification. India rubber was expensive and difficult to come by, particularly in any shape more complex than a ball.

Sophronia nodded in a significant way.

"You destroyed a dumbwaiter for it?"

"I'm not saying I did. I'm not saying I didn't, either." Sophronia was cautious. *After all, this woman wants to steal me away to finishing school. I'll be there for years and then foisted off on some viscount with two thousand a year and a retreating hairline.* Sophronia rethought her approach; perhaps a little less circumspection and some judiciously applied sabotage was called for.

"Mumsy wasn't lying, you understand, about my conduct? The climbing and such. Although it has been a while since I tried to climb up a person. And the footman and I weren't flirting. He thinks Petunia is the pip, not me."

"What about the taking apart?"

Sophronia nodded, as it was a better excuse for destroying the dumbwaiter than spying. "I'm fond of machines. Intriguing things, machines, don't you find?"

The woman cocked her head to one side. "I generally prefer to make use of them, not dissect them. Why do you do it? To upset your mother?"

Sophronia considered this. She was relatively fond of her mother, as one is apt to be, but she supposed some part of her might be on the attack. "Possibly."

A flash of a smile appeared on the woman's face. It made her look very young. It vanished quickly. "How are you as a thespian? Any good?"

"Theatricals?" *What kind of finishing school teacher asks that?* Sophronia was put out. "I may have smudges on my face, but I'm still a *lady*!"

The woman looked at Sophronia's exposed petticoat. "That remains to be seen." She turned away, as though not interested anymore, and helped herself to a slice of cake. "Are you strong?"

Down the hall, something exploded with a bang. Sophronia thought she heard her mother shriek. Both she and the visitor ignored the disruption.

"Strong?" Sophronia edged toward the tea trolley, eyeing the sponge.

"From all the climbing." A pause. "And the machine lifting, I suppose."

Sophronia blinked. "I'm not weak."

"You're certainly good at prevarication."

"Is that a bad thing?"

"That depends on whom you're asking."

Sophronia helped herself to two pieces of cake, just as though she had been invited to do so. The visitor forbore to remark upon it. Sophronia turned away briefly, in the guise of finding a spoon, to tuck one piece in her apron pocket. Mumsy wouldn't allow her any sweets for the next week once she found out about the dumbwaiter.

The woman might have seen the theft, but she didn't acknowledge it.

"You run this finishing school, then?"

"Do you run this finishing school, Mademoiselle Geraldine?" corrected the crow.

"Do you run this finishing school, Mademoiselle Geraldine?" parroted Sophronia dutifully, even though they had not been properly introduced. *Odd, in a finishing school teacher. Shouldn't she wait until Mumsy returns?*

"It *is* called Mademoiselle Geraldine's Finishing Academy for Young Ladies of Quality. Have you heard of it?"

Sophronia had. "I thought only the very best families were allowed in."

"Sometimes we make exceptions."

"Are you *the* Mademoiselle Geraldine? You don't seem old enough."

"Why, thank you, Miss Temminnick, but you should not make such an observation to your betters."

"Sorry, madam."

"Sorry, Mademoiselle Geraldine."

"Oh, yes, sorry, Mademoiselle Geraldine."

"Very good. Do you notice anything else odd about me?"

Sophronia said the first thing that came to mind. "The gray in your hair. It's amiss."

"You *are* an observant young lady, aren't you?" Then, in a sudden movement, Mademoiselle Geraldine reached and pulled out the small throw pillow from behind her back. She tossed it at Sophronia.

Sophronia, who had never before had a lady throw a pillow at her, was flabbergasted, but caught it.

"Adequate reflexes," said Mademoiselle Geraldine, wiggling her fingers for the return of the pillow.

Bemused, Sophronia handed it back to her. "Why—"

A black-gloved hand was raised against any further questions.

Mrs. Temminnick returned at that juncture. "I do apologize. How incurably rude of me. I can't comprehend what has happened to the dumbwaiter. It's making the most awful racket. But you don't want to hear of such piddling domestic *trifles*." She put a great deal of emphasis on the word *trifles*.

Sophronia grimaced.

Mrs. Temminnick sat down, rubbing at a grease spot on her formerly impeccable gloves. "How are you and Sophronia getting on?"

Mademoiselle Geraldine said, "Quite well. The young lady was just telling me of some history book she was recently reading. What was the subject?"

So, she doesn't want Mumsy to know she's been throwing pillows at me? Sophronia was never one to let anyone down when fibs were required.

"Egypt. Apparently the Primeval Monarchy, which follows directly after the Mythical Period, has been given new dates. And—"

Her mother interrupted. "That's more than enough of *that*, Sophronia. A headmistress isn't interested in education. Really, Mademoiselle Geraldine, once you get her started she'll never stop." She looked hopeful. "I know she's a terrible mess, but can you *do* anything with her?"

Mademoiselle Geraldine gave a tight smile. "What do you say to a probationary period? We'll return her in time for that coming-out ball of yours in a few months and see how she gets on until then?"

"Oh, Mademoiselle Geraldine, how perfectly topping!" Sophronia's mother clasped her hands delightedly. "Isn't this thrilling, Sophronia? You're going to finishing school!"

"But I don't *want* to go to finishing school!" Sophronia couldn't help the petulance in her voice as visions of parasol training danced through her head.

"Don't be like that, darling. It will be very exciting."

Sophronia grappled for recourse. "But she threw a pillow at me!"

"Oh, Sophronia, don't tell fibs—you know how unhappy that makes me."

Sophronia gawped, swiveling her gaze back and forth between her now-animated mother and the crowlike stranger.

"How soon can she be made ready?" Mademoiselle Geraldine wanted to know.

Sophronia's mother started. "You wish to take her away *now*?"

"I am here, am I not? Why waste the trip?"

"I didn't think it would be so soon. We must shop for new dresses, a warmer coat. What about her lesson books?"

"Oh, you can send all *that* along later. I shall provide you with a list of required items. She'll be perfectly fine for the time being. A resourceful girl, I suspect."

"Well, if you think it best."

"I do."

Sophronia was not accustomed to seeing her mother railroaded so effectively. "But Mumsy!"

"If Mademoiselle Geraldine thinks it best, then you had better hop to it, young lady. Go change into your good blue dress and your Sunday hat. I'll have one of the maids pack your necessities. May we have half an hour, mademoiselle?"

"Of course. Perhaps I will take a little tour of the grounds while you organize? To stretch my legs before the drive."

"Please do. Come along, Sophronia, we have much to do."

Frustrated and out of sorts, Sophronia trailed after her mother.

Accordingly, she was given an old portmanteau from the attic, three hatboxes, and a carpetbag. With barely enough time to ensure a nibble for the drive—to goodness knows where, at a distance of goodness knows how far—Sophronia found herself being shoved hastily into a carriage. Her mother kissed her on the forehead and made a show of fussing. "My little girl, all grown up and leaving to become a lady!" And that, as they say, was that.

Sophronia might have hoped for a grand send-off with all her siblings and half the mechanical retainers waving tearstained handkerchiefs. But her younger brothers were exploring the farm, her older ones were away at Eton, her sisters were busy with fripperies or marriages—possibly one and the same—and the mechanicals were trundling about their daily tasks. She thought she spotted Roger, the stable lad, waving his cap from the hayloft, but apart from that, even her mother gave only a perfunctory waggle of her fingertips before returning to the house.

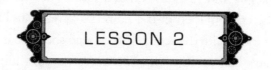
BEWARE FLYWAYMEN, FOR THEY ARE
ILL-DRESSED AND ILL-MANNERED

The carriage was amazing, outfitted with the latest in automated roof removal, retractable footstool, and collapsible tea caddy. It was a hired transport but decked out like a private conveyance, with walls of midnight-blue quilted velvet to reduce road noise, and gold-fringed blankets to ward off the chill.

Sophronia barely had time to take it all in before Mademoiselle Geraldine banged the ceiling with the handle of her parasol and they lurched forward.

More startling than the decoration was the fact that the carriage was already occupied—by two other students. They had, apparently, been sitting patiently the entire time Mademoiselle Geraldine took tea and Sophronia fell out of dumbwaiters and packed all her worldly goods into a portmanteau.

Directly across from her sat a bright-eyed, lively looking young lady, a little younger than Sophronia, with masses of honey-colored hair and a round porcelain face. She wore an enormous gilt and red glass brooch pinned to her bright red dress. The combination of the hair, the jewelry, and the dress made her look quite the scandal, as though she were in training to become a lady of the night. Sophronia was duly impressed.

"Oh, goodness!" said she to Sophronia, as though Sophronia's appearance in the cab were the most delightful thing to happen all day. Which, for one left to sit idle in a carriage with no distraction or entertainment, it might well have been.

"How do you do?" said Sophronia.

"How do you do? Isn't this a spiffing day? Really, quite spiffing. I'm Dimity. Who are you?"

"Sophronia."

"Is that all?"

"What, isn't it enough?"

"Oh, well, I mean to say, I'm Dimity Ann Plumleigh-Teignmott, actually, in full."

"Sophronia Angelina Temminnick."

"Gosh, that's a mouthful."

"It is? I suppose so." *As though Dimity Ann Plumleigh-Teignmott were a nice easy sort of name.* Sophronia dragged her eyes away from the girl to examine the final occupant of the carriage. It was difficult to make out what kind of creature lurked under the oversized bowler and oiled greatcoat. But, if pressed, she would have said it was some species of grubby boy. He had spectacles that were very thick, a brow that was very creased, and a large dusty book occupying the entirety of his lap and attention.

"What's that?" she asked the girl, wrinkling her nose.

"Oh, that? That's just Pillover."

"And what's a pillover, when it's at home?"

"My little brother."

"Ah, I commiserate. I have several of my own. Dashed inconvenient, brothers." Sophronia nodded, perfectly understanding the outlandish hat and coat.

Pillover glanced up from behind his spectacles and issued them both a *look*. He seemed a few years younger than his sister, who was, Sophronia guessed, about thirteen.

"He's slated for Bunson's."

"For what?"

"Bunson and Lacroix's Boys' Polytechnique. You know, the other school?"

Sophronia, who had no idea what Dimity was talking about, pretended to follow out of politeness.

The girl prattled on. She seemed to be a bit of a prattler. Sophronia was comfortable with this after living with her own family. They were big talkers, but with a lot less interesting things to say than Dimity. "Mummy and Daddy want him to be an evil genius, but he has his heart set on Latin verse. Don't you, Pill?"

The boy gave his sister a nasty stare.

"Pillover is terribly bad at being bad, if you take my meaning. Our daddy is a founding member of the Death Weasel Confederacy, and Mummy is a kitchen chemist with questionable intent, but poor Pillover can't even bring himself to murder ants with his Depraved Lens of Crispy Magnification. Can you, Pill?"

Sophronia felt as though she was progressively losing the thread of the conversation. "Death Weasel Confederacy?"

Dimity nodded, curls bobbing. "I know—can you countenance

it? I tend to look on the bright side; at least Daddy's not a Pickleman."

Sophronia's eyes popped. "Uh, oh yes, *rather*." *Pickleman? What in aether is a Pickleman?*

"But Pill here is a sad disappointment to poor old Daddy."

The boy in question put down his book, clearly driven to defend himself. "I made the articulated hassock that moved when someone went to sit on it. And there was that custard pot that never got cool enough for the pudding to set."

Dimity provided parenthetical information against this defense. "The hassock always ended up moving forward helpfully. And Cook simply used the Custard Pot of Iniquity for keeping her buns warm."

"Oh, I say. That's not on. Telling family secrets like that!"

"Face it, Pill, you're disappointingly *good*."

"Oh, I like that! And you're so evil? Why, you want to get married and be a *lady*. Who ever heard of such a thing in our family? At least I try."

"Well, finishing school should help with being a lady. Shouldn't it?" At least this was something Sophronia knew about.

The boy snorted derisively. "Not half. Not *this* finishing school. Wrong kind of finishing altogether. Or should I say right kind, but only on the surface? I'm sure you follow." Pillover made a funny little leer at Sophronia, then, seeming to have embarrassed himself, resumed his book.

"What could he possibly be implying?" Sophronia looked to Dimity to explain her brother's behavior.

"You mean, you don't know?"

"Know what?"

"Oh my goodness. You're a *covert recruit*? No family connection at all? I knew they took them, of course, but I didn't think I would get to meet one. How charming! Have you been under surveillance? I heard they do that sometimes."

Mademoiselle Geraldine interceded at that juncture. "That's enough of *that*, Miss Plumleigh-Teignmott."

"Yes, Mademoiselle Geraldine."

The headmistress went back to ignoring them.

"So where are we traveling to?" Sophronia asked, figuring that was a safe question, since they clearly weren't allowed to talk about the school itself.

"You don't even know that much?" Dimity's tone was full of pity. "Why, to Mademoiselle Geraldine's Finishing Academy for Young Ladies of Quality."

Sophronia shook her head. "No, I mean, where is the location of this school?"

"Well, no one knows *exactly*, but to the south. Dartmoor, or somewhere around there."

"Why so mysterious?"

Dimity shook her head, curls flying. "Oh, no, you see, I'm not meaning to be. It isn't, you understand, at a fixed location."

"What isn't?"

"The academy."

Sophronia imagined a building, filled with shrieking girls, scooting about the moor on tracks, like some massive, over-excited mechanical. "The school is mobile? What, on hundreds of tiny little legs?"

"Legs? Well, yes, moving, only not on legs. I think it's, *you* know." Dimity tilted her head back and looked to the ceiling.

Sophronia was about to inquire further when a terrific jolt shook them where they sat and the carriage came to a stop so abruptly that it pitched Dimity on top of Sophronia, and Pillover on top of Mademoiselle Geraldine.

Mademoiselle Geraldine screamed, probably upset by extended contact with Pillover's grimy coat, and flapped her arms and legs to get the boy off.

Sophronia and Dimity untangled themselves, giggling.

Pillover extracted himself from the headmistress with remarkable dignity for a boy of his age and dress and retrieved his bowler from the floor.

"What on earth is going on?" Mademoiselle Geraldine banged on the ceiling of the cab with her parasol. "Coachman? Coachman!"

The carriage remained still. Or at least it didn't appear to want to move *forward*. Every so often it would bob *upward*, as though it were afloat on the open sea.

The door to the carriage was yanked open to reveal not the coachman, but a bizarre-looking gentleman. He was dressed for the hunt in tweed jodhpurs, boots, red jacket, and riding hat, but he also wore goggles, with a long scarf of the type donned by arctic explorers wrapped around the lower part of his face.

The carriage lurched again. One of the horses neighed in alarm.

The strange man had a massive brass onion pinned to his cravat and was pointing a wicked-looking pistol at the occupants of the carriage. Sophronia's eyes, once caught by the weapon, remained fixed upon it. Never before had she come face-to-face with an actual gun. She was shocked. *Why, that thing could go off. Someone could get hurt!*

"Highwaymen!" squeaked Pillover.

"No," corrected Mademoiselle Geraldine, her teeth gritted. "Worse: *flywaymen*." There was something in her tone, felt Sophronia, that suggested she was not surprised. Sophronia was instantly suspicious of both Mademoiselle Geraldine and the flywayman.

The headmistress batted her long eyelashes. "Why, sir, what could you possibly want from us? I'm simply a headmistress transporting these children to their final destination."

Laying it on a bit thick, isn't she? thought Sophronia.

"We have nothing of great value. We—"

The flywayman interrupted Mademoiselle Geraldine. "Silence. We know perfectly well what you've got those pretty little mitts on. Hand over the prototype."

"I have absolutely no idea what you are on about." The headmistress's trembling smile was well executed, but apparently not convincing.

"'Course you do. Where is it?"

Mademoiselle Geraldine shook her head, eyelashes lowered prettily.

"Well, perhaps we'll simply have a look for ourselves."

The man stuck his head, briefly, back out the door and yelled something indistinguishable up to the sky.

There came a thump on the top of the carriage. Sophronia and the others could do nothing but watch, mutely, as their trunks, bags, and hatboxes were thrown from the roof to crash to the ground. There they fell open, littering the dusty road with clothing, hats, and shoes.

Two more flywaymen, dressed much like their leader, jumped down after and began rifling through the spilled contents. Whatever they were looking for appeared to be relatively small, as every piece of luggage—no matter what the size—had to be emptied. One of the men even used a knife to slash the bottoms of the trunks, searching for hidden pockets.

This was all highly embarrassing, to have one's private possessions strewn about in public! Sophronia was particularly mortified that Pillover could see all her underthings—*a stranger, and a boy!* She also noted that Mademoiselle Geraldine's trunks included some very salacious night garments. Why, there was a nightgown of purple flannel. *Imagine that!*

The flywaymen's movements became increasingly frenzied. Their leader, while still guarding the occupants of the carriage, glanced frequently behind him at the activity in the road.

After a quarter of an hour, the man's hand, the one holding the gun, began shaking from fatigue.

"Where is it?" he hissed at Mademoiselle Geraldine.

"I told you, young man, you will not find it here. Whatever *it* is." She tossed her head. *Actually tossed it!*

"Impossible. We know you have it. You *must* have it!"

The headmistress looked off to the far distant horizon, nose elevated. "Your information would appear to be faulty."

"Come with me. You, children, stay here." The man dragged Mademoiselle Geraldine from the carriage. The headmistress struggled briefly, but finding the man's strength superior to her own, she subsided.

"Where's the coachman?" Sophronia hissed to Dimity and Pillover.

"Probably overcome by physical assault," said Dimity.

"Or dead," added Pillover.

"How'd they get to us? I didn't hear any horses or anything."

Pillover pointed up. "Sky highwaymen. Haven't you heard of them?"

"Well, yes, but I didn't think they *actually* existed."

Pillover shrugged.

"Must have been hired by someone," Dimity said. "What do you think the prototype is for?"

"Does it matter?" her brother asked.

"You think she actually has it?" Sophronia wondered.

Pillover looked at Sophronia with something like pity in his dark eyes. "Of course she has it. Question is, did she hide it well enough?"

"Or did she make a copy?" added Dimity.

"Is it safe to let them think they've won?"

"And was she thinking that far ahead?"

Sophronia interrupted their speculation. "That's a lot of questions."

They heard Mademoiselle Geraldine say something sharp to the men rifling through the luggage. All three looked out the open door to see what would happen next. The flywayman with the gun struck the headmistress across the face with his free hand.

"Oh, dear," said Sophronia. "Violence." She suppressed panic and a strange urge to giggle. She'd never before seen a grown man actually hit a woman.

Dimity looked slightly green.

Pillover's small face became drawn behind his round spectacles. "I don't think she planned for *this*."

His assessment seemed correct, for Mademoiselle Geraldine proceeded to have a bout of hysterics, culminating in a very dramatic faint in the middle of the road.

"Quite the performance. My sister Petunia once acted like that over a mouse."

"You think she's shamming?" Dimity was inclined to be impressed.

"Shamming or not, she seems to have hung us out to dry." Sophronia pursed her lips. *I don't want to go to finishing school, but I don't exactly want to be kidnapped by flywaymen either.*

The carriage lurched up again.

Sophronia looked at the ceiling. The flywaymen's transport must be tied to the luggage rails above. She put two and two together: the flywayman's goggles plus his onion-shaped pin. *Balloon transport.* At which point Sophronia decided she had better do something about their predicament. "We need to cut the balloon's ties to the carriage and get to the driver's box and take command of the horses. Once we get moving, can we outrun them?"

Pillover nodded. "No scientist has figured out how to make air transport move as quickly as ground. Although there *were* some interesting dirigible prototypes in last month's *Junior Guide to Scientific Advancements and Amoral Superiority.* Something about utilizing the aether currents, but nothing on balloons, so—"

Dimity interrupted her brother. "Yes, thank you, Pill." Clearly, prattling was a family trait even Pillover was prone to indulge in sometimes.

"So?" said Sophronia. "Resources. What do you two have?"

Pillover emptied the pockets of his oversized greatcoat: some pine-sap gum, a monocle on a stick—*the Depraved Lens of Crispy Magnification, perhaps?*—and a long piece of ribbon that probably started life in his sister's hair. Dimity produced a box of sandwiches, a wooden spoon, and a knitted stuffed octopus out of the small covered basket at her feet. All Sophronia had was the piece of sponge she'd swiped at tea and stashed in her apron, now sadly crushed.

She split it into three and they ate the cake and thought hard.

None of the enemy paid them any mind. The three flyway-men had given up demolishing the luggage and now stood about arguing. Mademoiselle Geraldine was still firmly fainted.

"No time like the present," said Sophronia, grabbing Pillover's magnification lens. She climbed out of the small window of the carriage, the one on the side facing away from the flywaymen.

Carriages, as it turned out, were a whole lot easier to climb than dumbwaiters. Sophronia hoisted herself onto the top of the cab, unseen by the men below. There she found a large and colorful airdinghy tied to the roof. It wasn't made of one balloon, but four, each attached to a corner of a passenger basket about the size of a small rowboat. In the center of the basket sprouted up a mast, higher than the balloons, with a sail unfurled. Steering propellers were suspended below. These were moving slightly, hovering directly above Sophronia's head as she crawled across the carriage roof. They looked quite sharp. Keeping an eye on them, she made her way over to the mooring point.

The rope was tied firmly about the luggage rail and impossible to work loose.

Sophronia pulled out Pillover's magnification lens and, angling it to catch the sun, began to burn through the rope. The acrid smell of scalded fiber permeated the air, but her activities remained unobserved. It seemed to take forever, but eventually the rope burned away to a point where Sophronia could break it. The airdinghy bobbed up, caught a slight breeze, and drifted away.

Without pausing to survey the effects of her handiwork, Sophronia crawled over and lowered herself down onto the driver's box. The coachman lay slumped to one side. There was a large red mark on his forehead. She relieved him of the reins and clucked the horses into motion. She was perfectly well aware of how inappropriate it was for a young lady of fourteen to drive a coach, but circumstances sometimes called for extreme measures.

At that point, the flywaymen noticed what was happening and began shouting at her. The leader shot his gun rather ineffectually into a nearby tree. Another took off after the airdinghy, chasing it on the ground. The third began running toward her.

Sophronia whipped the horses up and set them a brisk canter. The cab behind her swayed alarmingly. It might be the latest design, but it was not meant for such a frantic pace. She gave the horses their heads for a few minutes before drawing them back to a trot. When she came upon a junction wide enough, she turned the carriage about and pulled up. She jumped down and stuck her head inside the cab.

Pillover and Dimity stared with wide, awed eyes back at her.

"All righty, then?"

"Tremendous," said Dimity.

"What kind of *girl* are you?" grumbled Pillover, looking rather yellow about the gills.

"Now I see why you were recruited," added Dimity. "I'm surprised they left it until you were so old."

Sophronia blushed. No one had ever praised her for such activities before. Nor had anyone looked upon her as *old*. It was quite the honor.

"How on earth do you know how to drive a carriage?" Pillover asked, as though this were some kind of personal affront.

Sophronia grinned. "I spend a lot of time in stables."

"Nice-looking stable boys?" suggested Dimity.

Sophronia gave her an arch look. "So what now—go back for the headmistress?"

"But we're safe, aren't we?" Pillover looked alarmed by the idea. "Is she really worth it?"

"It *is* the polite thing to do. Hardly fair to abandon her among criminals," pointed out his sister.

"Plus the coachman is insensible. And he's the only other one who knows where we are heading." Sophronia was all for logic as well as manners.

"But they have guns," replied Pillover, also logically.

Sophronia considered this. "True." She looked at Dimity. "Mademoiselle Geraldine—how useful do you think she is?"

Dimity frowned. "Did she fib with you?"

Sophronia nodded.

"I'm not convinced she can be relied upon to follow any kind of plan; you know how adults are. However, we must do something."

"Did I mention the guns?"

"Oh, stuff it, Pill." Dimity dismissed her brother, turning her attention entirely on Sophronia. "What do you suggest?"

"If I go in quick, could you and Mr. Pillover tie yourselves down and see if you can't simply grab her off the road?"

"Remember, ladies, the guns?" Pillover repeated.

Dimity was nodding. "It'll require both me and Pill. Mademoiselle Geraldine is slim, but not *that* slim."

Pillover would not let up. "What about the whole shooting at us part of the equation?"

Sophronia and Dimity said together, "Stuff it, Pill."

"We don't have any rope."

Sophronia dangled the long ribbon from Pillover's pocket. Dimity firmed up her mouth, grabbed it, nodded her head sharply, and went to work.

Sophronia shut the cab door and climbed back up onto the driver's box.

The coachman was blinking blearily and clutching his head.

"Hold on, sir," suggested Sophronia. "It's about to get a mite bumpy."

"What? Who are you?" was all he managed to say before the young lady in the blue dress grabbed up the reins of his horses and whipped them into a fast trot.

They dashed back toward the pile of clothing and luggage in

the middle of the roadway. Mademoiselle Geraldine now stood a short distance away from the head flywayman, wailing tragically over one of the hatboxes. The other two men had vanished.

Seeing the carriage charging toward him, the flywayman took aim and fired.

The bullet whined over Sophronia's head. She thought dark insults at the man—slander she'd learned from Roger, the stable lad.

The coachman, after a yell of horror, hunkered down. Luckily, he did not try to wrest the reins away from Sophronia. He probably thought he was in the midst of a bad dream.

She slurred the carriage around, bringing it up alongside the headmistress and pulling back on the reins at the same time. On cue, the cab door banged open and four little hands scrabbled for purchase on the black lace of Mademoiselle Geraldine's fabulous dress. They yanked. Something tore. Mademoiselle Geraldine squealed and fell forward and into the carriage. Her legs dangled.

The flywayman dropped his gun and dove for Mademoiselle Geraldine. The headmistress dropped her pathetic act and kicked frantically, eventually losing her shoes, but also the flywayman's grip. He fell to the road, clutching to his chest a pair of black satin slippers.

Sophronia turned to face forward, flashing the whip. The horses hardly needed the encouragement, as they were already terrified by the gunfire and the erratic driving methods of their new coachgirl. They sprang into a gallop.

HOW NOT TO MAKE INTRODUCTIONS

The coachman finally regained his senses, realizing this was not some nightmare. There really was a fourteen-year-old girl with mousy hair and a serious expression driving his carriage. He yanked the reins away from Sophronia and pulled the horses up short. They hung their heads, sides heaving.

"Well, then," said Sophronia to the coachman, sticking her nose in the air. She jumped down. A series of cries and wails emanated from inside the carriage. She opened the door to find Pillover sitting and reading his book, while his sister lay in a crumpled heap on the floor.

The boy gestured with his chin at Dimity. "She was shot." He sounded remarkably unconcerned for a brother with any degree of affection for his sibling.

"Good lord!" Sophronia climbed in to see to her new friend's health. The bullet had grazed Dimity's shoulder. It had ripped her dress and left a partly burned gash behind, but didn't look all that bad.

Sophronia checked to make certain Dimity had no other injuries. Then she sat back on her heels. "Is that all? I've had worse scrapes from drinking tea. Why has she come over all crumpled?"

Pillover rolled his eyes. "Faints at the sight of blood, our Dimity. Always has. Weak nerves, Father says. It doesn't even have to be *her* blood."

Sophronia snorted.

"Exactly. And the smelling salts were in her suitcase. Which is now some distance behind us. Leave her be. She'll come 'round eventually."

Sophronia turned her attention to the source of the wails. "What's wrong with her, then?" *Is Mademoiselle Geraldine also injured?* The headmistress was curled into a ball, hands covering her face, whimpering.

Pillover was as disgusted with the headmistress as he was with his sister. "She's been like that ever since we pulled her inside. Nothing damaged except her brain, so far as I can determine."

Sophronia looked closer and caught the headmistress watching them slyly from behind her hands. She was shamming. But why? *So she doesn't have to explain anything? Such a peculiar woman.*

It was then that Sophronia noticed that Pillover was looking unwell behind his sneer.

She turned her full attention on the boy. "And are *you* quite all right, Mr. Pillover?"

"I'm not a very good traveler at the best of times, Miss Sophronia. You might have taken that last half mile a little smoother."

Sophronia tried to hide a smile. "I might. But what pleasure would there be in that?"

"Oh, wonderful," said Pillover. "You're one of *those* kinds of girls."

Sophronia narrowed her eyes. "You could ride on the box next to the coachman. Fresh air would do you a world of good."

Pillover looked most offended. "Outside, like a peasant? I think not."

Sophronia shrugged. "Suited me."

Pillover gave her a look that suggested that her valiant rescue was no excuse and that she was, in fact, now quite low-class in his eyes.

Sophronia returned her attention to the whimpering headmistress. "What are we going to do about her?" And then, more directly, "You're not fooling anyone, you realize?"

Pillover evidently had been fooled. "She's shamming? Well, there's nothing we can do about her. The coachman knows where to go. He can get us to Bunson's. Someone there will know what to do."

Sophronia nodded and stuck her head out the carriage window. "Coachman?"

"Yes, little miss?" The man looked generally upset with life.

"You can drive us on to this Bunson's locale, can't you?"

"Yes, little miss. I know the school. But I'm not convinced I intend to continue on, now. Never been held up by flywaymen afore."

Blast it. How would Mumsy handle this? Sophronia looked the coachman full in the face and straightened her spine as stiff as she could. "You will if you wish to be paid. Keep a decent pace and an eye to the sky and it shouldn't happen again." The moment she said it, Sophronia became completely shocked by her own daring. She was also mildly impressed by how imperious she sounded.

So was the coachman, apparently, because he resumed his post without another word and set the horses a sedate trot.

Pillover glanced over the top of his glasses. "You do that rather well, don't you?"

"What?"

"Order other people around. I've not yet got the way of it myself."

Sophronia thought Pillover was, regardless, doing pretty well at snobbery, for a grubby boy. She was about to say something of the kind when Mademoiselle Geraldine's whimpering escalated.

"Oh, do stop it and explain yourself," Sophronia ordered, feeling she was on an autocratic streak.

Much to her surprise, the headmistress listened, transforming her simulated whimpering into outright ire, directed at Sophronia. "I didn't attend for this, you understand. Easy assignment, they said." Sophronia noted with interest that Mademoiselle Geraldine had lost her French accent. "Nothing to it but improvisational theatrics. Some on-point assessment of new candidates. Simply act older. Put on a bit of an accent and a pretty dress. Such an easy finishing. Others should be so lucky. You're certain to make it through. But no. Oh, no. I had to have a combination retrieval and recruitment undertaking with an unexpected attack from unknown counterintelligencer elements, and no second. How dare they send me on without a second? Me! I mean, did I ask for this? I didn't ask for this. Who needs active status? I don't need active status. This is ridiculous!" She seemed to be progressively building herself up to sublime self-righteousness.

Sophronia felt that there was something else undercutting the flood of words. "Headmistress, is there nothing we can do for you? You seem upset."

"Upset? Of course I'm upset! And don't call me headmistress. *Headmistress*, my ruddy arse."

Sophronia gasped at the shocking word. *Now, that's taking matters too far!*

Mademoiselle Geraldine sat up straight and glared, as though Sophronia were responsible for everything bad in the world. "My face hurts, my dress is in tatters, and I have no slippers!" This last and deepest offense was uttered in a positive wail.

"Then you're not our headmistress?"

"How could I be? I'm only seventeen years old. You can't possibly think I'm the headmistress of a finishing school. You're not that naive."

"But isn't that what we were meant to think?"

"I didn't think about you at all," muttered Pillover, returning to his book.

"Who *are* you, then?" asked Sophronia.

"I'm Miss Monique de Pelouse!" She paused, as though expecting the name to produce some sign of recognition.

Sophronia merely gave her a blank look. "So this begs the question: where is the *real* Mademoiselle Geraldine?"

"Oh"—Monique waved a hand in the air and sniffed—"she never leaves much anymore, and she's useless when she does. They always send impersonators."

"They do?"

"Of course they do. It's easier, and it's a good way to finish."

"And who is *they*?"

"Why, the teachers, of course. But we were talking about me and my problems."

Sophronia looked Monique up and down gravely. "I don't think we're going to solve those in the space of one carriage ride."

Pillover *tut-tut*ted at her from behind his book—but there was clear amusement in the reprimand.

Monique sneered. "Who do you think you are? *Covert recruit.* You're not that special. You're not that good. Proud of yourself and your little carriage rescue, are you? Well, I didn't need your help! I'm a top-level student, on my finishing assignment. Ordered to retrieve three useless *children.*"

Pillover's voice emanated from behind his tome. "I hardly think that was all."

"Of course it wasn't *all*," Monique snapped. "I had the prototype to collect as well, now didn't I?"

Pillover took interest at last. "The one the flywaymen were after?"

Sophronia asked, "What's it a prototype *of*?"

"Don't be daft. I don't know *that.*"

"Do you think you might at some point tell me what *finishing* actually means?" Sophronia was getting more and more curious about the particulars of this finishing school. It seemed Mumsy might have been misled as to the nature of the establishment.

"No." Monique gave her a decidedly nasty glare and then turned her attention out the carriage window.

Sophronia wasn't certain what she'd done to incur such loathing. *Should have left her with the flywaymen.* She looked at Pillover, who ignored her. So she sighed and sat back, frustrated. After a moment's consideration, she switched to the spot next to Pillover and attempted to read over his shoulder, ignoring his faintly goaty smell. All boys smelled of goat. So they passed the rest of the ride, until the carriage pulled into the sleepy little town of Swiffle-on-Exe.

As they ratted to a halt, Dimity blinked awake. "Ow. What? Did I fall asleep?"

"No, you fainted. Blood," explained her brother tersely.

"Oh, did I? Pardon." Dimity glanced down at her wounded shoulder. "Oh!" Her eyes began to roll back into her head.

Sophronia quickly leaned forward and clapped her hand over the injury. "None of that, now!"

Dimity refocused on her. "Ouch. Uh, perhaps we could tie something over it?"

"Good plan. Close your eyes." Sophronia worked the long hair ribbon loose from the grip rail inside the carriage door and wrapped it around Dimity's shoulder.

"Oh, I do wish I were more like Mummy. She's terribly fearsome. Wish I looked more like her, as well. That would help with everything." Dimity sat up.

"Why? What does she look like?"

"More like Pillover than me."

Sophronia, who had seen very little of Pillover's appearance, outside of his massive outer garments, could only say, "Oh?"

"You know, *dark* and *brooding*. I should dearly love to be *dark* and *brooding*. It's so romantic and fortune-teller-like. I couldn't brood if my life depended on it."

"Well, the ribbon around your shoulder makes for a certain fortune-telling appeal."

"Oh, does it? Splendid. You know, Sophronia, *you* could probably do it if you put your mind to it."

"Do what?"

"Be *dark* and *brooding*."

Sophronia, with middling brown hair and moderately green eyes set in a freckled face, would hardly have described herself as brooding. Or dark, for that matter.

Dimity's attention, lightning fast, shifted to a new topic. "Where are we?"

"Bunson's, finally," said Pillover, snapping his book shut. He made a show of organizing for arrival. Given that he no longer had any luggage, this was rather like the action of a mechanical without instructions, trundling idly in circles until he ran out of steam.

The carriage door was opened by a stiff domestic mechanical of some advanced outdoor nature.

"What is that?" gasped Sophronia. She'd never seen anything to equal the monstrosity. It was taller than Frowbritcher and conically shaped, with a wheelbarrow attached to its back. Where a face facsimile should be was a confusion of gears and cogs, like the back of a clock.

"Porter mechanical." Pillover stood, clutching his literary tome, and jumped down. "You two coming?" he asked, without turning to see.

"Where is your luggage, young sir?" asked the mechanical. Its voice was louder and brassier than Frowbritcher's. It wore a gray cap, backward, and a brass octopus pin on a cloth cravat around its neck. *That's too bizarre.* Sophronia had never seen a mechanical wear clothing before.

Pillover answered. "Oh, about ten miles back in the middle of the road."

"Sir?" The porter rocked side to side in confusion. It was riding on a set of rails, like a very small train.

Sophronia climbed out of the carriage to get a closer look, wondering if she could take the porter apart.

Dimity followed.

The mechanical's attention instantly shifted to them.

"No females, young sir." It made a whirring, hissing noise and ejected a puff of steam from below its cravat. The material fluttered up against its clockwork face and then flopped back down.

Pillover turned back. "What?"

"No females allowed, young sir." The porter puffed again. *Flap, flap,* went the cravat.

"Oh, those aren't females. They're only girls. They're slated for the finishing academy."

"They read as females, young sir."

"Oh, I say. Don't be difficult."

Sophronia took the diplomatic route. "We need to speak with an authority. Our carriage was attacked and our guardian is overset."

"No females!" The porter mechanical was quite firm on this. Its chest panel moved aside to reveal some kind of weapon, too large to be a gun.

As Sophronia stood, transfixed, it sparked and then *whooshed* to life, hurling blue flames that got close enough to singe Dimity's hair.

The girls dove back inside the cab, and the coachman, who was not having any more tomfoolery on his watch, drove the carriage away at once. The flame-throwing porter did not follow them.

The carriage halted outside the school grounds. Sophronia pressed her nose against the glass above the cab door and looked out. Bunson's was massive, but oddly hodgepodge—not like a respectable educational facility at all. A few of its towers were square, but others were round; some were old, others new; and some were positively *foreign* looking. There were wires stretching between the towers, and sticks jutting outward with netting dangling off their ends. An orange glow lit up various windows, here and there puffs of steam emanated forth, and one large smokestack belched plumes of black smoke up into the sky.

Sophronia looked at Dimity. "What now?"

"Well, my brother's no good. He'll have forgotten about us the moment he got inside."

"It's starting to get dark." Sophronia turned to their erstwhile headmistress. "She's simply going to have to do her job."

Dimity took a deep breath, sat down on the bench next to Monique, and shook the older girl's arm.

"What do *you* want?"

"We don't know the academy's location, and neither does the driver."

Monique de Pelouse said nothing.

Sophronia crossed her arms and glared at the older girl. Dimity looked back and forth between the two for a moment, then crossed her arms and glared as well. Though perhaps not quite so fiercely.

Finally, Monique relented. "Oh, very *well*!" She banged on the roof with her parasol handle. The cab door opened and the coachman stuck his head in.

Monique said, "Take Shrubbery Lane to the Nib and Crinkle Pub, turn left, and follow the goat path behind the hedge. After an hour, the path ends in a thicket of trees. Go around to the right and then I shall issue further instructions. And hurry. We must beat the sunset or we'll never spot it."

"But madam, that's straight out onto the moor."

"Of course it is. What could possibly have made you think we'd stop at the edge?"

"There are stories about Dartmoor. People get lost in the mist and never return. Or are eaten by werewolves. Or are taken by vampires. Or are murdered by flywaymen."

At which juncture Monique proved she could do "commanding" far better than Sophronia. "Stop arguing, my man. You heard what I said about the sun."

Looking very uncomfortable, the put-upon coachman resumed his place. The tired horses started up once more.

At first, everything seemed ordinary, but a few minutes up the goat path the carriage started to sway, buffeted by the most intense gusts of wind Sophronia had ever felt. She pressed her face against the window. Endless rolling grassland stretched around them, brown after a summer's heat, waving in the wind. The moor was mist-shrouded in the distance. Here and there a coppice of trees or a small winding spring disturbed the monotony with a bright splash of green.

"Is this all?" Sophronia was dubious.

Dimity shrugged. "Windy."

"Don't let it fool you," Monique said with an unkind smile. "This is the *only* nice bit. Soon enough the rocks will sprout up like broken bones, and the mist rises so fast you can't see where you're going or where you've been."

Sophronia was not spooked. "You think you can scare me with doomy talk? I've older sisters, I'll have you know."

Monique gave her a dirty look before rapping on the carriage roof again and issuing a new set of directions.

The carriage turned, this time following some invisible path out onto the heath. The mist began closing in around them, or they were moving into it—hard to tell which.

Sophronia actually began to feel a tiny bit of dread in the pit of her stomach. *What if there really are werewolves roaming the moor?*

And then, there it was. The mist broke. The last rays of the sun cast a long shadow out of the carriage and lit up Mademoiselle Geraldine's Finishing Academy for Young Ladies of Quality. And no, the school wasn't dashing around the moor on hundreds of tiny little legs. It was bobbing above it in chubby floating majesty.

LESSON 4

THE CORRECT CONFIGURATION OF
A FINISHING SCHOOL

M y goodness," said Sophronia. "It looks like a caterpillar that has overeaten."

And it did. It wasn't so much a dirigible as three dirigibles mashed together to form one long chain of oblong, inflated balloons. Below them dangled a multilevel series of decks, most open to the air, but some closed off, with windows reflecting back the dying sun. At the back, a colossal set of propellers churned slowly, and above them billowed a massive sail—probably more for guidance than propulsion. A great quantity of steam wafted out from below the lower back decks, floating away to join the mist as if responsible for creating it. Black smoke puffed sedately out of three tall smokestacks.

Sophronia was enchanted. It was the most fascinating thing she had ever seen, and entirely unlike any of the finishing schools she had ever heard of, which were mostly—according to her sisters—inside castles in Switzerland. She did not, however, want to admit to being enchanted, as this seemed childish, so instead, she said casually, "It's much bigger than I expected."

"It's very high up, isn't it?" added Dimity nervously.

As the carriage drew closer, Sophronia realized that the floating academy was moving much faster than she had initially thought. It was probably riding the stiff wind that seemed to rush over Dartmoor constantly, tilting small trees into lopsidedness. Just when she thought they might actually catch it, the horses screamed in terror and the carriage jerked to a stop.

The door burst open. A young man stood before them. He was a tall, swarthy fellow of the type that Petunia would swoon over; rakishly handsome in a floppy way. He was wearing a black silk top hat and a greatcoat that covered him from neck to ankle. *Papa would call him a "young blunt" in a disgusted tone of voice.* Sophronia was briefly afraid that this was some new form of flywayman—except that he wore no goggles and was grinning at them.

"Ladies!"

Monique colored becomingly. "Captain."

"Winds are fierce this evening. Can't float down for a pickup. You ladies will have to wait until after sunset, then I'll give you a lift."

"Oh." Monique's delicate little nose wrinkled. "Must we?"

The young man's cheerful expression didn't falter under the weight of her dissatisfaction. "Yes."

"Oh, very well." Monique gave the man her hand and he helped her down.

He did not turn to accompany her, instead looking inquiringly at Dimity and Sophronia. "Ladies. No time like the present."

Dimity gathered up her little basket, also blushing furiously, and put her hand into the man's large one.

He helped her down and returned for Sophronia. "Miss?"

Sophronia busily checked the cab for any forgotten items.

The young man observed this with a twinkle in his dark eyes. "Cautious girl."

Sophronia didn't dignify that with a reply. She hadn't pinpointed the particulars yet, but there was something odd about this man, aside from his being adorable.

Outside, the wind was biting, and the great airship was even more impressive. The horses were restless, rolling their eyes and straining against their traces. The coachman fought to hold them. There seemed to be no reason for their panic. The young man strode forward to pay the driver. This only terrified the animals further. The coachman managed to take possession of his fare and keep hold of the reins, but only by dint of real skill. Then he turned his steeds around and let them have their way, careening across the heath at a breakneck speed.

Dimity sidled up to Sophronia and whispered, "Isn't he simply scrumptious?"

Sophronia pretended obtuseness. "The coachman?"

"No, silly. Him!" Dimity tilted her head toward their new escort.

"He's a little old, don't you feel?"

Dimity considered the age of the young man. He was, perhaps, one-and-twenty. "Well, I suppose. But Monique doesn't believe so. Look at her flirting! Shameless."

The man and Monique were discussing the lack of luggage. With animated hand gestures, Monique described its loss, their recent attack, and their subsequent escape. She downplayed Sophronia's part and accentuated her own. Sophronia would have defended herself, but there was something about the way Monique told the story that was about more than ego.

"She's hiding something. Has been all along—and not only her real identity."

"A brain?" Dimity suggested.

"And *he* isn't wearing any shoes."

"Oh, I say! You're right. How peculiar."

"And the horses were afraid of him. Every time he got close, they shied."

"But why?"

"Perhaps they have equine standards—an abhorrence of bare feet."

Dimity giggled.

The man, apparently tired of Monique's tales, came to join them.

The older girl trailed behind him and finally remembered her manners. "Girls, this is Captain Niall."

Dimity bobbed a curtsy. "Captain."

Sophronia followed suit a second later with a much less tidy curtsy and a much less pleasant "Captain."

Monique said, "Miss Dimity Plumleigh-Teignmott, full credentials, and Miss Sophronia Angelina Temminnick, covert recruit." Her lip curled.

The man touched the brim of his top hat and bowed to each in turn.

Captain Niall had a nice smile, and Sophronia liked his boneless way of moving. But she had a sinking suspicion he wasn't wearing a cravat under the greatcoat. Also, it looked as if his top hat was tied under his chin like a baby's bonnet. Since she figured it might be rude to point out the man's deficiencies in attire to his face, she said instead, "I do hope the coachman finds his way back to civilization safely."

"Commendable conscientiousness, Miss Temminnick, but I shouldn't trouble yourself."

Behind them, the sun had completely set. The airship, drifting away, began to fade into the misty, purpled sky, becoming increasingly difficult to see.

"Back in a jiff." The young captain ambled down a little gulley, disappearing behind a large rock.

The ladies could still see his top hat bobbing, but nothing else, and that only for a moment. The hat began to melt down and out of sight. *Was he crouching?* It was difficult to hear anything above the wind, and Sophronia's ears were already starting to ache from exposure, but she thought she could detect a moan of pain.

Then, out from behind the rock, trotting up the gulley, came a massive wolf. A rangy beast with dark, mottled, black-and-brown fur and a fluffy, white-tipped tail.

Dimity let out of a squeak of alarm.

Sophronia froze, but only for a moment. *Werewolf!* said her brain, putting everything together in one split second. The lack of shoes. The full greatcoat. Now he was coming *at* them.

She turned and ran straight for the nearest coppice of trees, thinking only in terms of safety. She ignored Monique's instructions for her to stop. She didn't even think of poor Dimity. Her only instinct was that of prey: to scurry and hide, to escape the predator.

The werewolf leapt after her far faster than any normal wolf ever could. Not that Sophronia had ever met such a monster before. She had heard the rumors about supernatural speed and strength, but she had hardly given them credence. This werewolf proved all the fairy tales true. Before she had gone more than a few paces, he caught up to her and jumped over her head, twisting in midair and coming to rest facing her and blocking her path.

Sophronia crashed right into him and fell to her back on the rough grass, winded.

Before she could rise, a massive paw descended onto her chest, and a vicious wolf face appeared above her—black nose damp and teeth bared. The face descended and . . . nothing.

Sophronia screwed her eyes shut and turned her head away, waiting for the deathblow to come from his other massive paw, or for those glistening canines to close about her neck.

Still nothing.

I guess I'm not dead. She cautiously opened her eyes to look up into the wolf's yellow ones. They crinkled at her, and the beast lolled out his tongue, grinning. His massive, sweeping tail brushed back and forth behind him. She noticed then, much to her shock, that the top hat was still tied securely to his head.

This incongruity served to calm her as nothing else could have. Later, Sophronia was to wonder if this was the reason Captain Niall always wore a top hat, even when he changed—

to put people at ease. Or if he believed that, whatever the form, a gentleman should never be without his hat.

She made to sit up. When he refused to let her, she said, "I won't run again. I'm sorry. You startled me. I've never met a werewolf before."

With a small nod, he backed away.

Dimity offered Sophronia a helping hand up. "Sophronia's parents are conservatives," she explained to the creature. She moved cautiously, suggesting that she, too, was unfamiliar with werewolves, for all her progressive upbringing. *Or perhaps that is the way one is supposed to behave around them.* Sophronia decided to take her cues from her new friend, and stood very slowly.

Monique minced over. "If you are quite done making a fool of yourself, Covert?"

Sophronia snapped back, "I wouldn't want to make a promise I couldn't keep."

"No, I suppose you wouldn't. I'd better go first, Captain. Show them how it's done."

The wolf nodded his furry, top-hatted head.

Then Monique de Pelouse did the most remarkable thing. She sat down sidesaddle on top of the werewolf's back, as though he were a Shetland pony.

"One holds on, like so," she explained officiously, burying her hands in the wolf's thick neck ruff. "Then one leans forward as much as possible."

Sophronia thought she heard the girl's stays creak.

The werewolf trotted off, gaining speed until he was nothing but a blur racing across the heath toward the floating school.

Sophronia squinted, trying to follow his movements. He leapt impossibly high into the air, toward the ship. He was a supernatural creature, and clearly very powerful, but even were-wolves couldn't fly. It became clear, however, that he didn't intend to, for he appeared to have landed midair.

"Must be some kind of platform," said Dimity.

Sophronia nodded. "Suspended on long cords, perhaps?"

Monique dismounted, and Captain Niall jumped down and came racing back to them.

He looked expectantly at Dimity.

Dimity glanced at Sophronia and said, "Oh, dear."

Sophronia smiled. "If you're afraid of falling, you could ride astride. It's much easier to hang on to a horse that way."

Dimity looked affronted at the very idea.

"It was only a suggestion."

"You're very calm."

Sophronia shrugged. "I'm overburdened by strange occurrences at the moment. I'll go next, if you like."

Dimity looked relieved and gestured expansively with one hand.

Sophronia climbed onto the werewolf. Her mother would have had hysterics—leaving aside the whole werewolf steed aspect—at the very idea that a daughter of hers would ride *astride!* Sophronia merely wrapped both her arms and legs about the wolf. "I'm ready." His fur smelled of hay, sandalwood, and pork sausages.

He started slowly, accustoming her to his gait—which was not at all like that of a horse!—then picked up speed. Sophronia hunkered down, watching the grass and rocks rush by beneath them. They neared the airship, and with a tremendous bunching of haunches and a surge of power, Captain Niall leapt into the air.

For a brief, glorious moment, Sophronia felt as close to flying as she ever would. The wind lifted her hair and dress; the emptiness of space surrounded her; the ground was far below. Then the werewolf touched down lightly onto a small platform beside a bored-looking Monique.

Sophronia climbed off. "Thank you, sir, most enjoyable."

Captain Niall jumped back down to collect Dimity.

As Monique was ignoring her, Sophronia examined the workings of the platform. It was made of thick glass, hollowed on the inside like a box, and hung on four chains. These were looped about pulleys at each corner, which meant the whole thing could be raised and lowered as one unit.

She craned her neck, but saw neither hole nor docking structure in the underside of the airship.

A distant shrieking, getting louder and louder, heralded Dimity's arrival.

As soon as they landed, Dimity stopped screaming—embarrassed—and dismounted. Then she sat down on the platform abruptly.

Monique laughed.

Sophronia hurried to her friend's side. "Are you unwell?"

"My nerves are a little shaky, I must confess. No, please, leave me until I recover the use of my knees. That was a tad overwhelming."

"I thought it was quite a wheeze."

"I'm beginning to understand that about you. I'm not

convinced it is a good personality trait, but it certainly appears to be useful." Dimity pushed her hair out of her face with a trembling hand.

Captain Niall deposited Dimity's basket, which he had carried in his mouth, next to her and barked imperiously. He then tilted forward over one foreleg in a lupine bow.

Sophronia and Monique curtsied politely, and Dimity nodded from her seated position. Then he was away, jumping down to the moor below.

"Isn't he joining us?" Sophronia was confused.

"Oh, he doesn't *live* at the school. He's a *werewolf*. They don't float. Didn't you know?"

Sophronia, who did not know, felt unjustly chastised. And also strangely bereft. Now that she knew what Captain Niall had been hiding with his bare feet and oddities of dress, she rather liked the man. He might have made for an ally of sorts.

Still, she had Dimity.

As if in reply to this thought, Dimity grinned at her. "I'm glad you're with me. I was so nervous about coming in alone. Everyone will know one another already."

Sophronia crouched down and squeezed her friend's hand. She was glad she had crouched, for with very little warning, the platform rocked from side to side and began to rise toward the airship above.

Monique gave a squeak of alarm as the jolt almost tumbled her over the edge. Acting as if it were all her idea, she also sat.

The platform picked up speed until it was racing along briskly. The underside of the airship looked to be of solid wood and metal construction. *Our skulls would definitely not win any kind of encounter with it!* Sophronia resisted the urge to raise her arms above her head to shield herself. Monique was sitting, unflinching, and Sophronia wasn't about to give the girl any more ammunition.

She and Dimity exchanged terrified glances.

At the very last minute, a hatch snapped open directly above them and they sped inside the ship, out of the freezing evening air and into warm darkness.

The platform stopped. The hatch snapped shut behind them. All was black. After the violence of the wind, the sudden stillness was overwhelming.

Sophronia's eyes adjusted quickly. They were in a large, cavernous room, like a barn, with beams and supports indecently exposed all around them. It was curved, however, like the inside of a very large rowboat.

They heard the chattering first: amiable but argumentative female voices. Then across from them, a door opened, and a beam of yellow light spiked through. Three silhouetted figures entered, one after another, all garbed in the voluminous dress of a modest upper-class Englishwoman. The first was of medium size and medium build, with a halo of blonde curls; then came a tall woman; and lastly a short, dumpy female.

Miss Medium held a lamp and was by far the best looking, although this fact was well-hidden under a quantity of face paint that might embarrass even an opera dancer.

Dimity was charmed. "Look at her cheek rouge!"

"Her what?" Sophronia was shocked. One ordinarily didn't

expect such an application of powder, except from women of ill repute. *What kind of finishing school has a lady of the night on staff?*

"Rouge—the red stuff on her cheeks."

"Oh! I thought that was jam."

"Oh, really!" Dimity tittered obligingly.

The short, dumpy female was wearing a religious habit of some approximation. The robes had been cut and pinned into a facsimile of modern dress, full skirts, ruffles, and all. Over her head she wore a hat that was part lace floof, part wimple.

Miss Tall was the only one of the three who actually looked the part of a teacher. Sophronia adjusted her assessment from merely "tall" to "impossibly angular." *Like a human hatstand.* This woman was severely dressed, with a face that might have been pretty if all the lines resulted from smiling rather than frowning. As it was, she looked like a stoat with gastric problems.

Monique stepped down off the platform and approached the three women. "You said it was a simple retrieval operation. No danger!" She was not speaking in the manner of a student to her superiors.

The nun said, "Now, dear, please don't carry on."

"'No difficulty finishing, Monique.' That's what you said!"

"Well, dear, it *was* your exam."

"It's a very good thing that I can keep a cool head in a crisis! We were attacked by flywaymen! I had to take *measures* to get us out of there safely."

"Explain," barked the tall one. Her accent was French in a way that suggested it was not fake. "And take off that ridiculous wig."

"The coachman was incapacitated, and those two panicked." Monique removed her wig, revealing that she was a blonde, and gestured with it at Sophronia and Dimity. "I had to take charge of the carriage and enact a daring escape. Unfortunately, we had to leave our belongings behind."

Sophronia was flabbergasted by this parade of outright lies. Monique definitely had some kind of secondary agenda. *What's going on here?*

Dimity said, "Oh, I say! That's not *at all* what happened."

"Those two made consistent errors in judgment and protocol. They even fainted at the *wrong* moments. They're entirely at odds with me. I can't think why. I've been perfectly civil to them the entire time. I believe that they want to take all the credit for *my* intelligent actions. They clearly don't want me to finish!"

"What?" said Sophronia, so shocked she was moved to speak.

"Look at her, all innocence! She's the crafty one. I'd watch her if I were you."

"She's lying," said Sophronia flatly; there was no other response possible.

The painted woman interrupted. "The particulars matter not at this juncture. The question is, Miss Pelouse, do you have *it*?"

Monique gestured to her torn dress. "Of course I don't have it! I'm not so idiotic as to keep it on my person. As soon as I realized what it was, and that you'd given me a dangerous finish, I secreted it away in a private location."

Sophronia understood the undercurrent of that statement. *She expected us to be attacked by flywaymen all along.*

The bony female craned her neck forward and hissed, "Where?"

Sophronia frowned, trying to remember a time when Monique might have hidden something.

Monique shook her head. "Oh, no. When I'm properly finished, then I'll tell you."

The Frenchwoman stepped forward to loom over the girl. "You manipulative baggage, I ought to—"

The dumpy nun put a hand on her arm.

"Now, Beatrice, don't fuss. We have new girls here, don't forget."

Beatrice glanced at Sophronia and Dimity, and then snorted.

Gosh, thought Sophronia, *the French are every bit as rude as Mumsy always said they were.*

The painted woman said, "Beatrice, take Miss Pelouse away and see if you can't come to an arrangement."

Monique looked militant. "I'll summon reinforcements if I have to."

"Are you threatening me, girl? We shall see about that." The Frenchwoman did not look cowed.

Sophronia shuddered—she wouldn't want to be alone with either of them for any length of time.

She heard Miss Tall say, as the two walked away, "Properly finish, my dear? What makes you think there is any way for you to finish at all, now?"

Sophronia decided to forget Monique for the time being.

"Well, it certainly appears that you two have had a very exciting journey," said the nun.

"We didn't faint!" protested Dimity. "Or, rather, Sophronia

didn't faint. I did, but only after *we* rescued Monique from the flywaymen! She told it all backward!"

"Do you have witnesses?"

"Well, my brother was there."

The teachers exchanged looks. Apparently Pillover's reliability was questionable. "A boy? I don't know."

"And there was the coachman." Dimity would not let the matter rest.

"He was insensible for most of the event," Sophronia pointed out.

"You're a funny one, aren't you?" The painted lady looked at Sophronia closely. "Why aren't you defending yourself?"

Sophronia shrugged. "I have sisters. I know how this works."

"Do you indeed?"

Sophronia said nothing else. Monique was covering up her trail as well as self-aggrandizing her own actions. Perhaps she'd given the prototype away to someone else beforehand. Sophronia intended to find out. What was the prototype, and where was it, and why did everyone want it so badly? *Some new kind of device for producing tea inexpensively?* In the Temminnick household, nothing was valued more than good quality tea.

Dimity opened her mouth to protest further, but Sophronia elbowed her in the ribs.

The painted lady said, "Shall we get on with official business? Where was I?"

The nun whispered something in her ear.

"Yes, of course! Welcome to Mademoiselle Geraldine's Finishing Academy for Young Ladies of Quality. I understand one of you is a covert recruit?"

Sophronia raised a tentative hand.

"Welcome, welcome! I'm Lady Linette de Limmone. I'll be instructing you in music and several of the finer creative arts. This is Sister Herschel-Teape. She's head of household management. And you are?"

"Sophronia Angelina Temminnick," said Sophronia with a curtsy.

"Oh, dear," said Lady Linette. "We are going to have to work on that curtsy."

"Dimity Ann Plumleigh-Teignmott," said Dimity, with a better curtsy.

I must ask her to teach me the way of it. It seems a powerful weapon, thought Sophronia.

"Ah, yes, Miss Plumleigh-Teignmott, we have been expecting you. Sister, if you would kindly get Miss Plumleigh-Teignmott settled. She knows everything already. Miss Temminnick, you're with me, please."

Dimity squeezed Sophronia's hand. "Good luck." She followed the dumpy nun out of the cavernous room.

The painted woman raised the lantern and looked Sophronia over.

"Well, well, let me see. You're...how old, girl?"

"Fourteen, my lady." Sophronia couldn't believe that a woman with that much face paint was a *real* lady. Mrs. Barnaclegoose had a teacup poodle named Lord Piffle; perhaps Lady Linette's was a similarly spurious title?

"Good bones, average height. I suppose there's no hope of your growing into that chin?" Sophronia said nothing. "No? I thought not. Eyes, indifferent. Hair"—she tsked—"you'll be wearing curling rags the rest of your natural life, poor thing. The freckles. Well. The freckles. I'll have cook order extra buttermilk. But you are confident. Shoulders back, girl, when you're facing inspection. Confident is something we can work with. And Captain Niall likes you."

Sophronia withstood the criticism with only a slight frown. She put her shoulders back as ordered. What she wanted to do was comment on Lady Linette's appearance. So far as Sophronia was concerned, the woman's hair was too curly and her skin too white, and she smelled overwhelmingly of elderflowers. *I wager she wouldn't like it if I told her that to her face!*

What she said instead was, "How do you know what the captain thinks of me?"

"If he didn't think you'd suit, he wouldn't have jumped you up. He has very good judgment, for a, well..." She paused, as though hunting for the right word.

"Werewolf?" suggested Sophronia.

"Oh, no. For a *man*. Now, child, come along. We have much to do, and it is getting late. I suppose you're famished, and, of course, we'll need to settle your luggage and such."

"No luggage, my lady."

"What?"

"Had to leave it behind with the flywaymen."

"You did? Oh, yes, you did, didn't you? How tiresome."

"When I was driving the carriage."

"When *you* were driving the carriage? I thought Miss Pelouse said..." A short pause. "Where was Miss Pelouse during all of this?"

"Well, either fainted in the road or crying in the carriage, depending on which point of the story." *All of it faked, if you ask me.* But something kept Sophronia from volunteering that information.

"Interesting. Well, Beatrice will sort it all out."

"What does she teach?"

"Worried, are you? You should be. Professor Lefoux takes a firm hand. Although she's too fearsome for the debuts. You won't have her until later. If you stay, that is."

Sophronia noticed that Lady Linette had neatly avoided answering the question. *What is Professor Lefoux's subject? I still don't know.*

"Now, dear, we must press on. Do follow me."

They emerged from the darkness of a passageway into the open air of one of the main decks—a wide semicircle of rough timber planks.

The school had floated quite high since Captain Niall had jumped them on board. It no longer bobbed through the low mists of the moor, but was instead well above them. Below now lay a mass of white cloud tops, and above was the starry night. Sophronia had never thought to see the other side of clouds. They looked as solid as a feather mattress. She clung to the rail, staring down, hypnotized.

"Amazing," she breathed.

"Yes, dear. I assure you, you'll become quite accustomed to it. I am pleased to see you are not afraid of heights."

Sophronia grinned. "No, never that. Ask the dumbwaiter."

And that was when the maid mechanical ran straight into her. It was a standard domestic model. Looking down at her feet, Sophronia noticed that the deck was inlaid with multiple tracks. However, like the porter mechanical at Bunson's, this one had no face, but only inner moving parts, completely visible to the outside world. It also had no voice, for even after it bumped into her and stopped, confused in its protocols, it neither apologized nor asked Sophronia to move.

Lady Linette said, "Really, dear, do get out of its way."

Sophronia did so, watching with interest as the maid trundled on to the other side of the deck, where a hatch opened and it disappeared inside.

"What was that?"

"A maid mechanical, dear. I know you're from the country, but surely your family cannot be so backward as that!"

"No, of course not. My family has a butler, an 1846 Frowbritcher. But why doesn't yours have a proper face?"

"Because it doesn't need one."

Sophronia was a little embarrassed, but it had to be said: "But her *parts* are exposed!"

"Mmm, yes, shocking. But you had best get accustomed to the style. Very few of our mechanicals are standard household models."

They wended their way up several sets of stairs, into and out of long corridors, and over other decks—some of wood, a few of metal, and one that seemed, most illogically, to be made of stone. Sophronia had boarded the airship under the back section of the long dirigible caterpillar, and they now were crossing through its center.

The interior decoration looked much as Sophronia imagined one of the great Atlantic steamers, except that the entire place seemed to have been attacked by a grandmother—the kind of grandmother who knitted horrible small booties for workhouse orphans and made jelly for the deserving poor. Railings and finials supported crocheted antimacassars in mauve and chartreuse. A medieval suit of armor in the corner of one corridor was decorated liberally with ribbon flowers. Sophronia paused to examine it, only to find tiny mechanical devices hidden within the flowers. Suddenly, the outrageous chandeliers at each junction took on sinister aspects. *Are those glass baubles decorative or deadly? They are rather knifelike. Can one call a chandelier sinister?*

"The back end of the school grounds," explained Lady Linette, "is for group and recreational activities. That is where we take meals and regular exercise. The middle section is comprised of student residences and classrooms, and the front is for teachers and staff. That is where we are heading now."

"Uh, why?" Sophronia wanted to know.

"To meet Mademoiselle Geraldine, of course."

"The real one this time?" asked Sophronia, a little snidely. And then, when her stomach rumbled, she added, "Will there be food?"

Lady Linette seemed to find this funny.

Sophronia couldn't understand Lady Linette. She had a French name, yet her accent was English. Sophronia thought she detected a certain burr that suggested the north country, or possibly the East End.

"Now, be certain to remember which way we are going, Sophronia. It is easy to get lost. The school grounds are rather convoluted. The most important thing to note is that you must be on a middle level or higher to get between sections. Very high up, however, is not recommended. Once you get to the squeak decks, the way between the sections is not suited to proper attire. Ah, here we are. You see this red tassel here? It marks the teachers' section. You are not permitted to roam anywhere freely at night, and during lesson time you are restricted to certain areas. However, you can *never* enter the tassel section without an adult escort."

Sophronia nodded. She wondered *how* the restrictions were enforced. Which was the moment she realized she was intrigued enough to give this abnormal finishing school an opportunity to prove itself worthwhile.

"Very well, Miss Temminnick. Tell me a little about yourself. Are you well-educated?"

Sophronia considered this question seriously. "I don't believe so."

"Excellent. Ignorance is most undervalued in a student. And have you killed anyone recently?"

Sophronia blinked. "Pardon?"

"Oh, you know, a knife to the neck, or perhaps a cleverly noosed cravat?"

Sophronia said only, "Not my preferred diversion."

"Oh, dear, how disappointing. Well, don't you fret. We shall soon find you some useful hobby."

Lady Linette stopped in front of a fancy-looking door decorated in gilt and navy leather and boasting a particularly large number of tassels. She knocked sharply.

"Come in, do!"

Lady Linette motioned for Sophronia to wait, then went inside alone, closing the door behind her.

After determining that she couldn't overhear anything through the door, Sophronia nosed about the hallway. The lighting was fascinating. Gas pipes were inset into the wall, and little lamps hung all along the ceiling like so many tiny parasols. It must be expensive, not to mention dangerous, to run gas through walls. Essentially, every corridor they walked along was liable to explode.

Sophronia was near the end of the passage, up on tiptoe to examine one of the parasol-shaped lights, when another maid mechanical came trundling down the hallway. It carried a tray laden with tea and companion comestibles. However, upon sensing Sophronia, it paused and let out a little whistle of inquiry.

When Sophronia did not respond, it whistled again, imperiously.

Sophronia had no idea what to do. The mechanical was between her and the gilt door. *No Lady Linette to come to the rescue.*

The whistle turned into a very loud shriek, like that of a boatman, and Sophronia guessed that this was how restrictions were enforced.

Halfway down the hallway, a door banged open and a gentleman emerged. He was improbably mediocre in size, shape, and looks. His nondescript features were only emphasized by the addition of a fantastic crimson velvet top hat. The face under the hat, Sophronia saw, did not look at all pleased.

Never Hurl Garlic Mash at a Man with a Crossbow

Whot, whot?" the man muttered, as if hard of hearing. He was very pale and boasted an unassuming mustache, which was perched atop his upper lip cautiously, as though it were slightly embarrassed to be there and would like to slide away and become a sideburn or something more fashionable. He wore a pair of spectacles and squinted through them at Sophronia.

"Who goes there?" He had a funny way of talking around his teeth. *As if they pose an inconvenience.*

"Sorry to disturb you, sir," said Sophronia.

"What's that infernal racket? Maid!" He glared at the mechanical barring Sophronia's path. "Stop that immediately."

The mechanical continued to shriek.

"Maid," yelled the man, "this is Professor Braithwope! End alarm protocol gamma six my eye is pickled and the earthworm sulks at midnight, resume previous path."

The alarm stopped and the maid twirled away from Sophronia, swiveling on its tracks as though built entirely of ball bearings. It sped down the corridor.

The man left the confines of his doorway, passed by the maid, and came to glower at Sophronia. "What are you doing in this section of the grounds? No students allowed."

"But sir, Lady Linette brought me."

"Whot, whot? Well, where is she?" The mustache quivered in annoyance.

"She's in that room."

"Whot?"

"That one there. The one with extra tassels." As she pointed, the mechanical bumped authoritatively at that very door with the laden tray.

Lady Linette opened it and admitted the maid, plus comestibles. Then she looked around, blonde curls bouncing. "Miss Temminnick, what are you doing all the way down there? Was it you who alarmed the mechanical? I did warn you. Oh, Professor, I *am* sorry we disturbed you."

"Ah, no trouble. No trouble. I was stirring anyway, whot."

"This is a new student, Miss Temminnick. Covert recruit."

"Indeed?"

"Yes. Isn't that lovely? We haven't had one of those in years."

"Six, to be precise."

"As you always are, Professor. My dear, the professor here will be teaching you history, deportment, manners, etiquette, and genteel dress."

Which was when Sophronia finally tore her eyes away from the mustache and noticed that the man was indeed cutting quite the fitted dash, as Petunia might say. In addition to the hat, he was wearing the very latest in evening attire, as if he were about to attend a theatrical performance in one of London's finer theaters. Sophronia found this odd, as there couldn't possibly be any practical reason for such garb on board an airship. But she supposed one had to commend the effort. *Unless one regularly wears evening garb to finishing lessons?*

The professor said, "And I also teach coping with—"

Lady Linette interrupted him with a sharp shake of the head.

He coughed rather than finish his sentence. "Ah, covert recruit, ease them in slowly, whot? I suppose you've already met Niall?"

Sophronia nodded. "Yes, sir."

"Rest of it later, eh?"

"Miss Temminnick, do come along!" Lady Linette said.

"Nice to meet you, Professor."

"Likewise, Miss Temminnick. Covert recruit, remarkable. Well, carry on." With which the man slid smoothly back into his room.

Lady Linette placed one hand on the gold and lapis handle of the gilt door and paused, giving Sophronia a very odd look. Sophronia supposed she meant it to be significant and sultry; however, she looked as though she had a mild case of indigestion.

"Now remember, dear, discernment and discretion are of the utmost importance here. I shall be watching you carefully. You wouldn't want us to think we had made a mistake in our selection process, now, would you?" Sophronia rather thought that was a tad caustic. *After all, I didn't ask to come here!*

Still, Sophronia nodded, to indicate she was willing to try, and followed Lady Linette through the gilt door and into... paradise.

Behind the excessive tassels was a private suite of the kind one might find in any upscale boardinghouse. The peculiar, and wondrous, thing was that the walls were lined with shelves. On those shelves were sweets of all shapes and sizes: stacks of petits fours, bonbons, trifles, iced cakes, custards, and any and all other confections that one might desire. Sophronia gaped.

"Beautiful, aren't they?" said a voice.

"Are they... are they *real?*"

The voice laughed. "No, but they look real, don't they? Little hobby of mine." An older female approached. She had rinsed red hair, friendly dark eyes, and a generous mouth. However, one was not prone to noticing any of the aforementioned features *first.* Oh, no, what was initially striking about the woman was the fact that she was endowed in a manner that suggested operatic tendencies. Sophronia could think of no more delicate way of putting it—her corset was distinctly under stress.

The woman smiled. "Do you like them?"

It took Sophronia a moment to realize she was referring not to her endowments but to the fake pastries on display.

"They are very... realistic."

"But you would far rather taste than merely look? I understand. Would you take tea with me? I should dearly like to make your acquaintance. It has been so very long since the school took in an outsider."

"Six years," added Sophronia helpfully, figuring this was merely another way of saying covert recruit.

"Really, so long? How did you know?"

"Professor Braithwope told me."

"Have you met the professor? Such a *nice* man. Definitely *qualit-tay*. Well, Lady Linette, tell me about our newest addition. Is she qualit-tay?"

"I believe she may do. She has certain advantages."

"And a definite air of nobility. I like that! Oh, but dear me we're forgetting our manners already. I am Mademoiselle Geraldine."

"The real one?" asked Sophronia cautiously.

"Of course, child. Why shouldn't I be? As if anyone would want to impersonate me!"

"Oh, but—" Sophronia caught Lady Linette shaking her head slightly. *Oh, yes, discernment and discretion.* Sophronia switched topics mid-thought. "Pleased to meet you, Headmistress. I'm Sophronia Angelina Temminnick." She executed her subpar curtsy.

The headmistress blanched. "Oh, dear, we will have to do something about *that*. I'll be teaching you dance and toilette and apparel selections. How are your steps?"

Sophronia had only had one dance instructor. He'd been hired for all the Temminnick girls, but spent most of his time with the eldest. This had led to the hasty dismissal of said dance instructor. As a result, Sophronia managed to escape the protracted torture of quadrilles. "Absent, I'm afraid, Headmistress."

"Good! That's very good. I much prefer a fresh palate. Nothing to unlearn. Now, sit down, do. Have some tea."

Sophronia sat, and after a moment's hesitation, began stuffing her face with the little cakes and sandwiches arrayed before her. These proved to be real. And delicious. *Now, if finishing school is full of tea cakes, I could certainly grow to love it.*

"Well," said the headmistress to Lady Linette, watching Sophronia eat with ill-disguised horror, "we have our work cut out for us."

"Indeed we do."

Sophronia stopped chewing long enough to ask the one question that was still really bothering her. "What was the prototype of?"

Mademoiselle Geraldine looked deeply confused. "Prototype? Linette, what is the child talking about?"

Lady Linette gave Sophronia a fierce look, and then covered it up by toying with a curl. "I have no idea, Geraldine, no idea at all. You know these modern girls—they will have their little joke."

Oh, dear, thought Sophronia, *I might be failing Lady Linette's discernment and discretion mandate already. Exactly how much am I supposed to be concealing from the headmistress?*

"Ah, Linette, sometimes I feel as though I know nothing of what is going on with young persons these days. They seem to talk in cipher. Don't you find?"

"Indubitably, Geraldine."

Sophronia, for lack of any other option, gave a huge, guileless smile and stuffed her face with more tea cake.

A knock came at the door. It swung open, and Professor Braithwope's unstable mustache, followed by its unassuming owner, trotted in.

"Do pardon me, ladies, but Lady Linette, something musically related has come up. It requires your immediate attention."

Lady Linette stood. "You'd better come with me, Miss Temminnick."

Sophronia grabbed a handful of finger sandwiches. "Thank you for the tea, Headmistress. It was most illuminating."

"Very prettily said, my dear. At least we know we won't have any trouble with your elocution. No, dear, don't curtsy. I couldn't bear it—not twice in one night." With that, the head-mistress turned back to her tea. Sophronia surmised that they had been dismissed.

Lady Linette hustled her and Professor Braithwope out into the corridor. "What could possibly be so important, Professor?"

"The aetheric long-scan monocular sensors are picking something up. Possibly adversaries."

Sophronia said, "She doesn't know, does she?"

"Who doesn't know what?" Lady Linette's attention swiveled. *Discernment and discretion, indeed!* "The headmistress doesn't know what's really going on here."

"Oh, and what is that?"

"I haven't quite figured out the particulars myself, but you're keeping her in the dark intentionally, aren't you?"

"No, dear, *you're* keeping her in the dark intentionally. You students. It's part of the training."

"You're keeping me in the dark, too. Am I supposed to figure something out? Is this a test?"

"Lady Linette," interrupted the professor, "we really haven't the time."

"Oh, yes, lead on, do. To the squeak deck."

"Whot-ho."

"I suppose you'd better follow, Miss Temminnick. Can't have

you gallivanting about the tassel section on your own. The mechanicals are already overwrought."

They moved through a series of corridors. Professor Braithwope led the way with a kind of controlled speed that hinted at a truly heightened fitness level under those fancy clothes—he must be a sportsman. *Cricket, perhaps?* Exiting onto one of the observation decks, he veered off and felt around the back of a railing. There must have been a lever hidden there, for a secret door snapped down, revealing a set of stairs. The three of them climbed up. These stairs were not lit by gas, and there were no windows. It was only the regularity of the steps that kept Sophronia from stumbling.

Eventually, they emerged out onto one of the very top decks, directly under one of the three colossal balloons. This deck was a full circle, stretching from one side of the ship to the other. It was like being on a rooftop. Looking down over one of the railings, Sophronia could see various other sets of decks bulging out, like enormous semicircular steps leading down into cloudy nothingness. Looking across, she could see there were two other decks just like hers, one under each of the other two massive balloons. Out the far back of the ship was a crow's nest, raised up to be almost touching the underside of the last balloon. Turning about, she saw that at the front, near them, was another crow's nest. This one was enclosed. It looked like a bathtub overturned on top of another bathtub. There was no apparent means of access, as the only thing holding it up was a set of struts and one long beam.

She pointed. "What's that?"

"Pilot's bubble," Lady Linette answered from behind one of the several telescopes that dotted the edge of the deck.

Professor Braithwope merely stood, squinting, into the night sky. His mustache quivered, due either to the slight breeze or to agitation—it was difficult to tell which.

"How does it land?" Sophronia wanted to know.

"What?" Lady Linette was distracted.

"The school, how does it land?"

"It doesn't, dear. Not all the way. Mostly, we drift," replied Lady Linette.

"Then why do you need a pilot?"

Professor Braithwope turned piercing eyes upon her. "You ask a lot of questions, little bite."

"Well, Professor, sir, you are providing me with a number of curiosities."

He returned to scanning the skies. Suddenly he pointed. "There!"

Lady Linette swiveled her telescope around, following his pointing finger. "Ah, yes, I see. Oh, dear. Flywaymen."

"A direct attack? I hardly think that likely, whot?"

"Nevertheless, best warn the engine chamber. Have them wake up all the sooties."

"Of course." The professor straightened the shoulders of his fine-cut tails, touched the brim of his top hat at the two ladies, and was off. Instead of going down, as Sophronia assumed one would in order to contact an engine room, he did the most extraordinary thing. He ran up the beam to the pilot's bubble. He did it with perfect balance and complete fearlessness, despite the wind and the ground far below. He did it so quickly, like a spider, that Sophronia wondered if she'd really seen it at all.

"Can he teach me to do that?" she asked Lady Linette.

"I'm afraid not, dear. That is a skill that has taken him more time to master than you have."

That only caused Sophronia to look militant. *I wager he was in the circus.* But there was no time to argue, for the professor had already returned. His attention was distracted by a group of six airdinghies heading purposefully in their direction.

Lady Linette said, "Best to sound the alarm."

Professor Braithwope nodded and did his rapid scuttle over to a small brass box affixed to a railing. He opened this with a key from his waistcoat pocket, reached inside, and toggled something. A loud bell began clanging—a bell that seemed to have sister bells throughout the ship.

Lady Linette said, "When you hear that in future, Miss Temminnick, it means deck access is restricted and all students are to remain stationary and *not involve themselves.*"

Sophronia didn't say anything in response to that. In all her fourteen long years, she had never stayed stationary and uninvolved in anything. Nevertheless, she did end up following her new teacher's orders this once, for the squeak deck became suddenly covered in mechanicals. Sophronia was hard put to find a spot safe from being bumped.

In a synchronized movement, the mechanicals all settled back onto their rear wheels, locking down to the deck with a clunk, and altered *themselves.* Like the porter at the boy's school, these had open hatches in their chests, only much bigger ones, so that their whole upper torsos were sliding back. Each hatch ejected the barrel of what appeared to be a small cannon. Then, in one smooth motion, they all swiveled and pointed their little cannons at...Professor Braithwope. *Goodness*, thought Sophronia, *what did he do that was so bad?*

"Soldier mechanicals?" asked Sophronia of the air. At which juncture she noticed that the professor had a tiny crossbow in his hands. The bow was armed but pointing harmlessly down at the deck.

"Wait for it, Professor. We are an institution of high learning and higher manners. We simply cannot shoot first; it isn't done. Now, remember that, Miss Temminnick, do—a lady never shoots first. She asks questions, *then* she shoots."

"Yes, Lady Linette, I'll remember," said Sophronia, riveted.

The fleet of airdinghies was now near enough for Sophronia to make out figures in the carrier baskets. They were dressed as their compatriots had been earlier that day, in goggles and riding outfits. There was one odd man out, however. In the airdinghy farthest to the left. Standing at the back, in the manner of an usher at the theater, was a *gentleman*. Sophronia couldn't make out his features, but he was dressed in black with a stovepipe hat. His cravat was green, as was the band about his top hat. Despite his upper-crust dress, he remained in the background.

"Why aren't you firing, Professor Braithwope?" A French-accented and imperious question came from Sophronia's right. Professor Lefoux appeared out of a nearby hatch, all angles and disapproval.

"No just cause," explained Lady Linette.

"But those are criminals out there. Flywaymen. We need no other cause."

"Patience, Beatrice. We must understand what they want of us."

"We know what they want! They want the prototype!"

"Did you get the location out of Monique?"

"No, she's closed-lipped, that one. *Some* of our lessons she learned well."

"So?"

"So I punted her down to debut status. We shall see if the boredom of relearning everything with the new girls loosens her tongue." Sophronia did not like the sound of that. It meant Monique would be in all her classes!

One of the flywaymen hoisted something to the edge of his dinghy.

Professor Braithwope tensed and pointed the crossbow toward the activity.

"Not yet," said Lady Linette.

The flywaymen's object made a loud *sput* and fired. A white mass hurtled toward them and landed with a *splat* against the side of the deck near Professor Braithwope.

The professor began to cough and fan the front of his face frantically while backing away at the same time. He was wheezing and his eyes were tearing up.

The ladies, however, did not seem to feel any ill effects. Professor Lefoux approached and bent over to examine the white substance.

"Garlic mash," she said, without emotion.

"That's simply petty!" said Lady Linette. "Are you handling the exposure well enough, Professor?"

He sneezed at her.

Professor Lefoux occupied herself with kicking the mashed garlic into a pile and then covering it over with a handkerchief.

Through his wheezing, Professor Braithwope said, "Now can I target them?" His tiny crossbow was up. All the while, the mechanicals' little cannons remained trained on him. The mechanicals, at least, considered him the greatest threat. *Must be the mustache*, thought Sophronia.

"No, no. That was only a warning shot, meant to discombobulate."

"Whot? Warning, you say? *Achoo!* Well, it worked." Professor Braithwope rubbed at his eyes with his free hand.

Sophronia watched in fascination as one of the airdinghies hoisted a white flag on the end of a mop and approached even closer. The small airship wafted one direction and then the next, as if confused.

"They want to parley?" Professor Lefoux was incredulous.

"Let them. We shall see what they have to say."

When the dinghy was only a few lengths away, the flywaymen inside mounted a catapult onto the carrier basket edge and hurled something else at the squeak deck.

It landed with a clatter and rolled across the planks, coming to rest against the base of one of the mechanicals. The object unfurled, revealing that it was also a mechanical, only much smaller than the ones standing guard. It was not human-looking at all, nor any attempt at human-looking. It had four legs—four very short legs—and a small, spiky tail. Steam emanated slightly from its underbelly, and smoke came out from under its leather earflaps. It looked a little like one of those sausage dogs the Germans were so fond of.

"Mechanimal!" yelled Lady Linette. "Everybody hide!"

Sophronia took refuge behind one of the defensive mechanicals, as did the two female teachers. Professor Braithwope did not obey the command. He stood firm. His sneezing subsided and his crossbow remained trained on the airdinghy.

The sausage dog didn't seem to understand the fear it caused. It trotted hopefully up to Professor Braithwope, mechanical tail wagging back and forth in perfect clockwork rhythm—ticktock, tick-tock.

Upon reaching the professor, the mechanimal stopped, and then—Sophronia blushed—it squatted down and emitted a tube of glass out its backside.

Professor Braithwope stared and then bent down, retrieved the tube, and stood, all without relaxing his arm. He was clearly unwilling to let go of the crossbow, so he pulled the cork stopper out of the tube with his teeth. The stopper caught and stuck on one of them, but he didn't notice. Inside the tube was a tiny roll of paper with a printed message.

Deciding there was no apparent danger from the mechanimal, the two lady teachers reemerged.

"Well," demanded Lady Linette, "what does it say?"

Professor Braithwope began to read, but his words were garbled by the cork. "Ith sayth thath—"

"Professor, you have something stuck on your fang," hissed Lady Linette, clearly embarrassed for the man.

"Whoth? Whoth?"

Professor Lefoux reached forward and tugged off the offending cork.

Professor Braithwope read out, "It says that they want the prototype. They are giving us three weeks to produce it, after which they will return with reinforcements."

"Absurd! What kind of reinforcements could flywaymen possibly have?" Professor Lefoux blustered.

Lady Linette was not so dismissive. "If they were being paid enough..."

"You think the Picklemen are behind this, whot?" Professor Braithwope swirled the little note between his long white fingers.

"Who else?" said Professor Lefoux, and then she added, "On the positive end of things, if they are threatening us, it means they haven't got it. No one's got it. Wherever Monique hid it, she hid it from everyone."

"Trained her too well, whot?" Professor Braithwope let out a self-deprecating chuckle.

"Little pitchers have big ears," said Lady Linette, nodding to where Sophronia still skulked behind a mechanical.

Sophronia came out, wondering what was required of her. Nothing, apparently, as the adults went back to ignoring her. She remained wildly curious about the prototype, but unfortunately, nothing else about it was mentioned.

Professor Braithwope waved the message at the flywaymen in the airdinghy nearest them and then doffed his hat with a free thumb.

Taking this as a dismissal, the whole parade of tiny airships turned and drifted lazily away.

"Three weeks," muttered Lady Linette. "Suggested course of action?"

"Leave the real one be for now; the girl's clearly hidden it well enough, whot?"

"We might provide them with a temporary surrogate," suggested Professor Lefoux.

"That *is* a good idea. Do you think you could?" Lady Linette turned to her compatriot.

"I don't see why not. I have old sketches of a previous model."

"Capital. Put some of the older girls on to it, too, do them good, whot? Then we can ask Bunson's to put the beastie together." Professor Braithwope nodded, smiling a tight-lipped smile. He handed Lady Linette the tube and message and disarmed the dart from his little crossbow. The defensive mechanicals all around them instantly lowered their cannons and closed the hatches in their chests.

Professor Braithwope returned to the brass box, opened it, and switched the lever inside. With a whir of gears, the mechanicals all trundled away. He then returned to Professor Lefoux's side and offered her his arm. "What initial material approach do you think best?"

"Well, I suspect magnetized steel might be the most emulatory. Copper could also work. We should get the furnace heated immediately."

"Steel, whot? Capital idea. Capital."

The two moved toward the exit hatch, Professor Lefoux looming over her diminutive male escort. Sophronia watched them go in bemusement.

"Well, that was rather a plump. I do apologize, Miss Temminnick. I assure you things aren't generally this much—well, *much*. If you'd like to follow me, I'll see you settled." Lady Linette dismissed the whole occurrence with a little toss of her head.

Sophronia hesitated, and then—because everyone seemed to have forgotten him and he looked so forlorn—she scooped up the sausage dog mechanimal and hid him in her large pinafore pocket. Then she trailed after her new teacher.

Music teacher, she thought, looking at the full skirts of Lady Linette's lavender dress. *And I'm Queen of the Vampires.*

Of course, the next day, when it finally came time for lessons, Sophronia was to find Lady Linette sitting at a pianoforte, playing scales.

LESSON 6

The Real Meaning of Finishing

"Miss Temminnick, you share this parlor with the other debuts. Now, ladies," Lady Linette said, looking at the four girls before her, "this is Miss Temminnick. I'm certain you will make her welcome. She is now ready to learn more about our educational institution." With that, Lady Linette whirled away to devote her time to more pressing matters.

Sophronia stood awkwardly in the center of the room. Most of the girls before her were younger than she, and all of them were better dressed. For the first time, she actually felt a twinge of concern about the modishness of her attire. Critical sisters were one thing, but these young ladies were elegant, with opinions more important than those of mere sisters. She reached inside her pinafore pocket and produced the little sausage dog.

"Is that all you brought with you? A mechanimal?" This was said by a mocking voice with clipped elocution, as if each word were being prematurely assassinated.

The girl behind the voice was tiny, with a mass of tightly curled black hair and a heart-shaped face set in a morose expression. She was, unfortunately, beautiful. Sophronia's only consolation was that the girl had a decidedly *low* nose. Sitting next to her was a wholesome redhead with freckles quite beyond Sophronia's own—somewhat of a relief, that—who glanced with shy interest at the mechanimal and then focused her attention on her own shoes. Next to her sat Dimity. The last girl, who was not seated, was an angular, mannish creature, her posture slouched and her dress ill-fitting. She was occupied in chewing on a stick and sneering at them all from the far corner of the room.

"Sophronia! Where did you get that?" Dimity bounced to her feet and came dashing up to exclaim over the mechanimal. She had changed clothing, presumably having borrowed a dress. She'd kept on her garish jewelry, however, and found a gown of sea green that strained to balloon over her many petticoats.

"I happened upon him during a recent excursion to a squeak deck. I thought I'd call him Bumbersnoot."

"Goodness me, why?" Dimity patted the metal dog on the top of his head with two fingers, not convinced. Bumbersnoot puffed out some smoke, flapping his little leather ears. Dimity started back.

"Why not?" Sophronia looked over at the pretty girl with the mocking voice. "And, unfortunately, he is indeed all I have with me. We had a bit of an upset with the luggage on our way in."

"Which I told you *all about*," said Monique de Pelouse,

appearing in the room from one of the bedchambers. The room was set up like a proper drawing room, most unlike what Sophronia expected in a school.

Dimity looked like she'd swallowed something sour. Apparently Monique was still lying about the rescue.

"Oh, yes, indeed you did, Miss Pelouse," said the pretty one with the mocking voice. "So exciting."

"We aren't allowed personal mechanicals." Monique tilted her blonde head, eyes narrowing. Sophronia noticed her hair was now up and styled, and that without the wig and face paint she was quite beautiful, if a little aristocratically horsey. *Too many teeth.*

Sophronia put down Bumbersnoot, who began trotting around the room curiously. She walked over to the blonde girl, sidling in close. Monique looked uncomfortable with the proximity. "How about a bargain, Monique? You refrain from telling anyone important about Bumbersnoot, and I won't make a fuss about your rewriting history."

Monique's eyes narrowed, but she said, "Very well," with ill humor.

That was rather easier than I thought it would be. "Very gracious, Monique," said Sophronia politely.

"This is all your fault, you know. My being here, demoted, living with the *debuts!*" Monique said the word like it was something smelly.

"Very logical. All I did was rescue you. Are you suggesting Dimity and I should have left you to rot with the flywaymen? I'm sure that could still be arranged." Sophronia turned away.

The other girls had been distracted by Sophronia's new pet.

Bumbersnoot was cavorting about, puffing steam and bumping into furniture and shoes in a most buffoonish manner. His tail wagged the whole time with tick-tock precision.

"May we keep him?" asked the clipped-voice girl hopefully. They all turned to look at Monique.

"If we must." Monique, after a brief hesitation, no doubt unhappy that she must socialize with girls so far beneath her, took a seat. *But she's pleased enough to be the one to make all final decisions by right of age.* Sophronia was pretty certain she should try to nip that tendency in the bud.

She turned to Dimity, mystified. "Who *are* these ladies?"

Dimity blushed. "Ah, yes. Oh, dear. Introductions. Let me see if I can remember. I only recently became acquainted myself. You already know Monique; she's the oldest—which I guess gives her some status. But precedence, who has precedence?"

The young ladies looked about at one another, and then, as one, gestured to the tall girl in the far corner.

Speaking as though the words pained her, the pretty brunette said, "Sidheag, if you would believe it. She's a proper lady. Laird or something like."

Sidheag took a little more interest in the conversation once her name was mentioned. Not enough to move close—but her head came up. "Aye?"

"How do you do?" said Sophronia.

"Lady Bacon, this is Sophronia Angelica Tendency. Sophronia, this is Lady Bacon," Dimity struggled to say.

The girls all laughed.

The one called Sidheag said, in a profoundly Scottish accent,

"I'm Sidheag *Maccon*, Lady Kingair, by rights. But you can call me Sidheag; everyone else does."

"Sophronia *Angelina Temminnick*," said Sophronia, gently correcting Dimity.

Everyone laughed again.

"Oh, sorry." Dimity was mortified by her blunder.

"Perhaps if we skipped standards, this once, and introduced ourselves?" suggested Sophronia, trying to protect Dimity from further humiliation.

"Oh, I don't know about that! It isn't done," said the pretty one, looking with relish at Dimity. "I'd like to see her try the rest of us."

Lady Sidheag Maccon straightened up, revealing that she was a good deal taller than any girl of thirteen ought to be. She strode over to Sophronia. Her hair lay in a thick plait down her back. Her face was masculine in a way that no one would ever call attractive, but her eyes were a lovely tawny yellow color.

Sidheag turned those eyes, filled with flinty disregard, upon the pert brunette. "*That* is Preshea Buss. She thinks she's smarter than everyone, when really she's just meaner. As to ranking, forgive me, Preshea, but don't your parents engage in *trade*?"

Preshea made a face like a fish with a digestive complaint. "Daddy dabbles with the East India Company, thank you very much. That's *hardly* trade."

Sidheag turned to the redhead. "Agatha Woosmoss, daughter of the noted railroad baron." The chubby girl looked up quickly from her shoes, nodded, and then returned to her intense scrutiny of her own feet. Sophronia thought that, even at thirteen, poor Agatha looked like she ought to be someone's maiden aunt. All she lacked were spectacles and a lapful of ugly but philanthropic crochet.

"A lively and engaging bunch," said Monique nastily.

Sidheag shrugged, like a boy, upsetting the fall of her gown. "We've only just started. Give us time."

Preshea gestured primly with one thumb. "Sidheag here was practically raised by wolves. One need only look at the way she behaves."

Sidheag laughed. "Practically? What does that matter? I still outrank you."

"Lady Linette says style is everything; one's shoes are as important as one's thoughts, and possibly more powerful in the correct context," said Preshea, sounding as though she were reciting from a broadsheet.

At this, Monique stood up pointedly. "Well, this has been most scintillating. If you would excuse me? I must unpack." Her lip curling at the very idea that she must now live among the debuts, Monique left the room.

Preshea immediately gestured at Sophronia to join them and huddled forward. She lowered her voice. "We understand Monique failed to finish while retrieving you. Professor Lefoux demoted her. Did you witness it?"

"Did we ever!" Dimity had clearly been waiting patiently for ages to answer this very question. "We were the cause!"

The girls gasped in titillated horror. "No!"

"Oh, yes, yes! Well, it's more Sophronia who's the cause. She saved the day and brought down the flywaymen, while Monique fainted and cried in the street."

Preshea's dour face brightened. "As if Monique had no training at all. That's certainly not how *she* told the story."

"So I gathered, but if she did so well, why the demotion?" said Dimity.

Sophronia glanced warily at Monique's closed door. She figured she hadn't promised to keep Dimity quiet on the subject; only to hold her own tongue and not go whining to the teachers. And at least Dimity wasn't blabbing about the prototype.

Sidheag slapped Sophronia on the back, hard enough to cause her to lurch forward and cough. "Good on you! If you had to make an enemy of anyone, Monique is certainly a high-end choice. Top-quality bite on that one. And many thanks—now we're all stuck with her."

"It wasn't my idea! It was Professor Lefoux's," replied Sophronia. "What exactly does she teach, anyway?" It was a blatant effort to change the subject, but it worked.

Dimity, bless her, was ever eager to be of use. She was clearly full to bursting with useful information garnered while Sophronia had been otherwise occupied. "She's *modern languages*, but Preshea says that's not all."

"Of course not." Sophronia took a seat facing Preshea, looking as wide-eyed and innocent as possible. She imagined herself sitting at the feet of genius and tried to give the impression of profound admiration.

Sidheag looked Sophronia up and down. "You're good. I can see why they wanted you."

Preshea poured everyone tea from a nearby pot and then passed around biscuits. Dimity offered one to Bumbersnoot. He sniffed at it with his mechanical nose, then opened his mouth wide, revealing two cavities: one leading to a storage compartment and the other to a tiny boiler. Dimity popped the biscuit into storage, where it would no doubt grow stale. Bumbersnoot continued his explorations.

Preshea finished serving and began explaining. "Old Lefoux has charge of modern weaponry and technological advancements. She's an honorary member of the Order of the Brass Octopus. They don't allow women, not officially, but they certainly use her designs."

Bumbersnoot approached Agatha and opened his mouth impolitely. Agatha hesitated, reached into her reticule, and fed him a wooden clothespin. It went into the boiler, if the resulting smoke coming out of the mechanimal's ears was any indication. Bumbersnoot's tail wagged in approval.

"And Lady Linette is music and . . . ?" Sophronia prompted.

Preshea obliged, puffing up with self-importance. "Intelligence gathering, of course; principles of deceit; fundamental espionage; and rudimentary seduction. I wager you can't *wait* for seduction class, can you, Agatha?"

Agatha looked petrified at the very idea.

"Don't worry," said Sidheag. "Doesn't happen until fifteen."

Sophronia was not to be thwarted in her quest for information. "And Mademoiselle Geraldine—do we have any lessons with her?"

"If you've met her, you've already had one. Ostensibly she's dance and dress, but really she's diversion. You know she's the only one who doesn't know what this school is really teaching?"

Except for me, of course. Although Sophronia did feel she

had it down to two options, neither of them finishing school–related. *Intelligencers or assassins.* She hadn't been aware until now that either position was open to a female. Sophronia felt that, given her propensity for dumbwaiters and penchant for observation, she'd quite enjoy being an intelligencer, so long as she was spying on someone interesting. But she wasn't certain about being an assassin. She'd once caused Frowbritcher to run over a mouse, and she still felt guilty about it.

"And Sister Herschel-Teape is household management?"

"Well, that's *part* of it." Preshea smiled for the first time, showing perfect small white teeth.

"It's Preshea's favorite class already," said Agatha softly, speaking for the first time.

"Sister Mattie also covers medicinal cures and proper poisonings for every occasion." Preshea looked positively animated.

Agatha explained further. "Preshea can't wait until she gets to poison her first husband. She's a great admirer of Mary Blandy's work."

"Oh, you flatter me."

So we are being trained to be assassins? Or are they joking with me? Sophronia looked back and forth between Preshea and Agatha. Agatha didn't look like she knew how to joke.

"And Professor Braithwope. What does he teach?"

Preshea went quiet at the name, her face once again dour and sulky. Which was odd, because Sophronia had liked Professor Braithwope best of the bunch.

"He's history." Agatha plucked at a ruffle on her skirt. Her voice shook slightly. "Some deportment and etiquette as well."

"But in actuality?" Sophronia prodded.

"Well, vampire lore and defense. What else?" Preshea pretended impatience, but she was clearly a little scared.

Sophronia thought quickly. Professor Braithwope had said he was just getting up when she disturbed him, yet it was after dark. He'd sneezed at garlic mash. He'd got the cork stuck on his *fang*, not his tooth! *Of course. My first vampire*, she thought, disappointed in herself for not realizing it at once and in Professor Braithwope for not being more...well...*vampiric*.

Preshea stood. "Speaking of Professor Braithwope, we ought to get ready, ladies."

The girls began to rummage about, gathering up lesson books and putting on bonnets. Monique reappeared, looking lovely and pulled together in a sweeping day dress of rose silk. With a good deal of bustle they filed out of the room, following Monique, who assumed the position of preeminence without challenge.

Sophronia summoned Bumbersnoot with an imperious gesture. The mechanimal bumped into her shoe and looked up. "Stay!" she said firmly, and then, "Sleep." The mechanized dog sat back on its haunches and made a little whistling hum before relaxing down, all internal components stilled. *Gracious me, it worked!*

Sophronia trotted after the group, ending up behind Sidheag and next to Dimity. "Where are we going?"

"Lessons, I suppose." Dimity grinned at her.

"At night?"

"Apparently the academy keeps London hours. Might as well get us accustomed to the Season. Or so Sidheag says."

"I like Sidheag," said Sophronia, not caring if the tall girl could hear her. "She reminds me of my brother Freddy. Freddy never pinched as hard as the others."

Dimity lowered her voice. "She's not very *ladylike*."

"I don't think that is necessarily a character flaw. Some of the most disagreeable people I know are the most ladylike."

"Oh, I like that!" Dimity pretended offense. She clearly liked to think of herself as a proper lady.

"Present company excluded, of course. Look at Monique. Speaking of which, she and I have an agreement. She won't tell the teachers about Bumbersnoot if I don't correct her version of the flywaymen rescue."

Dimity did not look pleased. "Oh, but Sophronia, she's such a pollock!"

"I didn't say *you* would also hold your tongue. But if you could confine yourself to gossiping with students about it, that would mollify her. And it prevents everyone else from figuring out the real reason for her demotion."

"Oh, are we keeping the prototype secret, too?"

Sophronia slowed, forcing Dimity to fall back with her and allowing distance to develop between them and the others. "Did you hear the alarm?"

Dimity nodded.

Sophronia explained, "It was flywaymen again. A whole bunch of airdinghies this time, after the prototype. They gave the teachers three weeks to find it. Professor Braithwope and Professor Lefoux are trying to build a fake in the interim. Monique won't tell them the location of the real one. But I think the teachers are allowing her to keep it secret for some reason."

"Remind me, why are we so interested?"

"It lost us our luggage. Also, it would prove we were better than Monique if we could produce the prototype for the teachers, now wouldn't it?"

"But what if Monique stashed it before we even got on board the school?"

"Well, then, we will have to determine a way to sneak off and find it."

"Already? But we just got here! I haven't even had my supper."

All the while they talked, they wended their way through the hallways of the school. As the young ladies were dressed to the height of fashion, this had to be done two by two; any more than that would not fit in the passageway due to the fullness of their skirts. Only Sidheag had a narrow gown, one that looked like it properly belonged on a governess. Sophronia could respect its practicality. Her own Sunday best was not used to such activity as it had seen over the past day. It was beginning to chafe, and she could but wish she had something more sensible to wear.

"What does 'London hours' imply?"

Dimity grinned. "Breakfast at noon, morning calls around three, tea at five, supper at eight, entertainment all evening, and bed by one or two. Doesn't it sound the pip? I'd love to be a London lady. Do you think my parents would be awfully mad if I married a nice politician and gave up on a life of crime? Then I'd get to throw dinner parties all the time."

Sophronia, country girl, for all she was gentry, found the very idea of London hours shocking in the extreme. "Rise at noon, you say?" *Why, that sounds positively decadent!*

*　*　*

Much to her shock, Sophronia actually enjoyed the lessons. They were nothing like what she expected from either a finishing academy or an ordinary grammar school. She'd had, at varying times in her life, a host of indifferent governesses. They were either overwhelmed by the number of children in the Temminnick household or in possession of the remarkable ability to nap through most everything—including lessons. Education, therefore, had been a matter of Sophronia's own interest and access to her father's library, rather than instruction. Consequently, she knew a good deal of ancient history and mythology, something on the fauna of Africa and native hunting practices, and all the rules of cricket, but little else.

"When defending yourself against a vampire," said Professor Braithwope at the start of the lesson, "it is important to remember three things, whot? He is a good deal faster and stronger than you will ever be. He is immortal, so debilitating pain is more useful than attempted disanimation. He is most likely to go for your neck in a frontal assault. And he is easily distracted by damage to his clothing or personal toilette."

"That's four things, Professor," corrected Monique.

"Don't be pert, whot," replied the vampire.

"Are you saying," Sophronia ventured, "that it's best to go for the waistcoat? Say, douse it with tea? Or possibly wipe sticky hands on his coat sleeve?"

"Exactly! Very good, Miss Temminnick. Nothing is more distressing to a vampire than a stain. Why do you think containing blood is so important to us? One of the tragedies of any vampire's life is that in order to survive we must continually handle such an embarrassingly sticky fluid."

Sophronia wondered whose blood Professor Braithwope drank on board the school. It must be someone loyal to the professor, as if they were a drone. She felt self-consciously for her own neck and thought affectionately of shawls.

The vampire paced back and forth as he lectured, his movements fluid and quick. The room in which they sat in no way resembled a classroom, except that it was *called* a classroom. A series of brocade settees was arranged in a semicircle around an imitation fireplace, a small piano, and an articulated brass statue of a cow. There were plush carpets on the floor, side tables on which the girls placed their books, and a maid mechanical waiting patiently in the corner in case she was needed to fetch tea. It looked more like a drawing room than anything.

"Another weakness in vampires, of course, is the limited range. A vampire who is hive-bound must stay near his queen, and the queen cannot leave her house. Roves are similarly tethered to a place, although our range is larger. When swarming, of course, all distances are moot, whot. There are some notable exceptions; the queen's praetoriani has a larger range."

Monique was trying not to look interested. "Why?"

"Our scientists suspect he is in a constant state of swarm because he is responsible for the queen's safety."

This was all very confusing to Sophronia, who had heard very few of the terms he was spouting forth and knew almost nothing—beyond late-night parlor stories—about vampires. *I wonder what the professor's range is? That might be a rude question.*

She was just about to ask for clarification on the word "praetoriani" when an explosion shook the classroom.

The entire airship lurched to one side and then righted itself. An odd sensation, since, until that moment, Sophronia had quite forgotten they were afloat.

Several of the girls screamed.

Displaying the speed he had only recently described, Professor Braithwope dashed out the door. Rather than waiting to be told to stay put, Sophronia leapt up and followed him.

The hallway was in chaos, filled mainly with young ladies, most of them covered in some kind of soot. Apart from the soot, they were all dressed beautifully, and were chattering among themselves with more animation than distress. Sophronia estimated around two dozen or so; perhaps half the attendees of the school? She hadn't yet managed a firm grasp on the numbers, but Mademoiselle Geraldine's seemed to have fewer students than one would expect from a normal finishing school.

Professor Lefoux, taller than most by a head, was trying to control the chaos.

"Now, ladies, calm down, do! Is this any way to behave in a crisis? What has Lady Linette told you time and time again?"

The girls quieted and stood expectantly. One or two took out handkerchiefs and began trying to repair the sooty damage to gown and face.

"That was *not* a rhetorical question, ladies!" snapped the Frenchwoman. Professor Lefoux herself was far more soot-covered than any of the others, and less inclined to deal with it. She had her hair back in a tight bun that appeared to pull her skin away from her eyes. It made her look like a greyhound that had stuck its head out a carriage window.

"In a crisis, remain calm," called out one voice from the crowd.

"And?" Professor Lefoux gestured impatiently with both hands.

"Assess any damage to one's attire. A lady is never disreputable in public, unless intended for manipulation of sympathies."

"Good. Anything more?"

"Ascertain the nature of the emergency. See if it can be turned to your advantage or used as an opportunity to gather information," said another voice.

While all this was going on, Sophronia—unconsciously following the instructions being repeated dutifully around her—made her way through the crowd to the open door of Professor Lefoux's classroom. Professor Braithwope stood on the threshold, staring in. He had out his own handkerchief and was waving it about in front of his face ineffectually, trying to dispel the smoke still permeating the room.

Sophronia nudged up next to him and looked inside. A *proper classroom.* There were uncomfortable-looking chairs facing tables covered in interesting-looking apparatus and scientific instruments. The walls were tacked with sketches of complex devices. The room, like the hallway, was in chaos. It might have started life as some kind of laboratory or engineering chamber, but its contents were now overturned, smoked, and covered liberally in black powder.

"I suppose Professor Lefoux and her students haven't had

much luck in creating an alternate prototype," said Sophronia mildly.

"Whot?" The vampire sucked on a fang, looking thoughtful. He turned dark eyes on his newest student. "Appears as if they haven't. Wait a moment there, whot! Where did you come from, young lady?"

"Your class, sir. Remember, we were just there."

The vampire only looked at her, not even acknowledging her levity. "Tell me, Miss Temminnick. What was the first thing you wanted to know, just now, before the explosion?"

Sophronia saw no reason to prevaricate. If he really wanted a window to her thoughts, then any possible rudeness was irrelevant. "Your range, sir. Being that you're a rove, as I'm assuming this school is no hive, I was wondering how a vampire in a dirigible managed to float all over the place the way you do. Then I figured you must be bound to the school itself, or something like."

"Something like, indeed."

"*Then* I was wondering, since you were instructing us in defense against vampires, what would happen if you fell overboard. What would happen to your tether? Would it snap? Would you die?"

The vampire narrowed his eyes, looking down his nose at her. He avoided her question by asking her one of his own. "And the explosion—what do you make of it?"

"Perhaps Professor Lefoux should not have tried steel first."

"My goodness, you do pay attention."

"Will you be able to convince Monique to tell you where she stashed the prototype?"

He said nothing at that.

But she's only a student. Sophronia wanted to ask why they didn't torture Monique or something. After all, this seemed as if it might be *that* kind of school.

Professor Lefoux came bustling over. "Ah, Professor Braithwope. Sorry to disturb. Little problem with the you-know-what; probably shouldn't have used steel. Copper is obviously superior."

Professor Braithwope looked down at Sophronia, who gave the vampire an arch look and returned to his classroom and the other girls.

They were crowding the doorway, but had not followed her beyond leaving their own seats.

"What happened?" Dimity asked breathlessly.

"Someone seems to have exploded something black and powdery in a room near ours."

"Professor Lefoux and the senior girls," said Monique, no doubt preferring to have been among them herself, explosion or no.

Sophronia returned to her couch and took a seat, crossing her hands demurely in her lap.

Dimity plopped down next to her. "Was it the...?" she hissed.

"Yes."

"What could explode like that?"

"Lots of things, I suspect."

"Sometimes I wish Pill were still with us. He knows all about accidental explosions. Then again, he *is* my brother, so it's nice to be away from him."

"I managed to extract a bit of the black powder." Sophronia

showed Dimity the fingertip of one of her gloved hands, which she'd purposefully run along the wall inside Professor Lefoux's classroom.

"I wonder if we could send it to Pill for analysis. Or, uh, *drop* it to him, I guess is a better way of putting it."

"Do we get post on board this thing?" Sophronia wondered. "If no one even knows where the school is at any given time, how would mail find us?"

"Mummy said she would send me some of my favorite emulsified biscuits, so it must. She mentioned Pillover as well, so perhaps we pick ours up from Bunson's."

"Oh, dear, Sophronia, your glove is dirty! Let me help you with that." Preshea looked more distressed by the black on Sophronia's white fingertip than she had been by the explosion.

Monique said, "You aren't permitted to have a soiled glove, not at Mademoiselle Geraldine's!"

Sophronia quickly placed her hand in her lap and tucked the offending digit under a fold of skirt. "Oh, I believe I have the glove under control, thank you."

"Right, ladies, shall we get back to our studies?" Professor Braithwope said as he reentered the room. "We are going to try to address first the best and most deadly application of wooden stakes, hatpins, and hair sticks. If we have time, I will move us on to how to properly judge a gentleman by the color and knot of his cravat. Believe you me, ladies, the two subjects are far more intimately entangled than you might first suppose."

Sophronia straightened her spine and prepared to be *educated.*

LESSON 7

THE PROPER PLACE FOR SOOTIES

The rest of the evening proceeded in a much milder manner. They moved from classroom to classroom, each room having been arranged to that teacher's particular taste. Each time the lesson was more in the manner of a visiting call or an intellectual salon than any school lesson Sophronia's siblings had ever relayed to her.

Sister Mathilde Herschel-Teape's room, which led out onto a small deck, was half potting shed, half manor-house kitchen. Their lesson was on emulsification and the fine art of egg whites as applied to sugared violets, fake eyelashes, skin care, and poison control. She left them with the wise, if somewhat confusing, "Now, remember, my dears, a separated egg is worth two in the bush."

Lady Linette's room was a combination conservatory, boudoir, and house of ill repute. It featured a good deal of red; three chubby, long-haired cats with funny, scrunched-up faces; fringe wherever fringe might be stuck; and some highly questionable artwork. The girls sat in prim rows on long velvet fainting couches. A stuffed duck in a lace mobcap stared austerely down at them from the mantelpiece.

By the end of Lady Linette's lesson on how to faint properly at any event and in a manner to cope with varying types of undergarments, Sophronia was yawning hugely. It had, after all, been a long day full of travel, excitement, and now classes that persisted well past her regular bedtime.

"Ladies don't yawn in public," Monique said loudly, so as to draw Lady Linette's attention to the transgression.

"You'll get used to the London hours eventually, country girl," Preshea added.

"I suppose you're from London?" Sophronia had a countryside suspicion of towns.

"My parents keep progressive hours," the girl replied, avoiding the question in a manner that suggested this was a sore point.

"Miss Temminnick, Miss Buss, Miss Pelouse, if you're quite finished? Miss Buss, it is as embarrassing to remark upon a behavior as it is to enact it. Of course, Miss Pelouse is, as always, correct, Miss Temminnick. Perhaps, Miss Pelouse, as you know everything so well, you would like to demonstrate fainting in a crowded ballroom in a manner that might attract only the attention of a specific gentleman? Without wrinkling your dress."

Sophronia was enthralled by the odd way in which the teachers treated Monique. They made it clear her demotion was a punishment, yet sometimes it was almost as if Monique had a kind of control over them. *Which must tie into how she has gotten away with not revealing the prototype's location.* Then there were times like this, when she was called out and made an example of.

Monique stood and did as instructed.

Lady Linette critiqued the faint closely as Monique executed it.

"Note both hands raised to the forehead. A classic maneuver, but perhaps overly dramatic for a large crowd; you might draw too much attention. Try only one, pressed to the breast. That has the added benefit of drawing a gentleman's gaze to your décolletage. Not that you younger ladies have any yet, but we can hope. No, not pressed so hard. Miss Pelouse, you'll skew your gown's neckline. Very nice. Now, a short breath and a small sigh. Eyes rolling slightly back. Only slightly! Otherwise one looks like a dying sheep. Flutter the eyelashes. Flutter them! More fluttering. Lovely. And sag back slightly. Always backward, ladies, never topple forward. And be certain to situate yourself so that if the gentleman does not respond appropriately, you can pretend to catch yourself against the wall or mantelpiece and make a recovery. Very nice, Miss Pelouse. Very realistic."

Sophronia yawned again.

"Sophronia," Dimity whispered, "what are we going to wear to sleep in tonight?"

"Goodness knows. Our petticoats, I suppose." For all Sophronia knew, their luggage still lay scattered in the road leagues away.

Such was not the case, as it transpired. After being let out from Lady Linette's class—"Practice your eyelash-fluttering, ladies. Six rounds of one hundred each before bed"—she and the other girls went to supper in the back part of the school. The recreation section, as the others called it, was much the same as all the others, only with larger, grander, and fewer rooms. Supper completed, their manners closely monitored by the teachers and Sophronia's knuckles rapped twice for her misuse of a fish knife, they returned to their quarters. The debuts found Sophronia's battered portmanteau and Dimity's cases neatly stacked in their parlor.

The girls were divided into two per room, Preshea seeming honored to have been selected by Monique as the best of a bad lot of options. Sophronia was delighted to find Agatha willing to vacate her abode to settle in with Sidheag so that Sophronia and Dimity might share.

"Do you think Monique has some kind of control over the teachers?" Sophronia asked the moment they were left alone. Bumbersnoot had woken upon their return and followed Sophronia dutifully into her new room, then paced back and forth as she unpacked.

"How could she?" Dimity pulled out her underthings furtively and stuffed them quickly into a drawer.

Sophronia gave her a look.

"Her family, I suppose. Although I've never heard of them, so they can't be that important or that evil." Dimity moved on to less embarrassing apparel: dresses, pinafores, petticoats, slippers, and boots.

Sophronia unpacked her own bags. For the first time in her life, she was slightly embarrassed by her own wardrobe. Her family was largely considered, by the surrounding gentlefolk, to be one of means. But she was still the youngest of four girls, and with three older sisters to clothe, she found her own dresses deficient. She was already composing a begging letter home in her head.

"What if she didn't hide the prototype but gave it away?" Sophronia suggested.

Dimity was prosaic. "Well, no sense in speculating. We'll simply have to find out more."

Unpacking complete, the girls prepared for slumber—Dimity's nightgown was bright yellow!—and settled down for the evening.

Bumbersnoot sat next to Sophronia's cot with a little wheeze of distress. She picked him up and put him at her feet. He wasn't exactly cuddly, and she was sure to bark her shin if she rolled over, but the little mechanimal seemed pleased, and the mini steam engine within made him quite an excellent foot warmer, if nothing else. Sophronia wondered idly if he required a diet of coal and water, and if so, where she would get the coal. *The airship must have a boiler room.* The last thing she heard as she closed her eyes was the tick-tock of Bumbersnoot's mechanical tail wagging back and forth.

Unlike her fellow students, Sophronia awoke early in the morning and decided she might take the opportunity to explore. She supposed there would be mechanicals trundling about and sounding the alarm if they encountered her, so she determined to figure out a way around the massive ship that did not cross any tracks. She chose her most basic dress, with the fewest underskirts and the shortest top skirt, and pulled on her boots with the india-rubber strapping.

She had to use the hallway to get to any exterior decks, so she ran as quickly as possible, sticking to the sides of the passage, away from the tracks that ran down the center. Luckily, she didn't stumble upon any mechanicals. This allowed her to escape out onto one of the lower decks and over the rail to cling on the outside with no one, human or constructed, the wiser. She was left breathless and leaning out and in a manner she was certain would be thought most unladylike.

In the early morning, the moor below was still mist-shrouded, but there was no longer any other cloud cover. Sophronia looked down, considered for a moment, and then decided it was probably better not to look again.

She inched around the banisters and along the outside of the railing. The deck extended around the dirigible's side and then in, before another deck rounded back out again, like flower petals. The difficulty was how to get from one to the next, over the small gap in between. Sophronia had a system developed soon enough: a little twisting movement as she thrust herself willfully over the abyss.

Several of the decks, smaller and more like private balconies, did not have mechanical tracks. Sophronia climbed over the railings of these and explored, peering in at the round windows. It would be good to know, for secrecy's sake, which balconies were safe from mechanical spies, not to mention vulnerable to attack because they lacked mechanical defense. She was also nosy.

As Sophronia made her way, one deck at a time, around the edge of the ship, she eventually left the students' residential area and found herself in the classroom area. There the decks changed, some of them made of strange and mysterious materials, and they did not always have rails. She passed the one that featured Sister Mathilde's greenhouse, and another with long tassels and fancy wicker furnishings that must belong to Lady Linette's classroom. Funny; Sophronia hadn't noticed a door from the classroom out onto the balcony during lessons.

Lady Linette's was the last classroom before the next balloon. There was another balcony, almost touching it, in the forbidden section. There was a little walkway to that balcony.

Lavishly decorated, thought Sophronia, *so probably Lady Linette's private quarters*. She had, as yet, not determined how to get up or down to any of the upper or lower decks, but from the sculpted railing of that particular private deck, a tempting rope ladder hung down to the lower levels.

Sophronia hesitated. She couldn't see any tracks, and she guessed Lady Linette wasn't an early riser. It was a risk. She didn't want trouble on her second day. Then again, there was that rope ladder.

Sophronia made the switch to the forbidden section, shimmied along the outside of the railing over to the ladder, and began to climb down.

The ladder was pegged inward at the next level. Sophronia considered getting off there, but at the very bottom of the ship there *had* to be an engine chamber. She could see the steam emanating from below. And where there was steam, there would be boilers. And where there were boilers, there must be coal.

Bumbersnoot was probably hungry. So she kept climbing down. There were no decks at the bottom level; only small portholes which she could press her face against. The glass in these was too filthy to see through, and not from the outside world, but from something within.

The ladder ended at a hatch in the side of the ship. After a brief hesitation, Sophronia twisted the handle and climbed inside. *Boiler room!*

The boiler room of the school was loud, and hot, and as soot-covered as Professor Lefoux's classroom had been after the fake prototype exploded.

Sophronia's entrance caused little reaction. It had to have been noticed, for she let a blast of light and fresh air into the dark, musty interior. But there was a controlled chaos all around her, and very few bothered to acknowledge her presence.

There were a number of larger men, who must be the firemen or engineers, and two dozen or more very grubby boys, covered in black soot, running about with fuel and scurrying up and down stacks of boxes, piles of coal, and ladders to the upper levels. A few of these doffed their caps as they passed Sophronia, but none bothered to stop or properly greet her.

She simply stood, taking in the bedlam and the massive boilers and wondering why the place was not staffed by mechanicals. *Perhaps the tasks are too complicated? Or too vital to entrust to machines?* The work seemed to be quite labor intensive, yet once or twice a bark of laughter issued forth from one side of the room, where a group of boys were hard at work shoveling coal into an immense boiler.

Sophronia made her way cautiously over to them, bending to scoop up some small pieces of coal, which she stuffed into the pocket of her pinafore.

"What's that one run?" she asked, once she arrived at the group.

"Propeller," came the answer, and then, "What-ho! What's an Uptop doing messing about down south?"

"Only curious," replied Sophronia. "No lessons until the afternoon, so I thought I would explore."

"You mean, you're an *actual* student?"

"'Course she is, don't she look as like?"

"Naw, her dress ain't fancy enough by halves."

"Well, thank you very much," said Sophronia, pretending hurt.

"Asides, students ain't permitted south."

"Well, allow me to introduce myself. My name is Sophronia. And you are?" She figured introducing *herself* couldn't be considered impolite, given that these were manual laborers and, judging by their accents, from equally manual upbringings.

"Ships' sooties, us, miss."

A yell of "Oy, up!" came from behind them, and the boys scattered like a group of very excitable partridge. Sophronia followed their lead. A new sootie, riding astride a great pile of coal in some kind of wheelbarrow-like contraption, came hurtling toward them. The wheelbarrow rattled headlong at the maw of the boiler. The boy remained proudly atop it, whooping enthusiastically. The others hooted him on.

Sophronia gasped, certain the thing would go crashing right into the impossibly hot boiler, dumping both coal and boy inside. At the last minute, the sootie jumped off and somersaulted away, leaving the cart to rush forward; tip in, unloading all of its coal inside; and bounce off.

"Pips! It worked!" The boy jumped to his feet.

The others all returned and gathered around him, proving that he was taller than most.

"Takes you twice as long to load it full. We're still stoking more per hour," commented one.

"Yes," said the tall one, "but ain't this *invention*?"

"How'd it bounce back like that?" Sophronia asked, joining the crowd as if she had always been there.

The boy turned in her direction. In addition to being taller than the others, he seemed to be more thickly coated in soot. His eyes were startlingly white in a dark face. Her question solicited a flash of equally startlingly white teeth. "Ah, yes, a spring rebound mechanism without india-rubber fixings. Vieve worked a whole week on that. Wait a minute there.... They letting girls be sooties now?"

"She's an Uptop."

"Came exploring."

"Found us."

"Ah, not so good at exploring, then?" The tall boy hooted at his own joke.

"I beg your pardon!" Sophronia took mild umbrage.

"No offense meant, miss. We sooties aren't exactly upmarket chappy chaps."

"Yet that contraption of yours was rather topping. Not to mention your dismount. I'm Sophronia, by the way." Sophronia decided to practice a bit of her eyelash-fluttering lesson.

The tall one didn't seem overly impressed by the eyelashes. "How-d'ye-do, miss? I'm Phineas B. Crow."

Sophronia gave him a curtsy, and for the first time since she'd arrived at Mademoiselle Geraldine's Finishing School for Young Ladies of Quality, no one commented on its poor implementation.

"Though everyone calls me Soap," added Phineas B. Crow. "Because I needs it more than most."

Sophronia continued batting her eyelashes at him.

"You got some soot in your eye, there, miss?"

Clearly I haven't mastered the art yet. "No, practicing."

"What, miss?"

"Never you mind."

"That india rubber you got wrapped about them little stompers?" Soap's tone was full of avarice.

"Yes. Got it off a dumbwaiter. But you can't have it; I need it."

"What's an Uptop need with india-rubber shoes?"

"Climbing, of course."

"That how you got here? Never heard of a girl who climbed afore."

Sophronia shrugged, pleased at the compliment. *Soap,* she thought, *has a pleasant smile.*

A yell came from behind them. One of the large men—*Supervisor, most likely*—marched in their direction.

"Oh, blast it," said Soap. "Greaser. Scatter!"

The boys ran in various different directions. Soap tugged Sophronia after him, to crouch down together behind a huge mound of coal.

"We ain't got long back here afore they suss us out."

"Is this what you do all day—shovel coal?"

"Ain't a bad life. Used to work Southampton docks," replied Soap with one of his grins. "Still can't eat fish."

Sophronia said, "You know, it *is* nice to meet you, Mr. Soap. I got myself an unexpected mechanimal, so I imagine I might have to pop down here regularly."

"After the coal, are ya?"

"Rather. Poor Bumbersnoot; he must be starving by now."

"I thought them mechanimals weren't allowed."

"Said he was unexpected, didn't I?"

Soap let out a bark of laughter that was sure to attract attention even in the noise of the boiler room. "You're all right for a girl, Miss Sophronia. Pretty, too."

Sophronia snorted. "I only recently made your acquaintance, Mr. Soap. No need to fib."

"Whoa ho ho," said a booming voice, "what have we here?"

Soap stood immediately, his back ramrod straight. Sophronia followed his lead.

"Just taking a breather, sir."

"Soap, you ain't never doing *just* nothing. Who's that you got with ya?"

Sophronia stepped forward. "How do you do, sir? Sophronia Angelina Temminnick."

"An Uptop? Down 'ere? Best get her along right quick, before the Junior Sixth Assistant Engineer sees ya. I'll pretend you was never 'ere, shall I?"

"Thank you very much, sir," said Sophronia with a curtsy.

Soap led her back to the hatch. "He's not a bad kind of greaser, Old Smalls."

"It was a pleasure to make your acquaintance, Mr. Soap."

He twinkled at her. "Aye, it was, miss. Supposing I'll be seeing you again."

"Perhaps." Sophronia let herself out.

Before she could close the hatch, Soap's dark head stuck out. "Oh, miss, best change that pinafore. Wouldn't want people knowing you went south."

Sophronia looked down at her front. The crisp white of her apron was covered in smudges. "You're probably right."

In the bright light of the morning sun, Sophronia noticed something else about her new friend. He wasn't simply dirty; he was actually black. Sophronia had heard, of course, of people with odd-colored skin, but she'd only seen pictures in her papa's books. She'd never actually met one before. *But Soap is just like a normal boy!*

She wasn't certain it was polite to mention, but she couldn't help herself. "Why, you're all over soot-colored by nature!"

"Yes, miss. A creature from darkest Africa. *Wooo, wooo.*" He weaved his head around, pretending to be a ghost.

Sophronia had read about Africa. This was a subject upon which she was fully conversant. "Oh, my, is that where you're from?"

"No, miss. Tooting Bec, South London." At which he returned to the noisy, musty darkness of the boiler room.

Sophronia made her way back to her quarters safely from balcony to deck, spending only a brief time running through the hallway. No one was awake upon her return except Bumbersnoot.

He was absolutely delighted by the piece of coal and dish of water she placed before him. He nibbled and slurped away happily, tooting small gusts of appreciative steam. Sophronia changed her pinafore and checked the state of her face and hands. Luckily, the maids had brought in the washing water and, being mechanicals, had not registered her empty bed. After much scrubbing, most of the boiler room's smudges were eliminated.

She practiced batting her eyelashes in the small hand mirror for the next half hour, until Dimity finally awoke.

"You'll never guess what I did!" said Sophronia while her friend blinked blearily and stretched.

"No, probably not. Could I wake up first, please?"

"Certainly." At which Sophronia paused. She had no idea how to dispose of her dirty bathing water. At home, she would have simply tossed it out the window, but here there was no window to their chamber. She excused herself, took it to the privy, and returned to hand the basin to Dimity.

Dimity poured herself some fresh water out of the pitcher and said, "Well?"

"I visited the land of soot and fire."

"Sophronia, really. Do you mean to traumatize me with riddles first thing in the morning? If so, I should warn you, I'd consider that grounds for rescinding all offers of friendship."

"It's almost noon. I've been up for *ages*."

"A habit you may come to regret." But then Dimity put it all together. She emerged from washing her face with a gasp. "Sophronia! Did you visit the boiler room?"

"Yes!" Sophronia casually leaned back on both elbows.

"You aren't allowed to *do* that!"

"So I learned."

"But all the engine parts down there are *exposed*. A girl can see exactly how things work. It's undignified."

"It's full of boys."

Dimity paused, giving that statement its due consideration. "Yes, but the wrong *class* of boy, to be sure? I really wouldn't if I were you. Terribly bad for one's reputation. Then again, I don't suppose there are any *proper* boys on board this school at all."

"Not unless you count Professor Braithwope."

"Certainly not. Now, Captain Niall, mind you, I'd count him."

A knock came at their door. Sidheag stuck her head in. "Breakfast in ten minutes." The tall girl looked much the same as she had the day before—her dress dowdy and her hair in one simple braid. She positively lounged against the doorjamb.

Sophronia wondered how she would fare during posture class.

"We won't have him for a few days at least," said the Lady of Kingair.

"Have who?"

"Captain Niall, of course."

"Have him for what?"

"Lessons, silly. Did you think they only kept him on retainer for ground support?" With which the tall girl drifted away.

Sophronia and Dimity exchanged startled looks.

"What on earth could we girls possibly learn from a were-wolf?" Sophronia wondered.

"How to keep a hat on no matter what the circumstances?" hazarded Dimity.

* * *

"We need to nip to the post," Sophronia stated firmly as they left breakfast.

"We do?" Dimity was confused.

"My soiled glove, remember?" She produced the offending article from her reticule.

"Oh, yes, we were going to send it to my problematical brother for analysis. I should warn you, it's unlikely anything will come of it. He's very forgetful, my brother. Rather a nascent absentminded academic."

Sophronia hesitated a moment, and then approached one of the older girls. "Pardon me, could you point us in the direction of the postal service?"

The girl looked down her nose at her. "Head steward handles that."

"And where would I find him?"

"Steward's quarters, of course," she said and turned away.

I guess we have been dismissed. "Dimity, any idea where the steward's quarters might be?"

Dimity cocked her head. "Well, on a boat it's one of the upper decks, midship, you know, to catch people boarding and the like."

"But we boarded from below."

"True."

Sophronia frowned. The steward would be in charge of all the mechanicals for servicing and maintenance, as well as all the human household staff. "We need to find the main hub."

"Follow the tracks?" suggested Dimity, pointing down to where the single track became multiples at the entrance to the dining hall, allowing various maid and footman mechanicals to service the tables.

The servants' quarters of any house are an odd place to explore, full of derelict machinery and broken tracks, not to mention the personal items of the human staff. Not wishing to be late to class, Sophronia and Dimity moved along the main hallways quickly, following the track when it split off and delved to the side into what was clearly a servants' area.

"Uh-oh, look," Dimity said, pointing.

Ahead of them, rounding a far corner in the narrow hall, they could see the back of some very flowery skirts of the kind no human maid, and certainly no mechanical, would wear. It was a dress familiar to them both, for there had been praise of it over breakfast.

"Monique," hissed Sophronia. "I wager she's trying to get a message off the ship, too."

Dimity nodded wisely. "To tell her contacts the location of the prototype, perhaps?"

"Or warn them of the delay. If I were her, I'd wait until I was free to hand it over in person. Too many other people want it. Any message, even one in code, could be intercepted."

They drew back and followed the older girl at a discreet distance.

Peeking round the corner of the next corridor, they spotted her entering a large white door and closing it firmly behind her. After an exchange of glances, Sophronia and Dimity ran to the door. On it were written the words STEWARD'S OFFICE, COR-RESPONDENCES SENT AND RECEIVED, MECHANICAL MISBEHAV-IORS HANDLED, NO SILLINESS.

Sophronia cracked the door, and the two girls put their ears to the gap.

"But we must be going near Bunson's before then!" they heard Monique whine.

"Not for three weeks at the very least, miss."

"But I must get a message home to my mama. It is vital. This season's glove order!"

"I understand, miss, and yet, the float is away, nothing to be done."

"Couldn't Captain Niall...?"

"The captain is not your personal message boy, young lady."

Monique switched to a more wheedling tone. "Well, could I leave it with you, to send as soon as possible?"

"I can't make any guarantees, miss."

Sophronia pushed Dimity away from the door and down the corridor. It seemed like the conversation would be ending soon. They made it round the corner just in time to hear the door open and peek out to see Monique striding quickly, and in a most unladylike manner, back the way they had come. She was clutching a letter in one hand, clearly having decided against leaving the missive in the dubious care of the steward.

"I bet he has to report messages to one of the teachers," said Dimity.

"Or one of them has him on the payroll," said Sophronia.

"Bribery? How crass."

"Useful, though."

"Shall we still try to send the glove?"

Sophronia considered the dangers and implications. "Best not, I think. Try again later. We're late for class."

LESSON 8

THE TEACHING HABITS OF WEREWOLVES

The schedule proceeded much of a pace after the chaos of that first day. Sophronia came to accept the un-finishing-school aspects of Mademoiselle Geraldine's. The lessons were mostly un-lesson-like, the teachers were mainly un-teacher-like, and the routine was more that of a London dandy than that of any proper educational system.

The girls commenced their mornings—which were really early afternoons—with a light repast, nothing too heavy, on the insistence of Mademoiselle Geraldine. "Breakfast," she said, bosom heaving, "should *never* be luxurious." Thus all they had to select from was tea, bread and sweet butter, porridge, ham and broiled mushrooms, rabbit pie, fricandeau of eggs, mayonnaise of prawns, and spiced beef. "Now, ladies," said the headmistress every day from the front table. "I know this is quite the meager selection, but breakfast comestibles should be undisruptive, nutritive, and effortlessly digested. You must watch your figures. *Watch them!*"

Sophronia, uncertain how she might do such a thing, ate bites between staring down at her own chest, and selected only what she might have eaten back at home—a little porridge with molasses. They all ate meals together, although separated into tables by age or inclination. The dining hall was stretched to capacity with four dozen or so students, plus assorted teachers. The ship's complement and personal staff ate beforehand, of course, and the sooties and other menial laborers ate belowdecks.

After breakfast, all the girls stood to recite, with religious solemnity, the school motto—*ut acerbus terminus*—three times over.

"What does it mean?" Sophronia wanted to know.

"'To the bitter end,' imbecile," said Monique de Pelouse.

After breakfast they were separated according to skill level and drifted off to their first set of lessons. Three days a week the debuts took mathematics and household management with Sister Mathilde, along with a number of older girls. They learned more in the manner of lists and organization than sums calculated on slates. There were no apparent exams, and yet Sophronia found herself intrigued into learning simply by the puzzles Sister Mathilde proposed. Algebra was far more interesting when it was a matter of proportioning out mutton chops so as to poison only half of one's dinner guests and then determining the relative value of purchasing a more expensive, yet more effective, antidote over a home remedy. Sophronia was a mite disturbed by the context, but could not help being intrigued by the macabre nature of the calculations.

On the other two days, they had physical culture with Lady Linette during the first time slot. This involved, much to Sophronia's shock, climbing, running, and even some light tumbling—in petticoats. There were also battledore and shuttlecock, tennis, croquet, pass the slipper, and wink-wink. Sophronia had the advantage of brothers. *Who would have thought I should ever consider them an advantage?* Which turned her, as Monique pointed out disgustedly, into rather a sporting lady.

"Ugh, Sophronia, you're so very country," she said.

"Well, yes, I was raised there." *At least I don't have horsey teeth, like you!*

"Next you'll be crying out, 'Tallyho!' from the squeak deck."

"Oh, now, be fair. Only when I have the dogs out after you, dearest Monique." Sophronia grinned slyly, and Monique gave her a nasty look.

Lady Linette completed a somersault across the carpet, ending in front of them and causing Sophronia and Monique to snap their mouths closed and pay attention. She seemed almost embarrassed as she guided them through the steps. "Now, ladies, remember this is for use only when strictly necessary, and you must be absolutely certain not to muss your hair. For the most part, you should delegate physical exertions to a willing, or unwilling, accomplice. We will discuss bribery and blackmail techniques later. Alternatively, you might arrange things so that fleshy activity does not become necessary at all. However, a lady is always prepared. Speaking of which, show me your handkerchiefs!"

The girls all stopped what they were doing, which had been preparing—in various states of distress or, in Sophronia's case, delight—to try their own versions of the somersault, and began patting about for handkerchiefs.

"What did I tell you yesterday? A lady *always* has her handkerchief on her person. A handkerchief is endlessly useful. Not only is it a communication device, but it can also be dropped as a distraction, scented with various perfumes and noxious gases for discombobulation, used to wipe the forehead of a gentleman, or even bandage a wound, and, of course, you may dab at the eyes or nose if it is still clean. Dab, mind you! Never blow. I don't tell you these things for my own amusement, ladies. Now, books on heads while I do the inspection."

The girls produced handkerchiefs from various pockets and held them up, at the same time placing books atop their heads for balance and posture.

Lady Linette, blonde curls bobbing, marched among them examining the offerings closely.

"Very good, Monique. Perfect, as always. Next time, Sidheag, smaller handkerchief. A lady carries embroidered muslin, not—what on earth is that? A square of tweed? Really, girl! Dimity, watch your balance, and red? Dear, not *red*. You're not ready for red. Red is only for the advanced deployment of handkerchiefs. Preshea, why the discoloration? Have you been experimenting with poison again? Next time, don't use your good handkerchief. Agatha!"

Poor Agatha lost her balance while waiting, causing the books atop her head to tumble to the ground. She reeled into Sophronia. Both girls fell over backward.

Sophronia giggled.

Agatha looked both terrified and mortified.

Lady Linette tsked. "Ladies. Ladies!"

So the lessons continued, with Monique garnering the most praise, and even being excused from class early on occasion for her good behavior. It was all very vexing.

Once a week, the after-breakfast lesson was deceit with Mademoiselle Geraldine, which the headmistress *thought* was a "getting-to-know-you session" and which the girls knew was really training in the fine art of engaging in conversation without actually saying anything.

In the afternoon came tea and social discourse. After tea, they practiced various parlor games and played cards among themselves in the dining hall while the teachers either joined in or circulated, offering critique. Sophronia learned quickly that Sidheag was particularly adept at cards and that Agatha was no good at all. Preshea knew by heart all the different flavors of sherry and what ought to be stocked for gentlemen to imbibe, and Monique was a horrible whist partner.

Following this, they had the history of social discourse from one of any number of teachers, which seemed mainly to be comprised of reading in the library.

Then came dinner. This was followed by a seemingly endless round of dancing, drawing, music, dress, and the modern languages with Lady Linette, Sister Mathilde—whom everyone quickly began referring to as Sister Mattie—or, after the sun had set, Professor Braithwope. Incorporated into these lessons were the fine arts of death, diversion, and the modern weaponries.

Supper occurred promptly at ten each night. Then there was a small spate of spare time, which, due to the amount of extra work and rote memorization they were assigned throughout the day, Sophronia soon deduced was purely mythical. A few additional lessons, and the gas was turned off at two.

Sophronia came to realize that despite a near-constant exhaustion in mind and body, she was very much enjoying herself. She loved the lessons in espionage and deceit—so many possibilities!—and remained only a smidge disturbed by the analytical approach to murder. This kind of finishing school was rather more engaging than the one she had imagined, although she couldn't quite determine *why* she was there. It occurred to her that perhaps all finishing schools were like this—after all, Preshea discussed poisonings as if they were commonplace—but she rejected that idea. She may not yet be fully educated in the finer arts of being a proper lady, but she was smart enough to realize that her sisters wouldn't put much stock in finishing schools were they all this subversive.

After two weeks of such lessons, Sophronia drummed up the courage to ask Lady Linette about the matter of her unusual education. She waited patiently until after their lesson with Sister Mattie on buttermilk—for use in whitening lace and coating the stomach—in order to catch the teacher alone. Lady Linette had just finished with a group of the senior students on some mysterious French letter-writing technique that had even the oldest of the girls red-faced and tittering as they left the room.

"Lady Linette, may I have a moment of your time?"

"Oh, Miss Temminnick. Certainly. How may I help you?"

"Would it be terribly forward of me to ask quite a direct question?"

"Well, it would certainly be against your training thus far.

We haven't yet covered the manipulation of conversation by applying provocateur diplomacy. However, I suppose I might excuse an uncontrolled query this once."

Sophronia took a deep breath. "What, precisely, will I be expected to learn here?"

Lady Linette twirled one curl of blonde hair around the tip of one finger. "Information gathering and object retrieval, of course. But mostly, you should learn how to finish."

"Finish what, exactly?"

"Why, anything or anyone who needs finishing, my dear."

Sophronia shuffled her feet. When Lady Linette's forehead creased at the movement, Sophronia stilled and said, "Ah, yes, you see, it is not that I am unaware of the honor of your taking me in even though I haven't the connections of the other girls, but..."

"Go on."

"I'm not certain I could do *it*."

"Do what, dear?"

"Kill someone in cold blood."

Lady Linette's cornflower-blue eyes crinkled. "Ah, yes, but how do you know until you try?"

"I suppose that's true."

"Besides, dear, you don't have to do it face-to-face; there is always poison. And many of our graduates never harm anyone. It will depend on your particular situation after you leave us. It always does. For the ones who marry have a different path from the ones who don't."

"If you don't mind my asking, Lady Linette, how did you know to recruit me?"

"Ah, now, my dear, that is part of your training. You will have reached quite a level of comprehension if you manage to determine that truth all on your own." Lady Linette looked away.

Sophronia wanted to say something about the prototype, but she knew when she was being dismissed. She bobbed a curtsy. "Thank you, my lady."

Lady Linette winced. "Miss Temminneck, arrange after-hours lessons with Professor Braithwope, do. We really must work on that curtsy of yours, dear."

"But I have advanced eyelash fluttering to practice, and a mathematics problem concerning how to order strychnine *and* a lamb dinner on a limited budget, and three chapters on court etiquette to read, and my handkerchief to starch, and the qua-drille to memorize!"

"No one said learning etiquette *and* espionage would be easy, my dear."

At the end of the third week, after supper, all the girls in the entire school collected on one of the lower decks instead of going to evening classes. There was a general air of excited anticipation, and the massive airship began to sink slowly toward the bland green of the moor. Eventually it almost touched the heath, it was so low. *I thought it wasn't supposed to land*, Sophronia thought. She was careful to disguise her apprehension. From what little she had seen in the boiler room, she wasn't certain the school *could* land.

The girls all trooped down to the warehouse bay, where the

glass platform awaited them. It was not to be utilized, however. Professor Braithwope, demonstrating his vampiric strength with a kind of embarrassed deference, pushed the massive platform aside, exposing the large hole in the bottom of the ship.

Older girls first, the students sat down around the edge of the hole, legs dangling, and simply jumped to the grass below. Most landed with small graceful bends, like a deep curtsy. One or two tumbled forward and bounced to their feet in the manner Lady Linette had demonstrated. "From my days on the stage," she'd said.

Sophronia, Monique, and Sidheag jumped down without fuss, but the other debuts were nowhere near as committed to proving themselves. Both Agatha and Dimity had to be pushed.

Sophronia kept a careful eye on Monique in case she did, in fact, still have the prototype on her person and was planning to stash it behind some shrub or rock. This was, after all, the first time they had been to ground in weeks. But Monique remained a model student, in her way, surrounding herself with a group of stylish older girls and showing no indication of subterfuge beyond that normally required by lessons at Mademoiselle Geraldine's.

Captain Niall stood waiting for them. The girls all gathered around him in an excited, giggling throng. *Two score*, estimated Sophronia.

He raised up his hands, grinning amiably.

A number of feminine sighs were emitted at the cheeky twinkle in that grin. The werewolf once again wore a top hat tied to his head and a massive leather greatcoat, which flapped in the wind of the moor. As before, his feet were bare, and even though the coat was fully buttoned, it was clear he wore neither collar nor neck cloth underneath.

Sophronia suspected that many of the sighs and a good deal of the titillation resulted from the certain knowledge that he was entirely naked beneath that coat.

"Ladies, ladies, settle down, please. For the debuts among you, let me quickly say that as you only have me for lessons on an irregular basis, everyone is taught the same lesson together. And today we are addressing knives!" He said this last with a dramatic flourish.

A wave of murmurs and gasps percolated through the crowd.

The captain moved off to a low cluster of boulders, on top of which he had placed a long leather case. This he unrolled to display several knives of differing styles and materials. The girls gasped in appreciative horror.

He returned to face them, clutching three knives in one hand, displayed like a fan. "Don't like knives?" He pretended to fan himself with the blades and fluttered his long eyelashes at them.

Sophronia wondered if he might be slightly unhinged.

Dimity said, "But sir, aren't blades for gentlemen?"

"Ah, excellent starting place. In fact, no. Knives can be quite useful to a lady of quality. Swords are for men; they are too easily caught in the skirts. Knifework is far superior for ladies of your position. With fashion as it currently stands, there is always a way for a woman of style to hide a knife about her person. Over the next few months we will cover concealment and how to draw without mussing the trim of your dress. We will delve into blade sizes, applications, and materials. We will discuss silver versus wood and the best place to strike a vampire versus a werewolf. You will learn some hand-to-hand combat, subversive attacks, and, of course, how to throw. Questions?"

Sidheag's hand shot up.

"Yes, Lady Kingair?" Captain Niall did not look surprised, although this was the first time Sophronia had ever seen the tall girl show any interest in any lesson, be it feminine wiles, hidden messages, or deadly deeds.

"What about artillery?"

"Not my subject."

"But you must have had military service," protested Sidheag.

Captain Niall took that as a teaching point. "Will someone please explain why Lady Kingair made that particular assumption? Yes, Miss Pelouse."

"Because all werewolves in England are required to serve Her Majesty." Monique wore a simpering smirk.

Sophronia said, under her breath to Dimity, "Look at her, so smart! And the fact that he's called *Captain* Niall isn't a hint?"

Dimity hid a smirk.

Captain Niall gave Sophronia a look.

Oh, right, supernatural. He probably heard that. Sophronia could feel herself flushing.

The werewolf continued. "I would like you all to please spread apart and find yourselves a nice stick that will work for some preliminary fighting. Ten minutes, ladies, and we will reconvene over yonder."

Anticipating this relocation, the airship had drifted to hover over a flat rise and now floated several stories above the ground. The glass platform had been lowered and turned into a massive gas lamp. It utilized a kind of swirling yellow gas that lit up the heath, allowing the lesson to be conducted with all the grandeur of a ball under a chandelier.

The girls broke apart.

Sophronia and Dimity followed Sidheag's lead and made for a convenient shrub. There was no point in feeling about the heath in the dark for sticks. They all selected branches from the bush, ripping them off. Their selections were quintessentially to character. Sidheag wanted a nice big stick. Dimity broke off what she considered the most shapely branch and commented upon the bush's aesthetic qualities. Sophronia chose one that fit her hand relatively well but wasn't as big as anyone else's. Thus far all the lessons at this school had involved some element of subterfuge, and if the captain asked them to hide their sticks on their personages, she didn't want to be, well, stuck. She worried over this decision. *Sophronia,* she finally told herself firmly, *don't overthink the matter.*

They reassembled in a row. It was fascinating to see the whole school thus arrayed. Sophronia and the younger girls stood at one end in pinafores and pantalettes. The older girls, with their hair turned up and their skirts full-length, stood at the other. Except Monique, who stuck out like a very angry sore thumb among the debuts. Sophronia counted forty-five students in all.

Captain Niall walked along the row, examining the sticks.

When he got to Dimity he took the stick from her. "An interesting choice."

"I like the shape and smoothness," said Dimity.

"Not the best reason I have ever heard for choosing a knife, but not the worst, either. We will go over workmanship next week. Selecting a knife is like choosing a quality pair of gloves—appearance is important, but how it has been put together accounts for most of its function and duration."

Dimity nodded and he returned the stick to her.

He turned to Sophronia. "Why so small?"

"I thought you might ask us to hide it."

"Interesting reasoning." With no additional comment, he moved on.

Sophronia let out a shaky sigh. She told herself that this was because she was not yet accustomed to the fact that he was a werewolf. Professor Braithwope's vampiric nature was now routine, but Captain Niall was still wild and mysterious. *And he smells funny.* In actual fact, Sophronia wanted to impress him because everyone else seemed so taken with the man.

He took Sidheag's stick, one eyebrow raised. "Like large sticks, do you, Lady Kingair?"

Sidheag shrugged like a boy, but Sophronia could tell the tall girl was hiding a smile.

"Know how to use it?" Captain Niall sniffed. Not in the way that a lady might sniff when offended by a comment, but in the way of a dog, tasting the air.

Then he tossed the stick at Sidheag, causing Sophronia to flinch. Sidheag, however, caught it with one hand, as though expecting just such a violent action.

The werewolf produced a knife from his greatcoat pocket—a short-bladed, all-wooden weapon, carved from mahogany.

"Oooh," said Dimity. "How pretty!"

"For vampires, of course," said Monique, trying to impress, but Captain Niall wasn't listening to her.

Sidheag, grinning, stepped forward out of the line.

The girls murmured in confusion.

Sidheag lunged first. Using her stick as though it were actually a bladed weapon, she slashed out at the werewolf. It was not a wild slash, either, of the kind Sophronia and her brothers played at with fake swords.

Sophronia watched with interest, partly from a learning perspective and partly because Sidheag was exposing more of her character now than she had over the past weeks of intimate acquaintance. She'd been trained by someone who actually knew how to fight.

"Sidheag even moves like a boy!" commented Dimity.

"Yes, but she's *good*, isn't she?" Sophronia was favorably impressed. *Better than my brothers, that's certain!*

Preshea wanted to know, "What high-rank lady gets that kind of training?"

"A lady by title only." Monique crossed her arms and stuck her nose in the air.

Captain Niall was holding himself back. *He must be. He is a werewolf, after all, and twice as fast as even the most highly trained soldier.* He was also ten times as strong, if the legends were to be believed. *Nevertheless, Sidheag isn't at all bad. She keeps her stick in motion, always pressing forward, looking for a hole in her opponent's defenses.*

After a few minutes, Captain Niall called a halt to the impromptu match.

"Very interesting, Lady Kingair. I sense some of your"—he paused delicately—"*father's* training."

Sidheag inclined her head and resumed her place in line.

Sophronia, Dimity, Preshea, and Agatha all turned to stare at her, mouths slightly agape.

"I guess we found ourselves a teacher's pet," said Monique. "Then again, can you be a pet to a werewolf?"

"Oh, now, Miss Pelouse, I understand that playing favorites with professors is more *your* approach," Sidheag shot back.

"Now, ladies, what you really want is to never get into the kind of situation Lady Kingair and I just demonstrated. You *never* want to actually engage with a rival. Your greatest advantage is surprise. Make the decision to strike first and with intent, and—if you will excuse the pun—stick to it. Miss Pelouse, if you would like to demonstrate?"

Monique moved forward, head held high, a small smile on her face.

Captain Niall approached her.

Monique, instead of striking out in the manner of Sidheag, stepped in toward the werewolf. She commented on the pleasantness of the night and the beauty of the countryside. She fluttered her eyelashes in a way Sophronia had come to recognize as very advanced. *I should never have thought there would be a time when I would envy another girl's eyelash manipulation.*

Playing her game, Captain Niall leaned in. He flirted back. He looked deeply into her eyes.

Monique struck him hard in the side of the neck with her stick, behind and below the ear. A stick that she had, somehow, sharpened into a point.

It speared into the werewolf's body half an inch at least.

Blood leaked out around the stick.

Captain Niall winced and gave a little gasp of pain. "Ah. Yes. Very good, Miss Pelouse."

Sophronia gasped herself, raising a hand to her mouth in horror. A small, untraumatized part of her wondered why Monique had not displayed such skill when faced with flywaymen. *Had she wanted them to kidnap her?*

Several of the other girls gave little mewling cries of distress.

Captain Niall reached up and pulled the stick out of his neck. Blood oozed forth, but not of the color or quantity that Sophronia expected. It was darker, almost black, and slower. Then, right before her eyes, the wound began to heal and close.

The werewolf handed the bloody stick back to Monique, who took it with a little curtsy.

Dimity fell facedown into the grass in a dead faint.

Sophronia crouched over her friend and with a gesture signaled Sidheag to help.

The tall girl bent down, and under cover of the hum of confusion, Sophronia asked, "What did you mean by that? What you said to Monique?"

Sidheag looked at her, assessing. "Only that the rumor is she has an advocate among the teachers."

"Like a patron?"

"Very like."

"Who?"

"No one knows."

Sophronia nodded, then turned back to Dimity. Someone passed over the sal volatile, and soon enough, her friend's soft brown eyes blinked open. Sophronia helped Dimity to sit, and while she did so whispered in one ear, "Monique has an advocate on staff. I think that's how she's managed to keep the prototype location secret."

Dimity looked at her, still recovering. "Really, Sophronia, it makes me most uncomfortable how you manage to sort everything out every time I faint."

LESSON 9

How Not to Flirt

Sidheag, why does Captain Niall behave differently around you?" Sophronia had decided that her tactics with Sidheag ought to imitate those she used when handling her brothers. *Direct questions, lack of delicacy, and a general roughness of manner is clearly called for.* Consequently, the two girls were developing some kind of a relationship. It could not precisely be termed *friendly*, but Sidheag was less hostile to Sophronia than she was to most everyone else.

The girls were gathered in their parlor, practicing discarding gloves *with purpose*, during a moment of peace before bed.

Sidheag didn't even look at Sophronia. "I dinna ken your meaning."

"Oh, yes, you do."

Sidheag sighed. "I was raised by wolves."

"Yes, so Monique intimated."

"No, literally. Kingair Castle is a werewolf holding. Lord Maccon isn't my father; he's my great-great-great-great-grandfather. And he's still alive. He was bitten after he had already bred."

Sophronia blinked in startlement, and not in the correct eyelash-fluttering manner. Lady Linette would have been most upset. "That must be odd."

"You have no idea."

Dimity tilted her head. "Are they all soldiers? Like Captain Niall?"

"Of course."

"Well, that explains your conduct," said Monique snidely.

Sophronia looked at Monique. "I'd watch your tongue if I were you. Sidheag here is rather adept with weapons, and judging from our flywaymen experience, you are not."

"Why, thank you very much, Sophronia." Sidheag actually looked like she was trying to blush at the compliment. *Trying, mind you.*

"My," snipped Monique, "aren't you two chummy."

"I know the very idea is well outside of your capacities, Monique. Do you actually have any friends?" retorted Sophronia.

Dimity gasped and then jumped in to temper the insult by diverting the conversation. Dimity was, as a general rule, a very nice person. "Is Captain Niall like other werewolves?"

Sidheag's brow quirked. "How do you mean?"

Dimity only blushed. She, unlike Sidheag, had almost mastered the skill. Her round porcelain cheeks darkened, and no flush extended to any other part of her face. She did it so well she was under orders from Lady Linette to learn how to better control the timing. "When someone blushes as prettily as you do, my dear, one must become proficient at exact execution!"

Sophronia looked accusingly at Dimity. "I thought your parents were progressive!"

"They are, but that doesn't mean I've met many werewolves before now."

"No?"

"Well, any, even."

Sidheag laughed. "Believe me, they dinna act all wonderful en masse."

"His wound healing like that was remarkable," said Sophronia.

"Oh, *don't*, Sophronia." Dimity put a hand to her head and looked pale.

Preshea said, "I hear they make the best…ooh la la." She wiggled her torso suggestively.

Sophronia could feel her face heating at the very thought, and she knew for a fact that *her* blush wasn't pretty at all. It mashed in with her freckles and made her look feverish and blotchy. She was under orders not to blush at all if possible.

"Practice, I suppose," said Sidheag, deadpan.

"Had some personal experience, have you?" needled Monique.

"Dinna be disgusting. Pack is family!" Sidheag looked revolted, which only encouraged Monique.

"Wagging tails at you, were they?"

Sophronia jumped in to rescue Sidheag before the girl did something violent. "It must have been a fascinating childhood, being raised in a pack."

"It was more like having six assorted fathers with very decided opinions on upbringing."

Dimity perked up. "Really? Strict parents? Mine, too. What about your mum?"

Sidheag shook her head. "That's why they sent me here; all of them were between wives. Gramps decided I was getting a mite unfeminine and needed polish."

"Imagine that," said Monique. "Me agreeing with a werewolf."

Dimity said, "You might be better off not having polish. Mummy finished here, so there was no chance I could avoid it. But you're a lady already by rights; why not go off and have a proper ladylike life? Mummy says I daydream overmuch and I ought to learn to kill something once in a while. But you don't have to."

"Except you keep fainting," pointed out Sophronia.

"True. I'm afraid I'm doomed to be a terrible disappointment to her."

Sidheag grimaced. "There's my advantage. Old Gramps dinna know how a young lady ought to behave, so he's bound to be pleased by any improvement."

"Even if only a very minor one?" Monique added.

"Exactly!" Sidheag said with a grin, choosing to ignore the insult. She had quite a nice smile; it crinkled the edges of her strange yellow eyes. Sophronia wondered if those eyes had to do with her werewolf ancestry.

Bumbersnoot came waddling in.

The girls continued dropping gloves and indicating the drop with a slide of the eye and lowering of the lid. It quickly became a matter of then rushing to pick them up, as Bumbersnoot seemed to think this a lovely new game. He would try to get to the fallen gloves first and swallow them, at which juncture they would have to wait for him to emit them out the other end— that is, if they went into his storage compartment, and not his boiler.

"Oh, really!" exclaimed Preshea in distress when she was not quite fast enough. Bumbersnoot got to her lavender glove first and smeared it with a drop of boiling drool from his internal steam engine before she was able to pull it away.

"I don't know why you keep that thing around," said Monique. "It's a terrible nuisance, and I'm certain you're going to be in masses of trouble if anyone finds out."

"You going to tell?"

Monique took deep offense. "I'm not a snitch!"

"Your one redeeming character trait?"

"Oh, la," said Monique. "I happen to enjoy being flawless."

"Don't you think he's moving slower than before?" Dimity wondered, reaching down to pat the top of the little mechanimal's head. Bumbersnoot's tail began to tick-tock in pleasure, but it did seem less rapid than usual.

Sophronia frowned down at her pet in concern. "He probably needs to be fed." She'd not managed to visit the sooties again. Someone else had been thinking of Bumbersnoot's health, however, for last week one of the mechanical servants had appeared at their door with a platter. Upon lifting the silver lid, the girls found a small mound of coal and nothing else. Not even a note. Sophronia had surmised both whom the platter was for and whom it was from. She also surmised that it was now her turn to visit Soap to renew the acquaintance and extend her gratitude.

She'd not mentioned the sooties to anyone but Dimity, and even then not in any detail. Dimity had been rather dismissive, and Sophronia figured it was best to keep the sooties to herself when possible.

As they watched, Bumbersnoot's interest in the fallen gloves waned and the flow of steam from his underbelly began to slow. He sagged down, and his tail stopped moving.

"Oh, dear," said Dimity. "Poor little mite."

Sophronia waited until the others were asleep before climbing out of her cot, pulling on a dressing gown, and letting herself into the hall. The gaslights were doused for the evening, and it took valuable moments for her eyes to adjust to the gloom.

As soon as they did so, she made out a shape that caused her heart to pound in her breast. It was the conical metal form of a mechanical maid. The creature was stilled in its tracks, with no steam escaping from under the crude white pinafore someone had dressed it in. It was either dead or asleep. Nevertheless, the maid was between Sophronia and any possible access to the outer hull of the airship. *I wish I knew more about the workings of these faceless mechanicals. Can it see me, the way Frowbritcher could see me, or will it only notice when I'm in its way? Does it matter if I move slow? Or fast?*

Sophronia decided to simply proceed with as much caution

as possible. She flattened herself against the wall and inched toward the maid, attempting not to step on the tracks, worried that any vibration might transfer to the mechanical.

She moved closer and closer, and then, sucking in to make herself as skinny as possible—glad she was in her nightgown and not full skirts—inched past the maid.

The mechanical did not stir. Sophronia made it. Throwing caution to the wind, she took off down the hallway.

At that, the maid whirled to life and came after her, far faster than any household mechanical Sophronia's mother had on staff. No alarm sounded, however. Sophronia charged through a door and onto an outside deck, past another slumbering mechanical, and slid nimbly over the railing to hang suspended on the other side.

The mechanical on the deck also awoke as she passed. It was a footman model, faceless like the others, but wearing an old-fashioned manservant's white lace cravat. The cravat fluttered as the mechanical's internal steam engine puffed to life. It began trundling back and forth. However, it did not sound the alarm, either, and its tracks did not allow it to spot Sophronia on the other side of the railing.

Sophronia barely breathed. She noticed that the previous weeks' book-balancing, dancing, and lessons with Captain Niall had given her new muscles and better balance. She found this position far more comfortable than she had the first time around.

She also found that edging along the outside of the rails, jumping from deck to balcony to deck, was far easier. *This school really is training me.*

She flung herself, almost automatically, at Lady Linette's private balcony—the one with the rope ladder. From there she climbed down and into the hatch of the boiler room with a sense of relief. At least this part of the ship did not house any professors. She was liking the school rather more than she had thought possible and would prefer not to be asked to leave just yet. She was fairly certain that pursuit of food for an illicit mechanimal was not an acceptable activity.

The boiler room was far quieter at night than it had been during the day. But it was still active. The massive ship had to be kept afloat, and the balloons must be augmented by both heat and propeller action. Plus, Sophronia had to assume, much of the rest of the ship ran on steam power—the kitchens, the gas containment, the glass platform, the lighting, the heating, the tea.

She had intended merely to sneak in, liberate some coal, and sneak out—a plan far simpler to execute when the outside of the ship was as dark as the inside. But someone observed her stealthy entrance, and even as Sophronia was straightening up, the small, cherubic face of a young boy appeared next to her elbow, grinning.

"Well, well! Who are *you*, then?" The boy had a bit of a French accent and a very cheeky demeanor. He was also much younger than any of the other sooties, with remarkably twinkly eyes. Sophronia suspected those eyes of being green, but it was impossible to tell by the light of the boilers. He had dark, cropped hair, trousers that were too big, and an upmarket-looking cap. An incongruous character all round. He was also slightly less smudged than any sootie Sophronia had seen before. *Only slightly, mind.*

"Good evening," said Sophronia. "I'm a friend of Soap's."

"Who isn't?"

"Point taken. I'm Sophronia."

"I heard of you. The Uptop Soap's sweet on." The boy grinned at Sophronia again, showing dimples.

"How old are you?" was all Sophronia could think of to say to *that*.

"Nine," said the boy, sidling up to her.

"Are you a sootie?"

"Nope." The boy winked. Actually winked!

"Then what are you doing down here?"

"I like it here."

"How'd you get in?"

"Came in, like you."

"You from up top as well?"

"Sort of."

Frustrated, Sophronia said, "I only came for some coal."

"Well, let me go wake Soap."

"Oh, no need to disturb him."

" 'Course there's need. Why do you think I was set to watch the hatch? Waiting on the ghost of boilers past? He'll box my ears if I don't tell him you came."

"What's your name?" Sophronia felt no compunction about disregarding proper introductions with a child.

"They call me Vieve."

"Odd name."

"Suits me."

"Right. I'm going to go over there and get some coal. Does that meet with your approval, Vieve?"

Vieve gave her another one of his dimpled grins and scampered off, holding his trousers up with one hand. He returned moments later, before Sophronia had a chance to collect any coal, with a sleepy Soap in tow.

They made for an odd pair: the scamp of a nine-year-old in overlarge clothing and the tall, gangly sootie with shirtsleeves so short his wrists poked out the ends.

"Good evening, miss." Soap's face lit up with that wide, white-toothed smile.

"Are you well, Soap?"

"Well and good, miss, well and good. Got my little meal, did ya?"

"Yes, thank you. Bumbersnoot and I were most appreciative."

"Bumbersnoot?" wondered Vieve.

"The miss here's landed herself a mechanimal."

The young boy's face lit up. "You have a real live mechanimal! Can I see it?"

"Well, no, not right now. He's in my room, up in the students' section."

"No, I mean later. Can I see it later?"

Soap explained the boy's evident enthusiasm. "Vieve here is fixing to be the next great inventor."

Sophronia was shocked. "That's a grand ambition for someone your age."

"Not when your aunt is Beatrice Lefoux." Soap twisted his mobile mouth into a funny grimace.

Sophronia flinched at that statement, glaring down at the nine-year-old before her. "Your *aunt* is Professor Lefoux! Why didn't you say?"

Vieve shrugged in a way that managed to look particularly French. "Why should I?"

"You won't tell her, will you?"

"Tell her what?"

"About Bumbersnoot? Or my being in the boiler room?"

"'Course not. Why would I?" Vieve looked offended.

"Oh, thank you."

"So *now* can I see your mechanimal?"

Feeling as though she had been somehow trapped, Sophronia said, "Yes, very well. How will you get up to my room, though?"

"Oh, I get round most anywhere I wants."

"No one bothers to keep track of this scamp," Soap said, pulling off the boy's cap and ruffling his hair in a manner Vieve clearly found unnecessary and annoying.

"Are you not a real Uptop?" Sophronia felt a little silly using the word.

Vieve shrugged again. "I'm whatever I want to be, so long as alarms don't sound."

"That must be nice." Sophronia exchanged a look of amusement with Soap.

"Get a small stock of black for the lady, would you, Vieve?" Soap tilted his head in the direction of a mound of coal.

Vieve gave the tall boy a measured look and then trotted purposefully off.

"Arrogant little blighter," said Soap affectionately, once the lad was out of earshot.

"I suppose you'd have to be, if Professor Lefoux were your aunt." Sophronia was philosophical.

Vieve returned with his pockets bulging. Sophronia transferred the coal to her black velvet reticule. It was her very best evening bag, but it was the only one that wouldn't show coal smudges.

"Nice keeper," Vieve commented on the reticule.

"Thank you."

"Vieve here has an eye for accessories."

"I like a nice hat on a lady," was Vieve's dignified response, with which he trundled off about his own business.

"Nine years old, you say?"

"Well, when your only ma is French and a Lefoux, gotta develop some ways to cope. That barrow contraption of mine, the one you saw last time you was here? That's Vieve's."

Sophronia was impressed. "I thought you built it."

"Nope, I tested it. Vieve's got the brains."

Sophronia tilted her head and looked up at the tall young man. "I don't know about that."

Soap pulled at one ear self-consciously. "Why . . . miss."

Sophronia was trying to come up with a way to extract herself from what appeared to be an awkward conversation—*That'll teach me to try flirting outside the classroom*—when one of the boilers nearby sparked to roaring life and far away she heard the clang of alarm bells on the upper decks.

"Oh, blast it! Do you think they noticed I wasn't abed?"

Soap hustled her over to the exit hatch and held it wide while Sophronia climbed out. "No, miss, that's a perimeter alarm, that is. School's under attack. Technically, you're supposed to stay put, here with us."

"If I'm going to get caught, I'd just as soon it was outside. Better for my reputation."

"My thinking exactly. Good luck, miss."

Must be flywaymen, back for the prototype. Sophronia slung the reticule full of coal around her neck and climbed up the rope ladder. On the positive side, none of the teachers would still be in their rooms. On the negative side, she might well encounter any number of them on deck as she tried to make her way back to her own quarters.

She considered hiding out on Lady Linette's balcony until the alarm stopped, but if this was the promised attack from the flywaymen, she wanted to see what would happen next. They had threatened to return three weeks after the first aborted attempt, but the school must have eluded them an extra few days. The school's aimless floating on the winds of the misty moor made it as difficult to track from the air as it was from the ground.

Sophronia began to climb steadily up the side of the ship. It was tougher going straight up than moving around the side. She had to find handholds and footholds in the woodwork to get through the points where one deck met the hull and another jutted out again. She managed it, mainly by not looking down. Once past the midpoint, she consoled herself with the thought, *Even if I do fall, I'll land on a lower deck, with probably nothing more dramatic than a broken bone or two.* It was small consolation.

She looked up. She could see the squeak deck above her.

The soldier mechanicals were once more assembled, their little cannons out and pointed inward. Professor Braithwope no doubt stood in the middle with his crossbow. The attackers, if there were any visible, were around the other side of the hull, out of her view.

Sophronia climbed until she was on the level directly below the squeak deck. She used the outer railing method to slip around to the opposite side of the ship. As she rounded one last deck, she saw that indeed the flywaymen were back, this time with reinforcements.

She counted twelve airdinghies and behind them two larger airships. Nothing to the school's size, but full dirigibles of the kind that were rumored to be in production for overseas transport.

Sophronia scanned the occupants, searching for the shadow gentleman. *He must be there.* It was dark and she had to squint so hard she developed a headache, but she managed to make him out in one of the dirigibles. The silhouette of a man not dressed for riding, like the other flywaymen, but in full evening attire, including a stovepipe hat. Sophronia had no doubt that the band about that top hat was green. He was standing to the back—seeming, as before, to be an observer rather than a participant.

Sophronia wondered if he observed her, in her dressing gown, with an evening bag about her neck, clinging to the side of the ship.

She supposed the dirigibles must belong to sky pirates. Like flywaymen, she had thought them mere creatures of legend. *After all, how does a pirate afford a dirigible?* But there was no other explanation. The two dirigibles floating among the crowd of smaller ships, like mallards among the ducklings, looked as though they matched each other. It was as if the trappings of weaponry and flags were merely that, trappings, and the dirigibles were a stylish set intended for something far more grand than threatening a finishing school. Sophronia concluded that, like the galleons of old, these must have been stolen from the government.

One of the flywaymen put a bullhorn to his mouth. "Give us the prototype!"

The teachers said nothing.

One of the dirigibles fired, a flash of a cannon on the deck, and a large object came hurtling in their direction. It whizzed right by where Sophronia clung, only just missing the school.

Sophronia suppressed a shriek.

"Fire, Professor Braithwope," she heard Lady Linette order.

Professor Braithwope came into Sophronia's line of sight as he took two vampire-quick leaps to the front of the deck. He pointed his tiny crossbow at the fleet arrayed before them.

Sophronia doubted a crossbow of such daintiness would be very effective.

He fired.

As one, all the mechanicals, whose little cannons had been pointed at the professor the entire time, swiveled, tracking the arc of the crossbow bolt.

They target the bolt! Sophronia realized. *I hope Professor Braithwope is a good shot.*

He was. The bolt hit and stuck into the side of one of the airdinghies, well below the edge of the carrier basket, out of reach of its occupants.

Lady Linette came into view as she reached over the side railing and pulled at something hidden there.

The soldier mechanicals all fired at once in a tremendous boom of noise.

Sophronia winced and wished she could cover her ears, but she needed both her hands to hang on.

The squeak deck disappeared in a cloud of gunpowder smoke. The sweet, tinny smell floated down to Sophronia. When it cleared, she could see that one of the small airdinghies was listing to one side, two of its balloons collapsing. It started to spiral down and out of the sky. The ones to either side of it had also taken hits.

One of the dirigibles returned fire. This time it aimed higher. The cannonball tore a massive hole in the school's middle balloon. Sophronia tilted her head back, trying to look into the cavity and assess the damage. But the balloon was one deck over, and it was too dark for her to see anything. One side of the balloon looked to be caving slightly, and the whole ship listed in that direction.

"Get the sooties up there!" she heard Professor Lefoux yell, pointing at the damaged balloon.

Professor Braithwope did his fast scuttle out across the plank to the pilot's nest, presumably to call down to the boiler room.

Lady Linette stepped forward to the very front railing of the squeak deck. She needed no bullhorn, for she was very good at projecting her voice. *There is no doubt about it; she must have had considerable experience on the stage.*

"Stop firing. We will give you the prototype! Send over your ambassador."

They are giving up very easily, thought Sophronia. *Seems orchestrated, perhaps to pass along the fake prototype? Use it as a means to buy more time?*

The flywayman with the bullhorn shouted back over the intervening distance, "Agreed."

LESSON 10

THE CORRECT WAY TO GET CAUGHT

"What happened next?" Dimity was positively riveted by Sophronia's tale.

"Professor Lefoux gave the flywaymen a fake prototype. It looked like a shiny metal dodecahedron." It was the following morning, and they ought to be getting ready for breakfast, but instead they were lying in their beds chatting.

"I started to worry when you weren't back after the bells stopped sounding." Dimity's pretty face was somber with reprimand. "You could have *said* something to me about where you were going."

"I didn't want to get you into any kind of trouble. Bumbersnoot is my concern. Also, I hoped to return before anyone noticed. In the end, I had to wait while the teachers cleaned up after the battle. Did you know they brought sooties up top and had them climb inside the balloon to make repairs?" Sophronia was pretty darn certain, from a gangly silhouette, that one of those sooties had been Soap. She did not say this to Dimity. For some reason she felt very private about and possessive of Soap. Also a little embarrassed. She suspected Dimity might scoff. Petunia had always been very mocking whenever Sophronia befriended the stable lads. Then she hadn't minded so much. Now, after weeks of finishing school, she was beginning to concern herself with appearances.

"Regardless, I had to wait while everyone fussed over the balloon. I overheard the teachers talking."

Dimity's eyes widened appreciatively.

"Professor Lefoux said that the flywaymen would be back, because the prototype they passed over was a fake. She said it would fool them for a while, but that it was no guarantee of safety." Sophronia rolled over and pulled her black velvet reticule out from under the bed. She extracted a few lumps of coal. Bumbersnoot was asleep at the foot of her bed, barely warm. He was conserving all of his energy, his tiny internal steam engine almost completely shut down. She put him on the floor.

Sophronia tapped him on the head with a chunk of coal and then placed it in front of his face. He made a low whirring noise, heated up slightly, and then began to eat. Shortly thereafter, steam emanated from his underbelly, and he got to his four tiny feet with a few squeaks and clunks.

Sophronia continued her story. "Professor Braithwope said something about taking refuge in the mist—going gray, he called it—to buy us extra time."

Dimity looked thoughtful. "No mail drops for a while, then. Monique will be disappointed."

"As indeed am I. I was going to write to Mumsy for more clothes. And we were going to drop your brother that glove."

Dimity urged her on. "What happened next?"

"Sister Mattie asked about Bunson's. Professor Lefoux said something about them doing their best."

"I suppose that means Bunson's is trying to build a replacement prototype," Dimity suggested.

"Or a better-looking fake."

"I suspect we're heading in that direction, anyway," said Dimity.

"Goodness, how can you tell? The moor always looks the same to me."

"Well, the school will need proper repairs. I believe those are always conducted at Bunson's."

"Oh?" Sophronia was excited by this idea. She felt like they had been floating about aimlessly for an aeon.

"Well, the propeller is winding strong this morning." The girls looked up to see Sidheag, arms crossed over her bony chest, wearing a long pink flannel nightgown and slouching against the doorjamb. *Pink!*

"Is that what that vibration means?" Sophronia asked without missing a beat. She ought to have known someone would overhear their conversation. At least it was Sidheag, and not Monique. *Speaking of Monique, she's going to try to send that letter as soon as we arrive at Bunson's.*

"Indeed."

"How long have you been standing there?" Dimity wanted to know, drawing the covers up over her own red brocade nightgown.

"Long enough," replied Lady Kingair, coming inside their room. She bent to pat Bumbersnoot, who was working busily on his second lump of coal.

"So you managed to scarper back here without being discovered?" she asked Sophronia.

"Yes."

"Convinced of that, are ya?"

Sophronia felt a cold chill go up her spine.

"Yes, why?"

"Because Lady Linette is waiting for you in our sitting room, and she does not look pleased. She told me to tell you specifically, Sophronia, to dress and get yourself in there right sharp."

"Oh, bother," said Sophronia. "Dimity, will you keep an eye on Bumbersnoot for me?"

"Of course."

"Bumbersnoot, stay here with Auntie Dimity, please."

The mechanimal sat back on his haunches and sent a puff of smoke at her, tail wagging back and forth hopefully. Sophronia tossed Dimity another lump of coal, hoping to keep the dog's attention in their room, and climbed out of bed. In the interest of appearing as innocent as possible, she donned her simplest dress—a blue muslin with white flowers—and Sidheag helped her do up the buttons. Over this Sophronia pulled a white pinafore. She elected simply to plait her hair, as it was fastest. With Lady Linette such things were always a bit dodgy—take time to be particularly presentable, or dress quickly? She popped a lace cap on her head and went reluctantly into their drawing room to see how much trouble she'd gotten herself into.

"Miss Temminnick, good morning."

"Good morning, my lady." Sophronia bobbed a curtsy. She'd been working very hard with Dimity on the art of the curtsy—how to bend the knees without sticking out the bottom, a smooth dip and rise. Dimity had even shown her how to lower her eyes and glance up through her lashes.

Lady Linette, who looked rather irked, nevertheless noticed the improvement. "Much better, young lady. Not so much tilt to the head, not with a lady or a vampire. With another woman, it comes off as coy. With a vampire, it comes off as invitation. Otherwise a very commendable effort."

Sophronia rose from her curtsy. "Thank you, my lady."

"However, it does not make up for some very disturbing news I've recently had."

"Yes, my lady?" Sophronia's stomach fluttered ominously.

"I have been informed that you were seen *out* last night. You were spotted through one of the portholes climbing the exterior hull."

Sophronia narrowed her eyes. *Someone's ratted on me! That's certainly not in the spirit of this school.* "One of the teachers, my lady?"

"Oh, very nice. No defensive tone, merely a query for further information. You are trying to take advantage of my annoyance in the hope that I will be indiscreet about the informant. You are learning well, Miss Temminnick, very well indeed."

Sophronia widened her eyes hopefully, trying to look both nonthreatening and inquiring.

"Simply in honor of such a creditable effort, I will tell you that it was a student. And this is a concern. On the one hand, no one else saw you. On the other, you have made an enemy of one of your fellows in such a way as to cost you a covert operation. You should pay very close attention in your blackmail lessons in order to forestall such behavior in the future. Then again, so should the student in question. She might have used this information to manipulate you, rather than coming directly to us. A questionable choice of application, but perhaps she thought the matter was time sensitive."

"My lady?" Sophronia's heart was in her throat. *Please don't turn me out.*

"Yes, of course. So, for being seen, you are hereby ordered to report to Cook. She will have you cleaning the pots and pans after supper in the mess for the next two weeks."

Sophronia started to let out a breath of relief, but then Lady Linette continued. "For being told upon..." She paused, considering.

I'm being sent home when we get to Bunson's. I know it. Sophronia clenched her hands.

"For being told upon, you are being denied attendance at the upcoming stopover at Swiffle-on-Exe. There is an acting troupe in town. You will have to miss the show. And for being out during lockdown, you will not be allowed off the ship at all."

Sophronia let out a breath and relaxed her hands. "Thank you, my lady."

"Goodness, girl, what are you thanking me for?"

"You aren't going to expel me."

"Of course not! Don't be silly. None of the *professors* actually saw you, and you avoided the mechanicals during a high-order alarm. That's very good work indeed. And you've displayed untapped skills in climbing and night stealth. I'm considering extra lessons as a result. We were told you had gumption. Our mistake was in underestimating how much. Why were you out and about?"

"Curiosity." Sophronia lied without hesitation.

Lady Linette pursed her lips. "That's as good a reason as any. And now, girl, let us discuss hairstyles. I'm detecting young Lady Kingair's effect on your coiffure. It won't do, won't do at all. She is a lost cause, but she has the rank and title to be eccentric. You may actually need to look like a *lady* upon occasion. From here on out, you are to put your hair up in curling rags every night. Get Miss Pelouse to show you how. I do not wish to see you with a plait ever again. Is that clear?"

Sophronia considered this her real punishment—the very worst of the lot. *Curling rag training from Monique, indeed!* Still, she bobbed another curtsy of acknowledgment. "Very good, my lady."

"Good morning, Miss Temminnick."

"Good morning, my lady."

"Oh, and Miss Temminnick? You do realize you did not have to admit to your little excursion? It was your word against that of your accuser. Keep that in mind, in the future. Denial is always an option." With which Lady Linette swept from the room, her morning dress one of a particularly fluffy lavender, so wide it barely fit through the door.

"It has to be Monique!" said Dimity. She was pacing around their room, her hands and arms flying in annoyance, as though she were fending off a bee. The ruffles on the sleeves of her peach dress had an almost sea creature–like way of drifting about after her. "I wonder if Lady Linette is her *friend* on staff?"

Sophronia was charmed by how offended Dimity was on her behalf. "Of course it's Monique. And I suppose it could be Lady Linette; she's an actress, after all." Sophronia collapsed onto her bed with a groan. "Oh, but *curling rags!*"

"They can't be that bad."

"Easy for you to say—you'll never need them. Why did I have to be cursed with straight hair? And you know, I never cared much before now. What is this place doing to me? I'm coming over all frivolous."

Dimity had no solution to that particular problem. "I'm sorry you're going to miss the theatricals."

"In Swiffle-on-Exe? It could be worse."

"It *is* worse: all the boys will be attending."

Sophronia flopped onto her back. She wasn't certain whether to be upset or pleased by this. "That's all right, really it is. I don't think I'm quite ready for boys yet. My eyelash fluttering is subpar."

"Oh, but that's what Bunson's is for! Practice. I overheard Monique telling Preshea all about it. Some of the girls even keep score. They use what we learn to make as many boys as possible fall in love with them. They aren't allowed to encourage actual declarations, of course. If one of Mademoiselle Geraldine's girls takes a real beau, he'd better be a baronet at the very least."

"Isn't Bunson's training evil geniuses?"

"Yes, mostly."

"Well, is that wise? Having a mess of seedling evil geniuses falling in love with you willy-nilly? What if they feel spurned?"

"Ah, but in the interim, think of the lovely gifts they can make you. Monique bragged that one of her boys made her silver and wood hair sticks as anti-supernatural weapons. With amethyst inlay. And another made her an exploding wicker chicken."

"Goodness, what's that for?"

Dimity pursed her lips. "Who doesn't want an exploding wicker chicken?"

Sidheag opened the door and stuck her head in. "Are you two going to wallow in here all day? It's time to eat, and rumor is there's going to be a big announcement over the scones."

"We're headed to Swiffle-on-Exe. There's a play on. We'll be allowed to attend alongside Bunson's," said Sophronia.

"Gracious, aren't you in the know?" Sidheag arched an eyebrow and turned away. Today her dress was of plaid, as if she were a housekeeper.

Dimity sidled up to Sophronia and said, under her breath, "Plaid! Can you believe it?"

They followed Sidheag out to where the debuts stood waiting.

Dimity, with a mercurial gleam in her eye, said, "Sophronia claims we're headed to Swiffle-on-Exe to see a play with Bunson's."

Instantly the others all began to chatter excitedly.

"Really? What kind of play?" Agatha was, for the first time in Sophronia's experience, animated by the prospect. Agatha, so shy it was almost disruptive, never seemed to get excited about anything.

"Bunson's? You mean *boys*?" Preshea's pretty face narrowed into covetousness. Sophronia thought she looked like a partridge with a plucking disorder.

"Now, Preshea," reprimanded Dimity, "it's no good choosing your first husband from a school for evil geniuses. Much too difficult to kill."

"Why do you know any of this?" Monique demanded of Sophronia.

"Why, Monique, surprised I learned it first?" said Sophronia, minding her recent lesson on not revealing information unnecessarily.

They made their way through the passageways and out onto various decks toward the dining hall. Sophronia grabbed Monique by the arm, holding her back. Dimity gave her a confused look, but took the cue and concentrated on shepherding the other three forward, giving Sophronia some privacy.

"A word, if you would, Monique?"

"What do *you* want?"

"Shoddy business, tittle-tattling on me like that. I thought you didn't do that kind of thing. Did you go to your pet teacher?"

"I have no idea to what you are referring."

"Oh, very nice—denial. Lady L said I ought to have applied it better myself. I'll remember that in future."

"Do you think you might make sense at some point, or are you merely trying to annoy me?"

Actually, thought Sophronia, *she's pretty good.* Monique's blue eyes were guileless, even as they narrowed in exasperation.

"Not that I really wanted to go to the play," Sophronia added.

Monique shook her off. "You're mad, did you know that? But what can one expect from a covert recruit? Do refrain from socializing with me henceforth, will you?"

"With pleasure." Sophronia walked off.

"Well? What did she say?" whispered Dimity.

"She denied everything."

"Of course she did."

They arrived and took their seats at table.

The murmuring of talk and consumption of comestibles hushed when the headmistress stood and stepped forward, her hair a wild pouf of red. She took a deep breath and opened her arms wide, bracing her back and pushing her tremendous cleavage forward. "Ladies, ladies, your attention, please! We have changed direction toward that other school, Bunson and Lacroix's Boys' Polytechnique. There is a small troupe in residence at the moment, performing a highly instructional play, *An Ideal Bathtub.* We thought you ladies deserved a treat. Now, remember, if there is gossip to be garnered, garner it. If there are new dress styles to be imitated, imitate them. If there are hearts to be broken, break them. That's my girls."

"Gossip? I thought she didn't know about us, you know, gathering information?" Dimity was confused.

"I think she is actually implying social gossip," said Sophronia.

Mademoiselle Géraldine continued. "We will be on course for Swiffle-on-Exe for the next three days. Regular lessons will proceed smoothly during the interim. Now remember, ladies, this is a privilege, and attendance will be revoked at the professors' discretion. In one case, it already has been."

A flutter of *ooohs* swept through the hall, and everyone pretended not to glance in Sophronia's direction. *The thing about a finishing school that trains intelligencers,* thought Sophronia, *is that everyone knows your business, sometimes before you do. And occasionally they'll make it up simply for entertainment.* Whether she liked it or not, word was certainly out about her punishment, if not her crime. The speed of dissemination was impressive, if slightly embarrassing.

Everything was a fervor of excitement and preparation for the next three days. Despite what Mademoiselle Geraldine had said, things were not as before. Lessons changed to focus on proper dress and manners for the theater. Lady Linette spent two solid hours on opera glasses alone! Even Captain Niall switched from knives to garrotes. Much easier, he explained, to kill someone with a garrote at a seated event; only make certain you sit *directly* behind your quarry. "Very inconvenient," he said, "to try to kill someone when you are seated in front of him."

You'd think we were visiting the queen, thought Sophronia, watching Preshea try on yet another possible dress for *An Ideal Bathtub.*

The girls were assembled in their common parlor on the evening prior to their arrival at Swiffle-on-Exe. It was the only spare time they had, before bed, and they ought to be practicing walking properly in heeled boots. Instead, they were picking through each other's wardrobes and planning their accessories.

Sophronia was the only one practicing. She was tottering

about, pretending she wasn't interested in outfits, since she wasn't to attend. She was intrigued to find, however, that Agatha had the most expensive gowns and nicest jewelry, much to Monique's annoyance. Dimity's outfit, on the other hand, came in for pitying glances. It wasn't so much the fabric, although that was bad—purple and teal stripes—as the cut of the dress, which was nowhere near as elegant as current fashions dictated. Sophronia shuddered to think what they might say of her one and only evening gown. She was shocked at herself for such shallowness. *I'm turning out just like my sisters!*

Into the madness of a parlor strewn with dresses, wraps, and gloves, not to mention girls prancing about in assorted fripperies, came a loud knock.

Sidheag, who was standing off to one side observing the chaos with an eye to the ridiculous, went to answer it. Whoever was there was too short to be visible on the other side of Lady Kingair's lanky form.

A small voice with a French accent queried cheekily, "Is Miss Sophronia mucking about?"

Sidheag looked down for a long moment and then turned around, eyebrows arched, and addressed the room. "Sophronia, you have a, erm, caller." Then she resumed her languid pose, watching the other girls cavort with the look of a scientist observing the actions of a newly discovered species.

A few of the others glanced over to see who was at their door, but the visitor garnered very little attention after that first assessment.

Sophronia, still in the heels, teetered over.

"Good evening," said Vieve, grinning up at her. Vieve, as it turned out, did indeed have green eyes. His hair was pitch-black under his cap and he was looking quite at ease with the world, in the manner of most chronically ill-behaved children. He was dressed respectably, if a bit on the newspaper lad end of the spectrum, and was at least clean.

"Oh, Vieve, how are you?"

"Topping. I've come to meet your... you know..."

"Oh, yes, of course. I forgot." Sophronia turned around to face the other girls. "Would you mind if Vieve came in?"

Dimity said, "Who?"

The others barely looked up.

Vieve took off his cap, clutching it self-consciously to his chest, and sauntered into the room.

"I wouldn't pair that hat with those gloves, miss, if I were you," he said, rendering judgment on Preshea's choice of accessories.

The black-haired girl noticed him. "Oh, you wouldn't, would you? And what would you know of such matters?"

"I *am* French," replied Vieve with a shrug.

"Good point, that," said Dimity, grinning.

"You're nine years old and your guardian is an intellectual!" protested Preshea.

To be fair to Vieve, Sophronia privately agreed with him about the hat and gloves. The gloves were magenta and the hat pea green. "I wouldn't get involved if I were you," she said to the boy.

Vieve followed her through the chaos toward her room.

Dimity called after her, "Remember your reputation, Sophronia. Keep the door open!"

168

Monique let out a trill of unpleasant laughter. Agatha made her way over to Dimity to whisper something in her ear.

"I'm good with accessories," protested Vieve to Sophronia once they were safely away from the bedlam.

"I'm certain you are, but there is no point in arguing with Preshea. She always wins, even when she doesn't. And here is Bumbersnoot. Bumbersnoot, this is Vieve."

The little dog was sitting expectantly at the foot of Sophronia's bed, waiting for lights-out. He'd fled the parlor after Monique kicked him when he ate one of her hair ribbons. He now had a little dent in one side.

Vieve's green eyes lit up with pleasure at seeing the mechanimal. "May I?"

"Of course. Here you are." Sophronia picked up Bumbersnoot and presented him to the young boy.

The lad examined the creature closely, popping open various hatches and spending a good deal of time studying the tiny steam engine inside Bumbersnoot's stomach. "Incredible. Such intricacy. But he needs to be serviced, I think. Has he been squeaking at all?"

"As a matter of fact, he has."

Vieve nodded. "I'll come by tomorrow, when everyone is groundside, with some oil and bits of kit. Give him a spiffing up."

"That's very kind." Sophronia wasn't certain how she felt about a nine-year-old taking apart her pet, but she wasn't about to turn down the offer, either. If Bumbersnoot needed a looksee, Vieve was the closest she had to an expert.

"It'd be a pleasure. He's quite the little beauty, isn't he?"

Bumbersnoot had a long, sausagelike body, and while he was mostly bronze, it was clear he had some brass and iron parts, so that he was rather a patchwork. Fond of him though she was, "little beauty" was not a phrase Sophronia would have used to describe him. "If you say so."

Vieve put Bumbersnoot back on the bed and doffed his hat. "Until tomorrow, then, miss?" Such an odd child.

"Until tomorrow. Shall I show you out?" Sophronia fell back on her recent training in how to dismiss a gentleman caller without rancor.

"I think I can manage on my own." With which the boy left through the parlor, doffing his hat to the girls as he did so.

Dimity appeared in the doorway, glaring at her. "Who on earth is that? Or should I say, who in the *clouds* is that?"

"Vieve."

"So I gathered, but Sophronia, you never told *me* you had befriended Professor Lefoux's eccentric niece!"

"*Niece?*"

ON THE IMPORTANCE OF PROPER DRESS

Vieve was as good as her word. *Her* word. Sophronia still could not quite believe it. It seemed that Professor Lefoux's nine-year-old niece liked to dress as a boy and fraternize with sooties. And that apparently Professor Lefoux let her!

"What-ho, Miss Sophronia," said the girl, standing at the door and clutching a chubby reticule before her.

"Good evening, Miss Genevieve," replied Sophronia formally. "Won't you come in?"

Vieve didn't look at all embarrassed at being found out. "So you know, do you?"

"Why on earth would you want to go about as a *boy*?"

"Boys have it far more jolly." Vieve gave one of her dimpled grins. "I assure you, I find female dress fascinating. I simply prefer not to wear it myself. It's very confining."

Sophronia looked her guest up and down. This evening the girl was wearing her customary cap paired with an oversized man's shirt with the sleeves rolled up, a brown vest, and brown jodhpurs. "You'll forgive me if I don't entirely trust your judgment in matters of appearance."

Vieve laughed.

"There is your patient." Sophronia pointed to Bumbersnoot, who had taken advantage of the absence of Sophronia's fellow denizens to lounge in the parlor under the tea table in a position of prominence he wasn't normally permitted.

Vieve dumped the contents of her reticule onto the top of the tea table. Her kit appeared to be mainly mechanic's tools and a few unlabeled glass bottles with corks. The girl coaxed Bumbersnoot out from under the table, sat down on the settee, and lifted him into her lap.

"Can I do anything to help?"

"Don't think so. I take it you got caught climbing during shutdown and that's why they banned you from attending the play?"

"I didn't get caught; someone saw me and told."

"That's not on!" Vieve tipped the mechanimal upside down, opened up his stomach, and began tinkering and poking about with a sort of long squiggly stick made of iron. She picked up one of her little bottles, uncorked it, and poured a drop of some dark, viscous liquid down the stick so it went directly where she wanted it to. Vieve really was remarkably adept for a nine-year-old.

"So you're Professor Lefoux's niece?"

"That's what she tells me."

Sophronia sat back on the settee and tried to look casual. "Know anything about this *prototype*?"

"Now, miss, why would you think that?"

"You like mechanics and inventions, and so far as I can gather, the prototype is both."

The girl looked up and smiled, looking far more her age than when she was concentrating on Bumbersnoot. "It's for a special communication machine."

"A what?"

"Ever since the telegraph failed, stymied by the aether currents, they've been working on this new idea for communication over long distances—one station to another. Unfortunately, there seems to be some difficulty making them transmit back and forth. The researchers at the Royal Society in London came up with a new prototype to fix this. They made two: one for London, and one to come here, to Bunson's."

"Why Bunson's?"

"Well, that's where the other communication machine is located, of course. Anyway, something happened to that prototype."

"Monique hid it."

Vieve looked impressed. "Really? How do you know that?"

"I was with her at the time. That's when I was recruited."

"It was her finishing assignment?"

"Yes. And she failed."

"That explains why she's bunking down with debuts. And why she wasn't allowed to attend the play either." Vieve's dimples disappeared and she once more looked unnaturally serious for a nine-year-old.

That little bit of information was news to Sophronia. She'd sent Dimity off with strict instructions to keep a very close eye on Monique. Instructions that Dimity would find very hard to follow. "Monique didn't go? Why isn't she here in quarters?"

"Skulking about the teachers' section, ain't she? Nasty piece of work, that one. And gets away with it, what's worse."

Sophronia pursed her lips. She didn't have time for Monique's tomfoolery at the moment. "So do you know where it is?"

"The prototype?"

"No, the communication machine at Bunson's." *If I could get a look at it, I might learn why everyone thinks it's so important. Besides, I'd like to see inside Bunson's, where girls aren't supposed to go, on principle.*

Vieve looked up at that, her green eyes narrowed. "I can see why you keep getting into trouble. Are you sure you're a girl?"

"That's rich, coming from you."

"You don't act like a girl." Vieve cocked her head. "You want to go after it?"

Sophronia nodded. "See what all the fuss is about."

This didn't appear strange to Vieve. "We're going to need help. Can't get on and off this airship that easily."

"Good thing we're friendly with the sooties, then, isn't it?"

Genevieve Lefoux dimpled down at her work. "Good point. Right." She put Bumbersnoot back on his feet. "That should do it."

The mechanimal shook himself, like a wet dog might, and trotted about the room. His tail wagged excitedly, *ticktockticktock*!

Sophronia watched him. "He's moving much easier, and he doesn't seem to be squeaking. You do good work."

Vieve blushed. "I try. He might...oh, there he goes."

Bumbersnoot crouched down in one corner of the parlor and deposited a pile of ash in a small mound.

"Oh, dear. Bad mechanimal!"

Vieve defended the dog. "He *is* a tiny steam engine. There're bound to be a few deposits."

"What about his capacity as a storage device?"

Vieve said, "About the size of your fist. Any larger and it might get stuck."

Sophronia nodded, hoarding the information away for future use. "So are you any good at climbing?"

"Yes, but fortunately, we don't have to." The girl held out her wrist. On it she had strapped a wide leather band with what looked like a small brass jewelry case affixed to it. She flipped open the lid and held up the gadget for Sophronia to see.

At first Sophronia thought it might be a music box, but when she looked closer, she saw there were all sorts of dials and wheels and small knobs.

"What is it?"

Vieve grinned. "I call it my anti-mechanical mobility and magnetic disruption emission switch. Soap calls it *the obstructor*."

It took only five minutes for Sophronia to badly want an obstructor of her own.

Vieve simply marched out into the hallway, and when a maid came trundling threateningly in their direction, the girl pointed her wrist at the mechanical and clicked a switch with her free hand.

The maid froze in place. Steam stopped emanating from the base of its carapace, and the gears and dials where its face ought to be stopped moving. It was as though the mechanical had seen something scandalous and been seized by a fainting fit. *Ingenious!*

"Come on!" Vieve grabbed Sophronia by the hand and dragged her past the mechanical. "The effect wears off in six seconds. I'm trying to figure out how to extend it, but that's the best we've got at the moment."

They ran past the maid, pausing at a bend in the hallway and peeking around the corner in case there was another mechanical, or possibly one of the students who was being punished by confinement and had similar escapist tendencies.

So they proceeded through the sections and levels of the airship, engaging in a kind of transdirigible hopscotch. Anytime they happened upon a mechanical, Vieve froze the poor thing for six seconds while they dashed past and continued on.

They crossed the midpoint of the school and immediately headed down toward the lower levels. As Vieve explained, "There are still two teachers aboard."

"Professor Braithwope?" Sophronia said, hazarding a guess. "He can't leave the ship. And"—she paused to think—"your aunt?"

"Because she doesn't care for anything fun or entertaining," explained Vieve without rancor.

Eventually, they found themselves at the entrance to the boiler room. Sophronia felt odd approaching that room from above rather than below. They pushed aside two massive brass doors emblazoned with images of fire and all sorts of symbols of danger. Sophronia squinted. One of the symbols looked to be a badger with his tail in flames. Another was a skull like that on a pirate's flag, but with its mouth open and long vampire fangs. *If that's a vampire, perhaps the badger on fire is meant to be a werewolf?* Another, Sophronia could swear, was a robin in a bowler. *What,* she wondered, *is dangerous about a robin in a bowler?*

They climbed down a small flight of stairs out onto an internal balcony that overlooked the engine chamber. It was like being in a box at the theater. From that vantage, Sophronia and Vieve could see the entirety of the boiler room spread out below them: the four huge boilers with orange mouths agape, the mountain of coal over to one side, and smaller piles near the boilers. There were giant pumps and pistons, and rotary gears and belts, some cycling round, others moving up and down, and some utterly still. Lit by the flickering of the boilers, the colossal machinery glowed. Even all the coal dust and steam in the air had not dulled the shine. Sophronia wondered if they polished the metal regularly. Threading through and around and within the machines were the sooties, like ants. The larger forms of the greasers, mechanics, and firemen stood as points of stillness within this movement; fulcrums to which the sooties would periodically gather for instructions, as if those selfsame ants had discovered a nice crumb of cheese.

"Impressive, from this angle," said Sophronia.

"Beautiful." Vieve's eyes gleamed. "Someday I want a whole massive laboratory exactly like this all to myself."

"Oh?"

"I shall name it my contrivance chamber." She had clearly given this a great deal of thought.

"Excellent name. Perhaps we should move on before we're noticed by an engineer?"

"Well put." Vieve led Sophronia over to a set of steep stairs that spiraled to the boiler room floor. Vieve scuttled down. Sophronia, who was in a dark blue visiting dress with multiple petticoats, followed as nimbly as those petticoats would allow.

Vieve knew the way once they got down. She moved with purpose through the machines and around the coal heaps, in easy avoidance of greasers, sliding in and out of the sooties as if she were one. With her cap pulled low and her hands shoved deep into the pockets of her jodhpurs, she looked like a sootie, only shrunken and a little less dirty.

Sophronia, on the other hand, felt self-conscious. She stuck out like a puff pastry among meat pies in her prim dress. She was glad that when they stopped it was behind a massive rotary engine to one side of the room, mostly out of sight.

Vieve grabbed an impish towheaded boy by one elbow. "Rafe, fetch Soap, would ya?"

"Do it yourself, Trouble."

"Can't. I got important *company*. Couldn't leave a lady alone in this dangerous place, now could I?"

"Her?" The blond boy squinted into the shadows where Sophronia stood. "What's one of *them* doing down 'ere?"

"Same as everybody else: minding her own business. Now get Soap, would ya?"

The blond sniffed, but ambled off.

"Pleasant young man," commented Sophronia.

"They can't all be as charming as me," Vieve replied with a smile.

"Or as adorable as me," added Soap, coming up behind Vieve and nicking her cap. "Good evening, Miss Temminnick; Vieve. To what do we owe this honor? Shouldn't you be watching a play or something highfalutin in town?"

"Give it back!" Vieve made a grab for her hat, but Soap held it out of reach. "Can't stand the theater."

"And I'm not allowed," Sophronia added. "But Soap, Vieve and I were wondering if you could help us get out?"

"Out?"

"We want to pay a visit to Bunson's."

"But why? No one will be there."

"Exactly," crowed Vieve.

"They've got something we want to see."

Soap was suspicious. "What *kind* of something?"

"A communication machine," Sophronia explained.

Vieve nodded, grinning.

Soap looked back and forth between them. He ended with Sophronia. "Not you as well? Gone barmy over mechanics, have you? I should never have introduced you two. It'll all end in tears and oil."

"Not really. I'm more intrigued by this one's desirability."

"What?"

"Flywaymen want it, or parts of it. Monique failed because of it. I've seen two air battles so far over stray bits of it."

Soap latched on to the last part of her statement. "You saw what happened with the mid-balloon?"

"Yes, and I saw you repairing it."

"No joke. I was squeaking for nigh on an hour because of all that helium. Funniest thing, repairs up top. So?"

"Someone fired a cannon at us."

"Because of this communication machine?"

"Not exactly. Because of a piece that might make the communication machines actually communicate with each other."

Soap looked confused but willing to play along. "Well, very good, then, but I better come with you. Can't have you two scrabbling about groundside unsupervised."

Sophronia arched her eyebrows. "I assure you, I have been sneaking around with impunity for years."

Soap glowered at her.

"Oh, very well," said Sophronia, unwilling to waste any more time.

Soap enlisted a few off-duty sooties so that a small, dirty herd escorted Sophronia and Vieve over to yet another hatch in the boiler room floor. This was one Sophronia hadn't noticed before, in a corner behind what she assumed was a hot water pump for the school's serpentine room-heating system. Up top, in the residential rooms, the heating contraptions looked like grates in the walls, and they kicked in at night if it got icy, which it often did up high. The one in Dimity and Sophronia's room made such a rumbling and growling that Dimity named it "Boris the Indigestive." This, then, was Boris's origin.

There was a coiled rope ladder resting nearby. When the hatch flipped open, it became clear the airship was floating very low to the ground, perhaps only two stories up. They were also at the edge of the moor. Swiffle-on-Exe became visible after they let down the ladder and began to climb.

The school had stopped above a knoll off a goat path above the town, but it was far enough outside the village for Sophronia to be nervous that, should the moor mists rise up, they would not be able to find their way back. The moon was full, which explained both the revels in the town and the absence of Captain Niall. He would be a true monster tonight, uncontrolled and uncontrollable. Sidheag had explained that Captain Niall took himself off several days before the moon, far into the moor, away from civilization, so that his moon-mad werewolf self wouldn't be a danger to anyone. Sophronia thought this sad. Werewolves supposedly loved the theater.

They dropped down to the grass, Sophronia first, then Vieve, and then Soap. Soap saluted the sooties above and the ladder was pulled up. They would lower it again in exactly two hours, right before the performance was supposed to let out. Sophronia worried about the time constraint, but Vieve was confident that two hours was enough.

Under the bright moon, the path into town was well-lit. Swiffle-on-Exe was a silvery hodgepodge of thatched roofs, church steeples, and the looming monstrosity of Bunson's to the left. They moved at a swift trot and arrived at the gates to the boys' school in a little under a quarter of an hour.

Sophronia hid while Soap pulled the porter's bell rope. They had decided to let Vieve face the porter mechanical initially, both because she had the obstructor and to ascertain whether the porter would recognize her as a female. Vieve maintained that the identifier nodule apixiter, whatever *that* was, had to be the shape of the lower half of a human body and that if Sophronia would only don trousers like a sensible person...

Either Vieve was correct or some other aspect of her personality came off as intrinsically masculine, for when the gate was thrown open and the mechanical stood facing her, he made no objection.

Vieve stepped toward him and puffed up her chest. "Message for Mr. Algonquin Shrimpdittle from Professor Lefoux," she said in her high treble voice.

"Give to me, young sir," boomed back the porter from behind his faceless confusion of gears and cogs.

"Can't be done," replied Vieve. "Orders are to deliver it directly."

The porter let out a blast of steam in apparent annoyance. This flapped up the cravat pinned about his neck so that it momentarily obscured his clockwork face. He whirred and clunked, sending out a puff of smoke from a stack at the top of his head. Finally he said, "Very good, sir, follow me."

The porter made a wide loop on its tracks. It hadn't the pivot mechanism and nimbleness of the single-track mechanicals on board the finishing school. It began to trundle away, the wheelbarrow on its backside rattling side to side.

Vieve turned to Sophronia and whispered, "Go on! Hop in!"

"What, inside?"

"It hasn't any sensory nodules on its back."

Sophronia gave the young girl a look of doubt. *Then again, Vieve was correct about the porter not recognizing that she was a girl.* She exchanged a look with Soap.

The tall boy flapped his hands slightly in the universal gesture of "you decide."

Sophronia shrugged, jogged after the porter, and, with a flutter of skirts, hoisted herself inside the wheelbarrow. Soap sprinted after and jumped nimbly in next to her. He sidled in close, bumping up against her shoulder, and grinned. He smelled of soot. Sophronia thought it rather a pleasant odor, on him, and smiled back. Genevieve Lefoux was correct—the porter didn't register their presence.

Vieve walked alongside the mechanical, as though they were companions out for a stroll. It was rather comical, given that the porter was easily twice the young girl's height and three times her girth.

The mechanical's tracks ended at the front of the school's main building.

This was far more the kind of structure Sophronia had expected from Mademoiselle Geraldine's Finishing Academy for Young Ladies of Quality. Bunson's had an impressive staircase leading up to huge double doors of wood and iron, engraved with an intricate pattern. Sophronia crouched low in the wheelbarrow as the porter mechanical approached the steps. *How will he alert the interior as to the presence of a messenger?*

The porter touched up against the bottom step where his tracks stopped. This triggered a response. A tremendous amount of steam emanated from below the lowest step, and with a great creaking and groaning, the stairs closed in upon themselves. The whole front section of the building that housed the main doors compressed downward like a concertina. After only a few moments, the doors were at ground level and the stairs had flattened out in such a way that it allowed the porter's tracks to continue.

The porter proceeded toward the doors sedately and bumped autocratically against them with a clang. This was obviously a signal, for one of the doors opened, revealing a darkened corridor. The porter backed off of the collapsed stairs far enough to switch tracks, beginning another loop that would lead him away to commence a circuit of the grounds. As he did this, Sophronia jumped out. She dashed inside, flattening herself instantly on the back side of the unopened half of the door. *One never knows who might be watching.*

Soap and Vieve followed sedately after.

As she passed through the doors, Sophronia noted that the intricate pattern carved into them was that of multiple octopuses holding one another's tentacles in a long unending chain.

It was a good thing she'd chosen stealth, for on the other side of that door a new set of tracks started up, and waiting patiently was yet another faceless mechanical, this one smaller, wearing a white ruffled pinafore, and carrying a duster in its articulated forceps. It was different, more chunky-looking, than the maid mechanicals at Mademoiselle Geraldine's. This maid said nothing and did not react to Sophronia. Sophronia hoped that meant the creature could not make her out in the shadows.

Close on her heels, Vieve and Soap crowded in, intent upon coming to her rescue, if necessary, or her disguise, if not. They saw her hiding and confronted the mechanical maid, both talking at once and gesticulating wildly.

Sophronia hoped that this would confuse the sensory nodules Vieve had referred to earlier and took it as permission to inch past the maid and run down the hallway. Soap and Vieve followed.

They paused for a breather on a small staircase to one side of the hall.

Behind them, the front foyer of the building raised itself back up, filling with white steam as it did so.

"You should have worn trousers," said Vieve in a low but disgusted voice.

"I may not be a lady yet, by any account," said Sophronia with great dignity, she felt, "but I am not a boy, either!" She was finding herself far more concerned with attire now than before attending Mademoiselle Geraldine's.

Soap looked at her. "You look like a lady to me."

"Thank you, Soap." *Thank goodness it is dark enough for him not to see me blushing!*

"Of course, miss."

They continued down the next corridor.

There seemed to be fewer maids at Bunson's, or perhaps they were decommissioned while the students were out. Sophronia would have predicted that a school full of boys would require more maids, not fewer! Everything was going swimmingly, with Vieve leading them unerringly ever upward through the building.

"You've been here before?" whispered Sophronia.

"Many times. Auntie always has some matter to discuss with Mr. Shrimpdittle. Lady Linette won't let her leave me unsupervised on board. She used to try to get Mademoiselle Geraldine to mind me, but I'd always escape her."

"So you've *seen* the communication machine?"

"Not as yet. They leave me outside. 'Workshop's no place for a child.'" Vieve's voice was full of outrage as she repeated a phase she had clearly heard overmuch in her nine years. "But I know where it's kept. On the roof."

Both Soap and Sophronia paused, raising their voices in shock. "The roof?"

"Shush! We don't know who might *not* have attended the theater. They wouldn't leave the school with only mechanicals on duty." Vieve took a moment to roll up the long sleeves of her shirt, her exposed wrists small and bony.

Sophronia said, "But why stash a piece of delicate equipment on the roof?"

"Search me. Intriguing, isn't it?" Vieve dimpled at them in a way that made her look very young indeed.

We are being led into enemy territory by a child, thought Sophronia all of a sudden. *This is madness. Oh, well.*

At that moment, a door ahead of them opened out into the darkened hall. Bright unflickering light of the kind that could only come from high-quality gas spilled forth. Into the beam trod a dark blob of a boy—not a mechanical.

The boy was relatively stocky and, like Vieve, shrouded in clothing too big for him. He was bent over a large, antiquated book and humming to himself.

Sophronia, Soap, and Vieve froze in horror.

The boy looked up, caught sight of them lurking in the shadowed hallway, let out a shriek of surprise, and dropped his book. The door slammed closed behind him and all was once more dark.

LESSON 12

PROPER COMMUNICATION IN SOCIAL SITUATIONS

"Who's that?" came a querulous voice into the darkness. "I know you're there; show yourselves!"

Sophronia stepped forward. "Buck up, Pillover. It's only me."

Pillover squinted. "Miss Sophronia? What are you doing here? How'd you get in? Is that my sister with you?"

Sophronia dragged a reluctant Vieve and Soap forward. "No, but I do have company. Pillover, may I introduce Genevieve Lefoux and Phineas B. Crow? Vieve, Soap, this is Pillover Plumleigh-Teignmott, Miss Dimity's brother."

Pillover gave his two new acquaintances a very haughty look. "Riffraff?"

"Only on the surface. They're both good eggs. Vieve here is an intellectual, and Soap's, erm"—she paused, struggling—"an engineer of a kind," she managed to come up with.

Soap gave a little snort, but Vieve looked childishly delighted to be described as academic in any way.

Pillover looked Vieve over and seemed to accept her title readily enough for all that she was nine. Then he turned to look up at Soap, illuminated by a bit of moonlight. "But Miss Sophronia, he's colored!"

Sophronia tilted her head and contemplated Soap as though she had never noticed his skin tone before. "It's irrelevant. Or do I mean irreverent?"

"It is?" Pillover arched one brow.

Sophronia nodded firmly. "Yes."

Pillover bent and picked up his book. "If you say so."

"Pillover, what are you doing here, instead of at the theater?"

The boy shrugged. "I'm tired of dealing with Pistons. Oily pains, the lot of them."

"Pistons?" *He can't possibly mean roving bits of steam engines, can he?*

Soap sidled in. "Miss Sophronia, we don't have much time."

"Oh, of course. Want to come, Pillover? We're going to the roof to look at a transmitter."

"Rather!" Pillover's normally dour face brightened at the idea.

So the infiltration party increased to four, and they trotted onward.

"Is he going to be useful?" Soap asked Sophronia.

"You never know," replied Sophronia wisely. She turned to their new companion. "So, these Pistons?"

"Oh, they think they are something quite exclusive, skulking about in riding boots, and wearing black shirtwaists, and being all gloomy about the state of the Empire. They sew cogs on the breasts of their jackets in a non-useful manner. Really it's only an excuse to push everyone else around. And no one does anything about them, because half of them are supposedly the sons of Picklemen. I think it's all faked, but they've got most of the school stitched up. You'd think we were here to learn, but apparently not."

Sophronia was awed by Pillover's chatter. "Oh, I know what you mean. We've got Monique de Pelouse living with us."

Pillover wrinkled his nose. "Must be quite the lark."

"Indeed. She's already tattled me out."

"No?"

"Oh, yes."

"And how's my pestilence of a sister settling?"

"Better than I. Although she fainted again."

"Blood?"

"Blood."

"From what I hear of your school, that's to be expected."

"We had lessons in knife-fighting from a werewolf."

"Werewolf? Bully! We don't have any supernaturals here. It's quite a dearth in the deanship if you ask me. Any reputable school ought to have at least one vampire professor. Eton has three. You lot are only girls, and you've a vampire *and* a were-wolf. Jolly unfair, that's what I call it."

By this time they had climbed up several flights of stairs, getting ever closer to the roof, when they came face-to-face with a maid mechanical. Instantly, Vieve and Soap stepped in front of Sophronia and began bouncing about.

"What are you doing?" Pillover demanded.

"Keeping it from deducing that I'm a girl," explained Sophronia.

"Oh, of course, I forgot." After a hesitation, Pillover too began an awkward gyration. They all looked so ridiculous that Sophronia had to suppress a giggle. She managed to slip past the distracted maid and thought about reminding Vieve of her obstructor, but it was so much fun watching them dance she decided not to.

They climbed the last set of stairs up into one of the many turrets, only to be faced with a locked door. Sophronia rattled the handle hopefully. Nothing.

She looked around. "Anyone know how to pick a lock?"

"Some intelligencer you are," complained Pillover.

"I've only been there a month! I can curtsy now, and my eyelash fluttering is practically unparalleled."

"Well, why not flutter your way into the locked room, then?"

Sophronia ignored this and looked at Vieve hopefully. "Inventions?"

Vieve shook her head.

"Stand aside, ladies," said Soap gallantly. "I shall rescue you."

Pillover gave Soap a disgusted look at being included with the "ladies," but made room for him to approach the door.

The tall sootie pulled a tiny leather pouch from some mysterious inside pocket and unrolled it to reveal a set of variously sized metal rods. He examined the lock closely and then selected one of the rods. He stuck this into the keyhole, and after a good deal of fiddling, there came a click.

Before they could push inside, Pillover said, "Careful! It might be booby-trapped."

Everyone stopped and looked at him.

"Evil genius training school, remember? I'd booby-trap it, if I were them, and I'm only *discourteous genius* level."

Sophronia stepped forward. "This was my idea. I'll do it."

Acting on instinct—they had yet to cover contravention of houses, house parties, and seating arrangements—Sophronia opened the door a tiny fraction and ran her finger slowly down the crack. A handbreadth up from the ground, she encountered a taut piece of twine. She twisted her fingers around the door, following the string, feeling along the jamb for a tie point. She found it with some relief, as the trap would be impossible to thwart without knowing which end activated it.

She pulled out her sewing scissors, and keeping the twine taut with one hand, cut it with the other. *Is it activated by additional tension from the door opening, or a release in tension when the string snaps?* she wondered. She put her sewing scissors back in her pinafore and pulled out a hair ribbon. She had to give her teachers credit: they were right to insist all students carry scissors, handkerchiefs, perfume, and hair ribbons at all times. At some point she'd learn why they also required a red lace doily and a lemon.

She tied the hair ribbon carefully to the end of the twine and then, keeping the tension as steady as possible, pushed open the door, belaying the hair ribbon at the same time.

The boys and Vieve watched all of this in impressed silence.

Finally, Pillover said, "You *are* getting a good education!"

I suppose I am. By that time Sophronia was all the way inside the room, hand extended, twine and ribbon stretching toward a crouched toadlike device to the right, slightly behind the door.

Vieve bustled over to it. "Compressed tension vent with boiled beet projectiles. Ingenious! Not dangerous, but it would cause quite the mess and definitely identify any intruders. Just a moment; let me disarm the catapults."

The young girl made a few adjustments. There was a sad squelching noise, and the pull against Sophronia's hair ribbon relaxed. She untied it from the twine and put it back into her pinafore. *This is fun!*

The room in which they found themselves was built of gray stone and was bare of all furniture, even chairs. There were only the trap and a series of telescopes and other devices set to look up at the skies. These were spaced out, with one to each of the many slotted windows, none of which had glass. The place felt very old, as if they had stepped into some fairy tale. *Rapunzel, perhaps?* If Rapunzel were a particular fan of astral observation.

One of the windows was bare of devices, and outside it, someone had built an unstable-looking balcony.

"There we are," said Vieve proudly.

They all went over to the window and looked.

"Rickety," pronounced Pillover.

Sophronia pointed to a lever and pulley system on one side. "I think it raises and lowers, like a dumbwaiter. Follow me." She climbed out onto the platform.

"This is not a good idea," Pillover said, following her.

Soap only grinned and bounced after. Vieve came last and immediately went over to examine the pulleys.

"Looks sound to me," she pronounced.

Well, Vieve hasn't led us astray so far, thought Sophronia. "Shall we?"

Vieve turned a little crank. Nothing happened.

"You aren't strong enough," accused Soap.

Vieve looked frustrated and not a little offended. "Actually, I don't have enough mass. Being young is *so* terribly inconvenient!"

"On the bright side, you're only nominally young," consoled Sophronia. "You don't act your age at all."

Vieve blushed crimson in delight. "Oh, why, thank you very much!"

Soap went over to help her man the lever. He looked gangly, but with all the coal he had to move every day, Sophronia suspected him of being quite strong. So he proved.

The contraption raised them up to the roof, where they disembarked to finally face the infamous communication machine. It looked like a deformed cross between a potting shed and a portmanteau.

"That's it?"

"I guess so."

"It looks like two privies," objected Soap.

Sophronia elbowed him. "Don't be crass."

"Well, it *does*!"

They made their way over to the structure. It looked, if possible, even more odd up close, perched in embarrassed shabbiness atop the turret, which was all ancient stone and crenellated edges. They opened the door. The shed was divided into two human-sized compartments, each filled to bursting with a peculiar assortment of tangled machinery. There were tubes and dials, and what looked to be glass boxes filled with black sand, and here and there blank cradles in obvious want of further enhancements.

Vieve immediately dropped down and crawled in, squirming her small form under various compartments to examine the undersides and any attachment points.

Pillover looked around in a lackluster manner, poked at a few things, and then mooched away. Sophronia and Soap were more entertained by watching Vieve's antics than by the communication machine itself, which was utterly incomprehensible to both of them.

"Well, I'm glad we came all this way for this," said Soap eventually.

"I did think it might give us some kind of indication as to the nature of the prototype, and thus where Monique might have stashed it." Sophronia's tone was apologetic. It seemed like a wasted trip.

Vieve reemerged at that juncture, very animated. "This is amazing! This isn't like that benighted telegraph invention. I don't think it requires any kind of long-distance wiring!"

"Then how could it possibly communicate from point to point?" Sophronia's forehead crinkled.

"It looks like there might be an *aether* conductor in there!" Vieve came over, wiping her small hands on her jodhpurs, leaving greasy black streaks.

Sophronia frowned, wishing she'd read more on the atmospheres. "Do you think they might be trying to bounce directed messages through the aethersphere?"

"It would explain why it has to be on the roof—closer to the aether." Vieve dimpled at her.

"And why they would involve our school. If necessary, we could lift the whole thing right up inside the aether," added Sophronia.

Vieve's eyes glowed. "Can you imagine, point-to-point messaging, long distances? It would revolutionize the whole world."

Soap and Sophronia exchanged looks. Sophronia was thinking about the fact that she'd had no letters from her family on board, nor had she been able to write any. Theoretically, the students should have been asked for letters before arriving in Swiffle-on-Exe. But nothing had been said on the subject, and Sophronia was pretty certain her punishment, like Monique's, probably extended to communication off-ship. She wondered if Pillover had received anything since she saw him last. *I suppose it's possible parents simply ship us away and then forget about us.*

Soap was probably thinking about the nefarious applications for a communication device. Vieve, a true scientist, saw only the upside of any contraption. Sophronia could imagine why flywaymen might want access.

Sophronia said, "So we are thinking that the missing prototype must be a valve that somehow facilitates ... bouncing?"

Vieve nodded. "Which explains the dodecahedron shape you said you saw. Multifaceted for multiple directions and to sympathize with the aetheric humors, which we have always hypothesized are trapezoidal."

Sophronia looked at Soap and Pillover. "You understand any of that?"

Soap shook his head.

Pillover shrugged.

Sophronia said, "Well, I understand I can clean that glove of mine now."

"Come again?" Pillover looked at her in confusion.

"Long story, you were in it, and it was all for naught."

"Sounds exciting."

"Only if you're interested in the postal services."

Pillover looked as though he might be, but Sophronia was starting to worry about the time.

Vieve was practically vibrating. "This is so exciting!"

"Yes, well, that said, we had better return to the airship, now that we have a bit of a better idea what's going on."

"Yes, I think we better had," Soap agreed. He was looking at the position of the moon, clearly concerned.

They made their way safely back through Bunson's—well, mostly.

About halfway down, they rounded a corner and ran smack-dab into a maid mechanical. Literally. Sophronia hit up against her with an *oof* and stumbled backward, banging into Pillover and stepping on Soap's foot. This did not give them enough time to do the little dance of obscurity, nor for Vieve to use her obstructor. The maid identified Sophronia as female and instantly sounded the alarm—a high-pitched whistle. This, in turn, triggered a schoolwide alert.

Unlike the bells of Mademoiselle Geraldine's, Bunson's alarm seemed to be based on the noise made by a wobbling saw, only louder. It was an amusing *wob-woob* that vibrated through the entire hodgepodge building. The hallways were instantly filled with mechanicals, and one or two humans as well. Sophronia leapt for a nearby door, opened it, and dove inside. The other three crowded after, only to find they had trapped themselves in a broom closet with no possible avenue of escape.

"Simply marvelous. What do we do now?" wondered Pillover.

"Quiet," said Sophronia.

He ignored her, continuing gloomily, "We're damned. I'll be turned away, having achieved only *discourteous*. What will Father say? No Plumleigh-Teignmott has ever been lower than *spiteful genius*. The family honor is at stake."

"What're you still larking with us for?" Soap wanted to know. "You're allowed to roam free, remember?"

"Oh, good point." Pillover straightened out of his slouch and made to leave the closet.

Sophronia grabbed his arm. "You can't leave now! You'll give away our hiding place."

"It's only a matter of time." Pillover was unsympathetic. "They'll do a schoolwide sweep." Then he pointed to a nearby broom sharing the closet with them. "Sweep. Ha."

"Delightful. Now we're trapped in a closet with puns." Sophronia gave him a dirty look. "Wait, of course—you are *meant* to be here. Perfect! Everyone turn away from me for a moment."

The three others looked at her in confusion.

"Simply do as I ask, please?"

Despite being crowded into the closet, the other three all managed to turn their backs on her.

Sophronia shimmied out of one of her two petticoats. "All decent."

They turned back around.

She handed the undergarment to Pillover.

"Ugh. What's this for?"

"If you put it on and go out there, they will think it was all a false alarm."

"Absolutely not!"

"Oh, come on, Pill, please?" Sophronia tried batting her eyelashes.

Pillover appeared to be immune to eyelashes. "The indignity of it!"

"We could come up with a reasonable explanation for your wearing it. Would that help?" wheedled Sophronia.

"Justification for my trotting around wearing lady's undergarments? I hardly see how."

Soap's eyes were sparkling with amusement, and Vieve was dimpling openly at the very idea of Pillover in a skirt. Pillover stood holding the petticoat between thumb and forefinger as if it were contaminated with some dreaded chemical.

"Go on, pull it on over your clothes and go out there," Sophronia urged.

"You could say you were running some experiment dangerous to your nether regions," suggested Vieve.

"You could say you were testing the response time of the maid mechanicals," suggested Sophronia.

"You could say you like lady's undergarments," suggested Soap.

"I'm doomed." Pillover rolled his eyes and flapped the petticoat.

"Oh, go on, Pill," Sophronia pushed.

Pillover, grumbling, pulled the petticoat on and all the way up to his armpits, as it was far too long for him. Sophronia handed him her hair ribbon to use as a belt. Soap was clearly holding in laughter. Pillover took a deep breath and straightened upright with great dignity and aplomb.

Sophronia listened at the door, hand up to keep the others quiet. Then, when there seemed to be a lull in the activities outside in the corridor, quick as she could, she opened the door, dragged Pillover forward, and thrust him out, slamming the door closed behind him.

The rumbling in the hallway escalated for a minute and then quieted. Into the silence a deep voice boomed out, "Pillover Thaddeus Plumleigh-Teignmott, what *are* you wearing?"

They heard Pillover reply querulously, "A petticoat, Headmaster."

"So I see. You had better have an excellently malevolent explanation as to why."

"Well, you see, sir," Pillover started to say, then, "Ouch. Please, sir, not the ear."

"Come with me!"

"Yes, sir."

A clatter of mechanicals on rails and the thud of footsteps followed, leaving the hallway in silence.

"What do you know?" whispered Soap at long last. "He *was* useful."

After that, they managed to escape Bunson and Lacroix's Boys' Polytechnique without further incident. Running up the goat path, Sophronia turned back to look at it only once. She thought that the school looked like an ill-decorated, oversized mangle of chess pieces.

"Our academy is much nicer," she asserted between breaths

as they jogged along. The moor mists had not arisen, and the great caterpillar of multiple dirigibles pressed together that was Mademoiselle Geraldine's floated gamely before them, lit by a picturesque golden moon.

"You believe so?" Vieve tilted her head in the manner of one who rarely considered the aesthetics of buildings. "Well, ours floats."

"I mean, it's less cobbled together."

Vieve said, "I always thought it had a rather hatlike aspect—like a great floating turban."

Sophronia tilted her head, but did not quite see it.

They raced on.

Sophronia was worried. "Do you think we made our window?"

Soap nodded. "Yes, but there might be another problem." He pointed over at a distant hill on their right. There, under the light of the moon, was the shadowy form of a wolf. Wearing a top hat.

"Is that who I think it is?" Sophronia hoped despite herself that it might be some kind of very large dog.

"Know of any other wolves roaming the moors in evening dress?"

"He's not supposed to be near civilization at the full moon!" Vieve objected.

"Guess someone made a mistake somewhere," said Soap.

"This is *not good*," Sophronia said, stating the obvious. The wolf's muzzle was up and he was scenting the air. Almost as she spoke, his shaggy head turned in their direction.

"We're closer to the school than he is," Soap pointed out.

"Yes, but he's supernatural," said Vieve, who clearly had some experience in the matter of werewolves. Her little face, normally open and friendly, was pale with fear.

Sophronia took the lead. "Enough talk, everybody—*run!*" Hiking up her skirts, she suited her actions to her words, feeling no shame over the fact that she was down one petticoat and showing ankle to all the world.

Soap quickly outpaced her. His legs were longer, and he was unencumbered by skirts. When he reached the underside of the forward section, he began frantically hopping about and gesticulating wildly. Only then did Sophronia realize that the rope ladder from the boiler room had yet to be dropped down.

She and Vieve came panting up. "Are we too early?"

"Possibly."

Sophronia picked up a clod of dirt and threw it at the underside of the hull, close to where she thought the hatch might be. She missed completely; the ship was higher up than she thought. Soap and Vieve followed her lead. Vieve also missed, but Soap's clod hit and spattered against the hatch.

Nothing happened. The werewolf had nearly reached their hill.

At the last possible moment, the hatch popped open and the rope ladder dropped.

"Soap, you go first; you're fastest."

"But Miss Sophronia, you're a lady. Ladies always go first!"

Sophronia threw her shoulders back and looked him in the eye. "I am trained for this." She wasn't yet, but it was worth the lie. "Don't contest a direct order during an active intelligencer undertaking!"

Soap frowned, but he clearly hated to argue with a lady. Least of all Sophronia. He began climbing up.

"Vieve, you next."

"But—"

"Now!"

Vieve began climbing.

Sophronia started up last, and just as she did so, she snuck one last look at the werewolf.

With a vicious growl, he was upon her.

For the second time that night, Sophronia was grateful to have worn proper dress. Captain Niall dove for her in a tremendous leap of the kind described in countless gothic novels. His jaws were open, his mouth an angry cavern of teeth and dripping saliva, and when he struck he bit down hard, ruthlessly savaging her . . . other petticoat.

Sophronia screamed and kicked out.

The werewolf's teeth were stuck in the bottom reinforced hem. This was her strongest-starched underskirt, the kind designed to support a gown in a full and feminine pouf.

Sophronia kicked again and her foot struck the beast's sensitive nose.

Captain Niall shook his huge, shaggy head, partly in pain and partly to get loose from the petticoat. His top hat wiggled back and forth hypnotically. The combined weight and motion dragged the undergarment off Sophronia. Both the werewolf and the petticoat fell to the ground. Sophronia, remembering that amazingly high leap the captain had performed in order to get them up on board the ship originally, began climbing as fast as she possibly could.

Sophronia's under-petticoat was of good-quality horsehair, thick and very durable. It should be; it was a hand-me-down that had survived three sisters before her.

But the werewolf, with supernatural strength, tore through the thick fabric as if it were fine muslin. Captain Niall wrestled with the garment briefly before shaking himself loose from the tatters. He crouched down and leapt for Sophronia again.

Sophronia angled her bottom around and swung the rope ladder to one side, avoiding the werewolf by the narrowest of margins.

"Captain Niall," she said between pants, "I liked you very much better when you weren't trying to kill me!"

The werewolf landed, shook his head, and whined as from the hatch above someone pelted him with a handful of coal. One particularly large lump hit his already-abused nose.

He tilted his head back and howled.

Sophronia attained the safety of the hatch. Multiple soot-covered hands reached for her and dragged her inside. Meanwhile, Soap threw another handful of coal down at the werewolf. Next to him, a few of the larger sooties stood grimly clutching steel stoking poles, ready to fend off the beast if necessary.

There was no need, for as soon as Sophronia tumbled inside they hauled the rope ladder up after her and slammed the hatch closed. The wolf jumped up, crashing hard into the underside of the airship. Had the hull's wooden beams not been reinforced with iron bracings, Sophronia was certain they would have shattered.

"What does he think he can do?" wondered Vieve, while Sophronia recovered her breath and brushed herself off.

"I don't think he's *thinking* at all," replied Sophronia, rising from her hands and knees to her feet, panting and shaking. *That* was the werewolf of her childhood nightmares. "Someone ought to lock him up! He's dangerous," she said finally, when she felt her voice wouldn't shake.

"And he's ruined your other petticoat."

"Oh, goodness. How will we get it back? Someone might realize it was mine!"

"Not a chance. See?" Soap pointed down out of the hatch, which the sooties had cracked open slightly. He had his eyes pressed to the gap.

Sophronia went over and joined him. She looked down.

Captain Niall, having apparently resigned himself to losing his quarry, was savaging her horsehair petticoat into teeny, tiny shreds.

"Really, what did my poor petticoat do to offend?"

Vieve said, "I can see now that your insistence on ladies' dress is very useful, in its way."

Sophronia looked the nine-year-old over. "You going to give it a try, then?"

"I didn't say it was *that* useful."

Sophronia had a sudden, terrifying thought. "Oh, goodness, the other students! They don't know Captain Niall is here, do they? What if they happen upon him on the way home from the play? We *must* warn them!"

"But how to warn them without explaining that you were out?" wondered Soap.

"I'll claim I saw him out the parlor window. I must go." Sophronia stood. She was covered in soot, her face smudged, her skirts flat, and her hair loose.

"But Miss Sophronia, *look* at you!"

"Can't be helped, have to chance it. Lives are at stake."

"But who are you going to tell? Everyone is at the theater."

"Not *everyone*. Come on, Vieve! The last thing I need is to be trapped by mechanicals again. I need you and the obstructor."

LESSON 13

ATTACK OF THE FAN AND SPRINKLE

Sophronia and Vieve dashed through the airship ever upward and forward, making their way to the forbidden tassel section. They paused in front of Professor Braithwope's door.

"You had better make yourself scarce, Vieve. There's no point in both of us getting into trouble."

Vieve looked up at her, then nodded. "We must do this again soon."

"Perhaps without the werewolf attack and the loss of petticoat life?"

"Perhaps."

With which the young girl tipped her cap at Sophronia and retreated down the hall, one hand in her pocket, obstructor pointed out in front of her, whistling some French tune in the tones of the deeply satisfied.

Well, I'm delighted someone had an enjoyable evening, Sophronia thought before knocking loudly on the vampire's door.

There was good deal of clattering, a wet slurping noise, and the sound of india rubber squeaking, and then the door was opened a crack and Professor Braithwope peeked out.

"Whot, whot?" He had something dark about his mouth.

Oh, dear, thought Sophronia, *have I interrupted him at tea?* She tried to peek around him and catch a glimpse of whomever he might be supping with. But while the vampire was modestly sized, he occupied all of Sophronia's line of sight.

"Professor, I do so hate to disturb you, but I have urgent business requiring your immediate attention."

"Student, whot? By George, how'd you get into this section without setting off the alarms?"

"That's not important, sir."

"No, I think it might be."

"Not *now*, sir. There is a problem, please, sir. It's Captain Niall."

"Werewolf, whot? What's that to do with your getting into restricted areas of the school without a chaperone?"

"No, sir, he's loose."

"Of course he's loose. Loose and leagues away, as he should be."

"No, sir, he's *here.*"

"On the ship, whot? Not possible. Werewolves don't float."

"No, sir, below. He's here, on the moor, directly below, and the others should be returning from the theater soon. I saw him out my window."

"Girlish fancies."

"That's possible, sir, but wouldn't it be better to check and make certain?"

"Whot, whot? Yes, well. I suppose you're right."

"Quickly, sir. They're due back at any moment."

"Yes, yes. Where's my hat?"

The vampire vanished for a split second and then pushed his way out into the hallway.

He was looking a tad disheveled, but he'd pulled on a great-coat and buttoned it closed to disguise any possible fashion transgressions, and he had boots on his feet, which was more than might be said of a werewolf. Sophronia wasn't certain, but she believed she might be coming down in favor of vampires as a general rule.

"Where is the blighter?"

"Below the boiler room area, sir. Last I saw."

"Miss Temminnick." The vampire tipped his hat and then sped away.

There was no point in even trying to keep up; he moved faster than any human could.

Oh, great, thought Sophronia. *Now how am I supposed to get back to my quarters?*

Vieve's head reappeared around a bend in the hall. "Need a helping hand, or should I say wrist?" She waved the arm with the obstructor.

Sophronia grinned.

"So there we were, in all our evening's finery, coming up the path toward the ship, and you will *never* guess what we observed!

It was almost more exciting than the play itself. Although it *was* a very stirring performance of *An Ideal Bathtub.*" Dimity's eyes were shining, her hands clasped together passionately, as she was thrust into the wondrousness of reliving the evening recently passed.

Sophronia, only slightly smudged, in a clean pinafore and her second-best set of petticoats, pretended rapt attention.

They were seated tête-à-tête on the settee while the other girls milled about, nattering about the finery of dress, the play, and the handsomeness of some boy or another—not necessarily in that order.

"Oh, what did you see?"

"Professor Braithwope, in a greatcoat!"

"Presumably he owns outerwear."

Dimity left off clasping her hands to fiddle at something hanging about her neck.

Sophronia leaned forward. "Dimity, are you wearing *two* necklaces?"

"I couldn't decide. But don't distract me. Where was I?"

"On Professor Braithwope's greatcoat."

"Oh, yes. Don't you believe greatcoats are rather a werewolf's provenance? Not to mention the fact that vampires aren't supposed to feel the cold. Anywho, where was I? Oh, yes. Professor Braithwope and his greatcoat were fighting a *werewolf!* Captain Niall!"

"Oh, how horrid." Sophronia arranged her features into an appropriately shocked expression. Or what she hoped was appropriately shocked. She wasn't doing very well in her acting lessons so far. *I probably look more like a stuffed squirrel.*

Dimity didn't appear to think so. "Unfortunately, I didn't see very much of the confrontation."

"Was the exchange of fisticuffs that rapid? Supernatural speed, I understand." Sophronia nodded wisely.

"Oh, no, there was blood, so I fainted."

Preshea came over and stood before them, hands on hips, in nothing but her stays and drawers. *So immodest!*

"Sidheag caught her. Such a shame, Dimity, that you hadn't arranged to faint earlier in the evening, when young Lord Dingleproops was paying you so much attention."

Dimity blushed. "His parents are friends of the family, that is all!"

Sophronia ignored Preshea and looked to the other girls to continue the story where Dimity had fainted out of it. "What happened with the fisticuffs?"

"Not so many fists, actually. More fang and claw," said Agatha.

"Very well, what happened with the fangicuffs, then?"

"Oh Sophronia, you're *so* droll." Dimity prodded her playfully with one thumb.

Sidheag only smiled dryly and retreated. Monique was pointedly absorbed in examining a small tear in the trim of one sleeve, and Preshea turned away to do her hair in rags for the night.

Agatha came timidly to Sophronia's rescue. "Mademoiselle Geraldine also fainted. That freed Lady Linette to order some of the older girls into covert action. They've had lessons in group tactics for coordinated social rebuttal. She had them do the fan and sprinkle maneuver, to good effect."

"Fan and sprinkle?"

Monique snorted. "Oh, really, Sophronia, don't you know *anything*? Fan and sprinkle is for young ladies coping with werewolf attack while gentlemen are away. There have been *pamphlets* published!"

Sophronia looked to Agatha for further explanation, but the portly girl had lost all her pluck and retreated to a corner with a book on the language of parasols.

"Dimity, do you know what this maneuver is?"

Dimity hedged. "Well, I've heard of it, of course, but never seen it applied."

"And you didn't this evening, either. Really, Dimity, you must learn to time your faints with greater accuracy." Preshea's tone was condescending; rooming with Monique was turning out not to benefit her character.

Monique tsked. "It's very simple, really. Distract the werewolf."

"In this case, with a well-applied vampire," interjected Preshea, to Monique's annoyance.

Monique continued. "Then approach to within sprinkling distance. Sprinkle the werewolf, or his near proximity, liberally with noxious perfume—anything herbaceous does the trick, though basil is best, of course—as well as smelling salts, to encourage the inhalation. They have a heightened sense of smell, werewolves. Then everyone takes up their fans and blows the fumes in the direction of the beast. The creature begins to sneeze uncontrollably, allowing one to escape. Voilà!"

"And is that what happened?" Sophronia looked to Preshea for confirmation. After all, Monique hadn't been on the theater excursion, either.

"Essentially. Although poor Professor Braithwope also got a

big dose of perfume. But still, it distracted Captain Niall long enough for the professor to get the upper hand and drag him away. We managed to board the airship with impunity using the grand stairs."

Stairs? thought Sophronia. *This ship has stairs?*

Preshea concluded, "A very exciting end to the evening. But that's enough rough talk. Did you ladies see how many beaux I had surrounding me at the theater?"

"Not nearly so many as I might have had," shot back Monique. "I've already managed to make half of Bunson's fall madly in love with me; this year I shall get the other half." She looked about magnanimously. "Of course, you are allowed some, Preshea. I'm no glutton."

Preshea smiled in a way that had nothing to do with pleasure. "And then there's Lord Dingleproops; he's clearly in Dimity's pocket."

"I know, so peculiar. Well, I suppose there is no accounting for taste. No offense meant, of course, Dimity."

Dimity could clearly think of nothing to say to that. She looked as though she had swallowed a live eel.

Monique and Preshea continued to chat about the young men Preshea had met at the theater. Boys whom Monique already knew and about whom minutiae of appearance, financial situation, and social connection had to be told to Preshea in a most condescending way.

With the other girls thus distracted, Sophronia turned to Dimity and said in a low voice, "*Do* you like this Dingle personage?"

Dimity blushed in such a manner as indicated she might.

Either that or she didn't like him at all. "He is quite tall for his age."

Sophronia tried to be sympathetic. "A good start, I suppose. Has he any other qualities of note?"

"He has a very nice nose."

"Good, a nose, excellent."

Dimity, who was rarely silent, fell quiet again at that juncture.

Sophronia tried to think of some other attribute a boy of interest to Dimity might possess. "Was he wearing anything sparkly?"

"He had a brass pin on his hatband." Dimity looked a little disappointed, as if this were the merest of seeds before the great tree of her own adornments.

Two necklaces. Two! "And, um, is he smart?"

"Oh, Sophronia, that is hardly a desirable quality in a beau!"

"No? Is he a beau, then?"

"I am not allowed followers until I'm sixteen."

"Well, then."

The conversation paused.

Finally Dimity said, "Did you know my revolting brother wasn't there? Scarpered off from the play. Apparently, he's a bit of a pustule so far as the other boys are concerned. Not that I'm surprised. He's probably going around correcting silly little mistakes and making himself unwelcome."

"Or it could be they are browbeating him out of spite."

"Oh, come now, I hardly think *boys* are like that."

"Oh, no?" Sophronia, who had several brothers of her own, was startled at this outrageous statement.

"Girls, yes; boys, no. They are much more forthright."

"Have you heard of the Pistons?"

"Yes; how did you . . . ?"

Sophronia shrugged. "I'm learning my lessons at this school."

"Pistons is some kind of Bunson's school club, I gather. Lord Dingleproops is a member."

"Is he indeed?"

"Yes, an engineering concentration. They put smudges of coal about their eyes. Very dark and brooding."

"How sootie of them."

Monique, whose own conversation had paused and who had taken to listening in on theirs, seemed unable to help interjecting at this juncture. "Sophronia, don't even say such a thing! Imagine comparing highborn lords to, well, the lowest of the low. *Really.*"

"Sooties aren't as bad as all that," Sophronia protested, rather more loudly than she ought.

Preshea, Monique, and Agatha all stared at her in dumbfounded horror.

Sophronia was truculent. "They can hardly be blamed for their station!"

Monique said with confidence, "Yes, they most certainly can!"

"Oh, come now, the poor sooties only require some social reform and a little charitable assistance with their wardrobes," said Dimity staunchly, no doubt thinking she was supporting Sophronia's unusually progressive social stance.

Sophronia closed her eyes in horror at the very idea of Dimity trying to reform Soap. Or worse, taking him on as a *charity case.*

A loud knock sounded on their door.

Lady Linette's voice said, "Gas out soon, ladies. You need your beauty rest. Well, most of you do, and there's no cause to risk any of the others."

"Yes, Lady Linette," replied all the girls in singsong unison.

Lady Linette moved on without coming inside. It was school policy for the students not to be disturbed unduly during their spare time. Even children, Lady Linette said, must be allowed some time to conspire together.

Dimity leaned in as close to Sophronia as possible and whispered, "Why are you defending sooties? How do you even know them with any intimacy?"

"Information gathering, Dimity, remember? It's what we do now."

"Yes, but sooties? They can hardly be of any use. They live in the boiler room."

Sophronia came up with her best excuse. "I need to feed Bumbersnoot, don't I?"

Dimity blinked at her in silence, the concept of befriending sooties as alien to her as having to choose between two necklaces. "If you say so. Come on, let's go to bed."

But before they could leave the sitting room, another knock sounded, startling the girls. This was not part of their normal routine.

A male voice said, through the door, "Miss Temminnick, a word, if you would be so kind, whot?"

Preshea let out a little gasp and dove for her room, she being still in her underthings.

Sophronia glanced about. "Agatha, pick your gloves up off the floor. Dimity, you aren't wearing shoes." Once the others were back in reasonable order, Sophronia opened the door.

"How can I help you, Professor Braithwope?"

The vampire was looking once more like his dandy self: no greatcoat. "Ah, good, you are not abed yet. Take a little walk with me, if you would, Miss Temminnick?"

Sophronia curtsied and reached for her wrap from a nearby hat stand. The other girls watched in dumb silence. Sophronia gave them all a quelling look and followed the vampire.

As she was in the company of a professor, none of the mechanicals were aggravated by Sophronia roaming the ship after hours. Professor Braithwope led her up and out onto a small balcony that bridged the gap between the middle and forward sections. They stood staring out at the clouds and the moon setting over the moor.

Finally Sophronia said, "Sir?"

"You understand, Miss Temminnick, that I am a vampire."

"Yes, sir, I had noticed the fangs."

"Don't be pert, young lady."

"Yes, sir."

"Yet I am tethered to this roaming ship far from all meaningful society."

"Yes, sir. But you did go down to the ground to fight Captain Niall."

"I am not a vampire queen to have so short a tether as all *that*."

"I see, sir." Although she didn't. *Why did that make him defensive?*

"Tonight when you came to my room..."

Sophronia cocked her head, remembering what must have been blood around his mouth. "I didn't hear or see anything. Although I have been wondering, sir, *how* you eat? Or should I say *who?*"

The vampire said nothing.

Have I revealed that I saw too much? Quietly Sophronia added, "And the soot on my dress, sir?"

"I didn't see anything." Professor Braithwope smiled down at her, showing a small hint of fang.

Sophronia grinned back. "I'm glad we understand each other, sir."

The vampire looked out into the night. "This is the right finishing school for you, isn't it, whot?"

"Yes, sir, I think it might very well be."

"A piece of advice, Miss Temminnick?"

"Sir?"

"It is a great skill to have friends in low places. They, too, have things to teach you."

"Now, sir, I thought you didn't see any soot."

Professor Braithwope laughed. "Good night, Miss Temminnick. I trust you can make your own way back to your room without causing an alarm? It seems to be a particular skill of yours."

"Actually, sir, I could use your escort tonight."

"Whot, whot? Interesting."

"Even a vampire can be surprised on occasion?"

"Miss Temminnick, why do you think I became a teacher?"

They turned together and walked back toward the students' residential section.

Sophronia thought hard about what it must be like to live forever. *I suppose one would get bored easily. That's one thing about Mademoiselle Geraldine's. So far, it's not been remotely dull.* What she said was, "It can't be all that bad, being away from cities. You're one of the few vampires who gets to travel."

"So long as we don't go too high."

"Really?"

"Whot, whot, there goes that curious mind of yours, Miss Temminnick. I think perhaps there has been enough of *that*, for the time being."

They arrived back at her door.

"Good night, Miss Temminnick."

"Good night, Professor."

School life carried on course after that, as did the school itself, except that it did so in the gray, as Lady Linette called it. It turned out mail had been retrieved from Swiffle-on-Exe when they stopped over for the play. Sophronia's loot was comprised of a package of clothing, including her winter cape, and one uninformative letter from her mother. They were told they could not send replies. Swiffle-on-Exe was already leagues behind them. The school's deadline from the flywaymen had been exceeded and they were now on the run and in hiding.

The great airship floated deep into the gray of the wild moor. The mists were more common and longer lasting now that autumn was upon them. Mademoiselle Geraldine's Finishing Academy for Young Ladies of Quality did not go low; lessons with Captain Niall were canceled for the time being. They had enough fuel and supplies for a good, long stint away from civilization. So they floated, shrouded by cool, wet gray, hidden from friends and enemies alike—for *three whole months.*

At about a month in, Sophronia overheard Monique complaining to Preshea about the ban on outside communication. Clearly the restrictions had finally gotten to her, and she hadn't managed to get her message out on the night Sophronia, Soap, and Vieve had infiltrated Bunson's.

"I cannot believe they won't let me—*me!*—send a message."

"They aren't letting anyone, Monique. I heard Sophronia complaining about it only the other day."

"But mine is *terribly* important."

"Oh, really? Is it an order for next summer's hats?"

"Oh, yes, of course. Something like." Monique neatly avoided Preshea's interest. "Gloves and a few fans as well."

Sophronia discussed the conversation with Dimity later that evening.

"I really do think that Monique was hoping to get information to someone about where she hid the prototype. Do you suppose the teachers actually imprisoned her on the evening of the theater jaunt in an effort to prevent this from happening? I mean to say, I saw neither hide nor hair of her all evening."

Dimity's round porcelain face scrunched up in suspicion. "That's a terribly medieval approach. I can't imagine they'd be that strict with her."

Sophronia lay back. "Dimity, we are missing something."

"On board? Decent cheese," suggested Dimity.

"No, I mean, if Monique hid it somewhere, why did we never see her do it? Is it still in the carriage, do you think? Were you ever separated from her during the beginning of the journey?"

"Only when she went to interview you."

"Of course! Dimity, you're brilliant!"

"I am?"

"While I was packing, she asked Mumsy if she might take a turn about the grounds. The prototype must be hidden at *my house!*"

"Goodness gracious, I suppose you're right. Oh, Sophronia, what if the flywaymen figure that out? Or what if Monique is working for someone else even more sinister, and *they* figure that out?"

Sophronia's stomach twisted in panic. "Then my family might be in danger. I must get a message to them somehow!"

Of course, Sophronia could no more send out a letter than Monique could. She and Dimity even made an abortive attempt at pigeon training. The pigeon was *not interested.* Sophronia began to see the appeal behind the transmission machine and the prototype. She tried to talk herself down. *I am, after all, the only one who knows Monique was alone for that small space of time. And even if the flywaymen do figure it out, they will, hopefully, use nonviolent stealth to retrieve the prototype, and leave my parents and siblings alone.*

LESSON 14

On Intermingling the Classes

Professor Braithwope took on some of their weapons training, giving them tips on how to wield a cane versus a parasol versus an umbrella, and the correct application of each to the skull or posterior as occasion demanded. Like Captain Niall, he seemed particularly pleased with Sidheag's abilities in this arena.

"Some slight advantage to being raised by soldiers." After lessons, Sidheag was self-effacing about the extra attention.

"So sad there don't appear to be any other advantages." Monique sniffed.

Sidheag's shoulders slumped.

Sophronia and Dimity exchanged a look and caught up to the other girl, one on each side.

"Don't let Monique bother you. You know how she gets," said Sophronia sympathetically.

Dimity was more direct. "She's a pollock."

Sidheag looked back and forth between the two of them. Then she shrugged. "I don't intend to be here much longer, regardless. She may do as she pleases."

Sophronia decided at that juncture that she'd had enough of Sidheag's recalcitrant nature. She'd put up with it for months. Preshea and Agatha were hopeless. But Sidheag had the makings of a decent friend if she would only open up a bit. Sophronia grabbed the taller girl by the arm and steered her out onto a balcony, rather than to their next lesson.

"What are you—?" The Scotswoman was clearly startled.

So was Dimity, who, with a little *eep!* noise, followed.

Sophronia braced herself, put her hands on her hips, and faced Lady Kingair. Mademoiselle Geraldine's did not encourage unequivocal confrontation under any circumstances. But Sophronia had a feeling that it was necessary with Sidheag.

"You must stop being so afraid of us," she said.

Of all the things Sidheag had been expecting, this was clearly not one of them. The taller girl actually sputtered. Finally she managed, "Afraid? Afraid!"

"Sophronia, what are you doing?" hissed Dimity, backing away from both girls.

"Sidheag, whether you like it or not, you are stuck here for *years*. Slouching about like a grump won't get you anywhere. You might as well learn what is being taught and attempt to get along with some of us."

"It's all chattering behind one another's backs. I dinna ken how females manage it."

Dimity said, timidly, "Like it or not, Sidheag, you are actually a girl."

"For my sins."

Sophronia had an idea. *Perhaps Sidheag simply wants to be included in something.* With a guilty look at Dimity, she asked, "How good are you at climbing, Lady Kingair?"

Sidheag was startled by the change of topic. "Do ya ken that's what I mean? Why ask me an obscure question? Why not tell me forthright what you think we should do and why it might help?"

Sophronia wondered, what with Vieve skulking about, how she ended up at a finishing school surrounded by girls who would rather be boys. *Well, except Dimity, of course.*

Dimity said, even though the conversation had already moved on, "What's wrong with liking girly things? I like petticoats and dancing and perfume and hats and brooches and necklaces and—" Her eyes glazed over slightly as she contemplated sparkles.

She seemed likely to continue in this vein for some time, so Sophronia interrupted her. "I have someone I think you should meet, Sidheag. By way of a coal supplier."

Dimity blinked. "How could coal possibly help, Sophronia? Are you cracked?"

"Have faith, Dimity. Well, Sidheag, *can* you climb?"

"Of course."

"Tonight, then?"

Which was how Sophronia ended up introducing Lady Kingair to a group of sooties.

"Good evening, miss!" Soap grinned at her as she climbed

up through the hatch. She'd tried to visit once every other week ever since the school had gone to gray. Soap, as a result, was only becoming more and more familiar, and more and more captivating. Sophronia would rather she didn't enjoy his company so much—he was so very dirty, and so very unsuitable, and so very boy, but there it was: liking him couldn't be helped.

"Good evening, Soap, how's the boiler room treating you?"

"Topping, miss, topping! You've brought a friend. You've never brought a friend afore now. I figured you didn't have any. Save us, a'course." He chuckled.

"This here is Miss Maccon. Sidheag, this is Soap, and these are the sooties." Sophronia made a wide gesture to include both the small collective hovering around Soap and the others scurrying back and forth behind him. She didn't give out Sidheag's title, afraid Soap and the others might be cowed by rank.

Sidheag didn't object to the demotion. She'd climbed up through the hatch and inside and was looking around with eyes as big as saucers. "What *is* this place?"

"Boiler room, miss. Ain't it grand? Lifeblood of the ship down 'ere. How-d'ye-do? I'm Phineas B. Crow. But most calls me Soap."

Sidheag grinned at him. A real grin, with no caution or stiffness to it. *That's more like it*, thought Sophronia.

While Soap pointed out the wonders of the boiler room to their new visitor with great pride, Sophronia turned to the other sooties. She emptied her pockets of the treats and nibbles she'd filched at high tea the day before, passing them out to the waiting group. It had taken her a few visits to realize the sooties were not, in fact, fed so well as the students, instead subsisting mainly on porridge, bread, and stew.

She pretended to be fully absorbed in distributing tiny lemon tarts so that Soap could work his inexplicable charm on Sidheag. No one could help but like Soap. Anyone not immediately set against him for the color of his skin or his station in life was bound to enjoy his company. And Sidheag might be many things, but Sophronia didn't think her particularly bigoted.

The tarts were Dimity's idea of reform. Sophronia had agreed to distribute them to the sooties so long as Dimity agreed not to try anything else altruistic. Nevertheless, Dimity had watched her creep out that night with an expression that was part fear and part jealousy. "Why take Sidheag, but not me?"

"But Dimity, you can't climb."

"I could try!"

"And you don't like getting dirty."

"I could wear my oldest dress."

"And you aren't interested in boiler rooms."

"But they clearly need my help! If I am to be a proper lady I must practice charitable endeavors as soon as possible. I want to be *good*."

"Be sensible instead!"

Dimity had only pouted.

So Sophronia was stuck passing out lemon tarts. She was paying so little attention to Sidheag and Soap that when the scuffle started, it took her a moment to react. They were fighting! *Oh, no, did I misjudge Sidheag?*

But a quick observation proved the fight was not with any real intent.

Sidheag and Soap were squared off, fencing, each with a stoking pole and a fierce expression. They were almost matched to each other by height, and they were also causing a stir of excitement. The sooties about them began to place bets, wagering the lemon tarts Sophronia had taken such care to distribute fairly.

"What are you two up to?"

"This is brilliant, Sophronia. Did you know this boy knows proper streetside fisticuffs?" Sidheag's dour face was animated with delight.

"Does he?" *Streetside, but he lives in the air?*

"Dirty fighting. It's capital! Look at this!"

Soap ducked in under Sidheag's swing and kicked her ankle.

Sophronia was shocked. *One is not meant to ever kick during a fight! It isn't gentlemanly, isn't proper, isn't done!* "Soap, that's unscrupulous!"

Soap stopped and turned to grin at her. "Yes, miss, but it works."

While he was distracted, Sidheag poked him in the side with her pole.

Soap let out a *woof* and doubled over.

Sidheag came up next to him, and after he managed to straighten, threw a companionable arm around his soot-covered shoulders. She was more relaxed than Sophronia had ever seen her. "It makes sense. Why should we fight like gentlemen? After all, as you keep reminding me, Sophronia, we *aren't* gentlemen. We aren't even soldiers. We're supposed to be intelligencers. We should learn to fight dirty. We should learn to fight any way we can."

Sophronia tried to put her doubts aside and be sensible. It

was more difficult than she thought. "That's reasonable, I suppose. But kicking?"

"Well, miss, not to be rude, but you ladies aren't sooties or soldiers. You don't have much in the way of arm muscle. You ought to be kicking more; you've got more power in your legs, don't ya? And you're usually wearing them sharp-toed boots."

Sophronia nodded. "Good point. But we're also wearing lots of skirts."

"Could get special boots made with metal reinforcements and attachments," said Sidheag.

"Sidheag Maccon, did I just hear you mention designing a fashion accessory?" Sophronia made her tone all-over appalled, but she was thinking, *Vieve could do something along those lines.*

Sidheag grinned. Another one of those genuine smiles that made her look, if not pretty, at least less plain. It crinkled up her remarkable caramel eyes and softened her normally harsh features. Sophronia, at that moment, decided that the idea to bring Sidheag among the sooties was a resounding success.

But then a looming shadow appeared above them and said, "What's this, what's this?"

"Greaser—scatter!" yelled Soap.

Sophronia and Sidheag did as directed, running hard alongside the sooties down and around the back of one of the coal piles and squeezing into a crevice.

Soap, who was a noble idiot, intercepted the greaser.

"He isn't going to get booted off school grounds for this, is he?" Sophronia asked, her heart sinking.

"What, Soap? For stopping and engaging in some mock swordplay?" One of the other sooties scoffed.

"So long as they didn't mark you ladies as Uptops, the most he'll get is an ear-boxing," added another.

"Greasers like him. He keeps us all in line, and he works harder than any two of us put together," explained the first.

Sophronia and Sidheag both let out sighs of relief.

Sidheag turned to her. "This is fun!"

"Finishing school's not all bad, now, is it?"

"It's not fair. I'm your first friend here! Why is it you persist in skulking off with Sidheag all the time?" Dimity was clearly trying not to whine.

"I hardly persist; we only go off once a week or so."

"And you two keep giggling together about things."

"I do *not* giggle without purpose. Lady Linette says you should never misapply a giggle. And Sidheag never giggles at all."

"Well, it's definitely not fair." Dimity was perched on the edge of her bed, looking down at her feet sadly.

"She's been helping me with fighting techniques."

"I could use extra fight training."

"Dimity, you don't even *want* to learn. You told me you decided to entirely give over that subject. That you really only wanted to be a lady."

Dimity sighed. "I suppose you're right."

Bumbersnoot, who was snuffling around the bed frame looking optimistically for a stray lump of coal or perhaps a small spider he might incinerate, came waddling over.

Dimity patted him on the head, and he blew a little blast of smoke out one ear.

Sophronia nibbled a fingertip in thought. "I tell you what—how about you help me with etiquette in court and ball settings? You're much better at remembering the order of precedence than I."

Dimity brightened.

Which was how Dimity and Sophronia ended up doing extra practice in the evenings. After some initial reticence, Sidheag joined them. Dimity managed to recover from her jealousy and, as a result, attacked the Scottish girl with her customary rapid-chatter teasing, which prodded Sidheag out of her awkward ways. In exchange, Sidheag started showing Dimity some of the easier knife tricks. No blood, of course. Nothing further was said about mysterious late-night jaunts.

"I don't feel like I'm really contributing to our little study group," Sophronia said to Dimity one night before they went to sleep.

"Don't be silly, Sophronia; you're the best of any of us."

Sophronia could feel herself blushing. "I'm not!"

"'Course you are. We simply haven't covered your subject yet in classes."

"Oh, really, and what's that?"

"You see opportunities. And you learn things and combine them in ways the rest of us don't."

Sophronia contemplated this. "I do?"

"I wager you've made a million connections in that brain of yours that I've never even considered. You say things to teachers that I know you've never told me. You've gone places on this airship I don't even know exist. Then again, you aren't always the most ladylike about it."

Sophronia remained silent.

"For example, your two best petticoats are missing. They vanished the night of the play."

"You noticed that?" *How embarrassing. If Dimity noticed my lack of proper foundation garments, why, anyone else might have as well—Monique, or Professor Braithwope!*

"I *always* notice clothing. I can't imagine you sat around all evening in this room alone that night, either."

"But...!"

Dimity lay back on her pillow and sounded self-satisfied. "I know you think I'm only paying attention to the etiquette side of our training, but I can't help picking other stuff up along the way. I may want to be a lady, but I'm learning how to be an intelligencer whether I like it or not. And you *are* my closest friend."

"So you spy on me?"

Sophronia could only just make out the movement of a shrug under Dimity's covers. "I'm not Monique. I'm not going to use it against you."

"She hasn't done anything to me directly since she turned me in."

"I know. Doesn't that worry you?"

"Yes. I think she's still trying to get a message off the ship. Luckily, she's as stymied as I am." Sophronia felt, rather fancifully, that they were lost forever, floating in the mist. Time had taken on an atmospheric quality.

"Do you think she knows that we know?"

"I certainly hope not."

The two girls went silent.

Finally Sophronia said, "You really do care about clothing and fashion, don't you, Dimity?"

"Very much. It's important—even Lady Linette says it's a method of manipulation. You can dictate what people think of you simply by wearing the right gloves, not to mention jewelry."

Sophronia was lost in remembering that second flywaymen battle. "What would you say of a man who went *floating* in fine evening dress and a top hat with a green ribbon about it?"

"Run," Dimity answered instantly. Her voice, normally full of bright fun and mockery, had taken on a completely sober tone.

"Why?"

"I don't know about you, Sophronia, but I'm certainly not ready to meet a Pickleman face-to-face. Not yet."

"Ah, of course. And what, exactly, is a Pickleman?"

"You don't know?"

"How would I?"

"Oh, I'm sorry. I keep forgetting you're a covert recruit. You seem to be so very much one of us."

"That's kind of you to say."

"Careful—wouldn't want Monique finding out you like it here. She'll make it her business to get you turned out. Anyway, Picklemen are sort of in charge of all kinds of important things. Not exactly legally, and rarely nicely. They like to collect money and power. That's pretty much all I know. Oh, and their leader is called the Great Chutney."

Sophronia's eyebrows arched. "Well, if you say so."

Dimity sat up, looking worried. "Do you think Monique might be working for *them*?"

"No, they're clearly backing the flywaymen, or employing them. And remember, Monique refused to cooperate. If she were working with them, why the theatrics in the road? Why not just hand over the prototype? Why hide it at my house?"

"So if she's not working for them and she's not working for our school, who is she working for?"

"Herself? Her family? I don't know—the vampires, maybe? Even the werewolves. Or perhaps one of the teachers is a traitor. We already know she has one of them defending her."

Dimity looked nervous. "Are you sure we should be involving ourselves? Isn't this something for the adults to sort out?"

Sophronia gave an evil little grin. "I'm thinking of it as training. Besides, if the prototype is at my house, I *am* involved. Monique involved me."

Dimity only nodded. "I still don't like how quiet she's been. We should be on our guard."

"Agreed."

Dimity's warning came none too soon, for having finally given up on trying to send a message, Monique turned her unwelcome attention once more to being a plonker.

Sophronia was minding her own business and running late to luncheon, as was her custom. She'd yet to learn the advantage of punctuality. As she told Sister Mattie the third time she was late to household potions and poisons, nothing interesting happened until *after* an event commenced. Her natural tardiness was compounded by the fact that she was trying to find time for all her classes; extra work in fan languages and how to plan a five-course meal; visits to sooties; and practicing with Sidheag and Dimity when no one was watching. There never seemed to be enough time.

So she was late to the dining hall, dashing in through the door, when someone stuck out one booted foot and she went flying.

Luckily, they'd learned some tumbling. Sophronia went head over heels, landing in a crouch on one knee with the other bent in what might be considered a mockery of a full court bow. It could have been graceful, except she tore her hem as she tried to rise, tripped to the side, and crashed into an unsuspecting senior girl.

By that point, the entire school had turned to watch her, and a wave of giggles rippled through the hall.

Sophronia was absolutely mortified. She'd been trying so hard to learn to at least pretend to be proper and well-mannered.

Mademoiselle Geraldine said, "Miss Temminnick! Is there a problem?"

"No, Headmistress." She could feel herself blushing furiously. It reminded her of the incident with the dumbwaiter and the trifle—only now she cared. *Stupid finishing school,* she thought, *teaching me to care about such things.*

"Where is your poise, young lady?"

"I seem to have misplaced it on someone's boot, Headmistress."

Professor Lefoux glared at her. "What was that? Excuses? Don't be smart, young lady."

"No, Professor. Apologies, Headmistress."

Lady Linette said with quiet firmness, "Miss Temminnick, go back out and reenter the room properly."

"Yes, my lady." Sophronia turned and marched from the room, and then came back in. This time she kept her eyes firmly to the ground, even though she knew everyone was watching her and they had recently had lessons in how to walk with one's nose in the air.

She saw a boot twitch as if it wanted to head out and trip her a second time. The boot was of peach-colored kid leather, with pink ribbons for laces and a shockingly high heel. The person attached to it was Monique de Pelouse.

Monique smiled sweetly at her and then turned and said in a very loud voice, "Isn't it *so intelligent* of Miss Temminnick to wear blue? With her complexion, it really is the only safe color. How unfortunate the dress couldn't be cut a tad more modern, poor dear."

Sophronia, stewing gently in annoyance, went to sit at the other end of the table. *Why does Monique impose upon us,* she wondered, *just for torture? I know she's been demoted, but I'm certain she could still sit with the senior girls. Give them the benefit of her scintillating conversation.*

"Don't worry, Sophronia," said Monique, "I'm sure no one saw your gaffe." At which Preshea tittered obligingly.

Sophronia didn't point out that Monique had tripped her, as she knew it would only sound defensive.

Dimity said, "You're not usually that clumsy."

"No, that's *my* role," added Agatha with a shy smile.

Sophronia looked down the table at Monique. "You're right, I'm not."

Monique wasn't finished, either. After tea, distracted by the prospect of a quadrille lesson with Mademoiselle Geraldine during which they had been instructed by Lady Linette to try passing secret messages without being caught by the headmistress, Sophronia and the others neglected to notice that Agatha wasn't with them. The poor thing wasn't *exactly* a friend, but they did try to keep an eye on her, as they might Bumbersnoot.

When Agatha finally joined them, some ten minutes late to class, her eyes were red. Mademoiselle Geraldine gave her a stern talking-to on the subject of tardiness, which started her crying.

"Now, dear, there is no use wasting tears on me; I'm not a man. Besides, you are clearly not the kind of young lady to cry with any form or grace. Your skin becomes blotchy."

Monique slid into the room gracefully at that juncture and glided to the back of the assembled girls without being observed. She was used to manipulating Mademoiselle Geraldine.

"Yes, Headmistress," Agatha replied, trying to stop her tears.

"No, no, not with the sleeve. Dear, how many times do I have to tell you? You must never wipe any part of your face with your sleeve. That is what a handkerchief is for. And even then we dab. Ladies *dab*! Where is your handkerchief?"

Agatha fished about hopelessly in her reticule.

"No handkerchief, Agatha Woosmoss? What kind of young lady of *qualit-tay* are you?"

"I am sorry, Headmistress."

Mademoiselle Geraldine turned to face the class. "Ladies, where do we always stash a spare handkerchief?"

"In our décolletage," sang out everyone in unison.

The headmistress smiled brightly, tossing her red curls and thrusting her own substantial décolletage forward as if in agreement.

"She could stash a whole cotton mill in hers," Sophronia whispered to Dimity.

Dimity pursed her lips to stop herself from laughing.

Mademoiselle Geraldine continued, "Show me, ladies!"

Obligingly, all the girls reached into their cleavage and pulled out squares of fine muslin. Being only thirteen or fourteen, few had sufficient cleavage to fish handkerchiefs out of, except Monique. Sidheag was a veritable beanpole. Sophronia felt her own wasn't bad. Preshea, of course, was perfect. Dimity said she thought the smaller girl stuffed. "You understand. With rosemary sachets." Dimity described herself as "lamentably undersized."

Sidheag seemed to be having difficulty following Mademoiselle Geraldine's instructions.

"Lady Kingair, where is your handkerchief?"

"Well, blast it. I put it in. It seems to have slipped down inside my corset."

Mademoiselle Geraldine fanned herself. "Lady Kingair, there is no need to go into detail. A lady of *qualit-tay* does not mention such a thing out loud."

"What? What did I say?" Sidheag was genuinely confused.

"Corset," hissed Sophronia.

"Miss Temminnick! Not you, too."

"I beg your pardon, Headmistress." Sophronia executed an almost perfect curtsy. This seemed to mollify Mademoiselle Geraldine.

"She doesn't have enough to hold it up, Headmistress," said Monique.

"Hush now, Miss Pelouse. We do not talk about another lady's endowments in public. Lady Kingair, my dear, did you put the handkerchief in before or after you laced this morning?"

"Before; otherwise I forget," Sidheag answered promptly.

"Well, you must wait to put it in after. Then it won't disappear on you. Miss Temminnick, lend Miss Woosmoss your spare, please? Then at least she will have something. Now, ladies, where was I? Oh, yes, the quadrille."

Agatha took her place in the set with Sidheag and Dimity. Sophronia stepped in to be her partner and passed her the handkerchief. Agatha stuffed it down her bodice with a muttered "thank you."

"Ladies, we begin with the *Le Pantalon*. And a one, two, three, four. Step forward, salutation to your partner—no, Miss Buss, you're playing the man, remember? You bow." The headmistress was making up the fourth in the other set with Monique, Preshea, and a mop dressed in a hat. They were having a much more difficult time trying to pass notes back and forth without her noticing. The mop, of course, was of absolutely no help.

"What happened, Agatha? Are you feeling quite the thing?" Sophronia asked when the dance permitted conversation.

"It's nothing to concern you."

"Let me guess—Monique?" While she talked, Sophronia

slipped Dimity a small, folded bit of paper. There was nothing on the paper; it was only for technique.

Sidheag said, "I saw that."

Dimity whispered, "Perhaps note-passing is better done during *L'été?*"

Agatha said, answering Sophronia's question, "She's evil. And not in a good way."

"What did she say?"

"Nothing of import." Agatha's face was red. "Not for *you*, anyway." The way she said it implied that Sophronia was somehow to blame.

They moved on from *Le Pantalon* to *L'été*. As Dimity had predicted, it was easier to pass the notes, but Agatha kept dropping hers. Every time she did so, everyone had to stop the pattern while she looked under her full skirts to try to find the scrap of paper. It was decidedly *not covert*. They had to pretend she was lacing her boot.

At the end of the hour, Mademoiselle Geraldine clapped her hands to get their attention. "That was adequate, ladies, but only adequate. You are to practice the first two sections of the quadrille ten times over this evening. In our next lesson, we will move on to the *La Poule*, so I expect you to have the *Le Pantalon* memorized."

"Do you think," Sophronia wondered to Dimity as they left the headmistress's classroom, "that she realizes she is saying 'the' twice?"

Dimity raised an eyebrow. "Why, Sophronia, are you implying Mademoiselle Geraldine is not actually French? Shocking suggestion."

"Any more than Lady Linette is a lady?" added Sophronia.

"Oh, come now, she could be a lady, you can't be certain of that. After all, Sidheag is a lady, and no one would ever have guessed *that*."

"Oh, thank you very much, Dimity," said Sidheag from where she stalked along behind them.

Dimity tilted her curly head back and over one shoulder, looking up at the tall girl with a cheeky grin. "Oh, don't pretend to be offended. I've figured you *all* out now. You'll take that as a compliment. You don't really *want* to be a lady. That's your whole difficulty."

Sidheag muttered something about who would want to be a lady when she could be a werewolf, which everyone politely ignored. Such an idea was patently ridiculous. Everyone knew girls couldn't be werewolves.

It was Dimity who found out what happened to Agatha. Dimity might not be very good at finding out anything about prototypes, or world domination, or next day's tea cakes, but she certainly had an ear for gossip.

"Did you hear Monique cornered Agatha in the hallway this afternoon? Apparently she said she wondered how someone of Agatha's vulgar proportions even got admitted to Mademoiselle Geraldine's. She said that Agatha probably wouldn't be asked back after the winter break, even if she did come from a long line of intelligencers. She said you would take Agatha's place, since there was no one better."

"Oh, dear, no wonder Agatha was mad at me. It's not true, is it?" In normal finishing schools, the general attitude was the more students the better, but this one was different. *Perhaps on an airship number restrictions have to be followed.*

Dimity chewed her bottom lip. "It's possible. Not that you'd take her place, but that she might not make it through. I don't mean to be unkind, but she really isn't very good. She might be better off at a real finishing school, and even then... I mean to say, have you *seen* her? It's not so much her figure as her confidence." Dimity shook her curly head in sympathy. "If only her posture were improved."

They heard a little gasp from the doorway and looked up to see Agatha's round, crestfallen face as she ducked away.

"I thought you closed that!" Dimity said to Sophronia, horrified.

"I thought I did, too. Perhaps she's not so bad an intelligencer as you thought."

Dimity was clearly upset with herself. Dimity was many things, but no one would call her mean-spirited. "Should I go after her, do you think?"

Sophronia sighed. "Perhaps we both should."

They went to knock on the other girl's door. Sidheag opened it, wearing a sour expression. *Well, more sour than usual.* "She doesn't want to talk to you."

"We came to apologize." Dimity looked hopeful.

"Well, it's a bit late for that." Sidheag crossed her arms over her bony chest and glared at them.

"Oh, don't take that attitude with us, Sidheag Maccon. We know you're not so bad as you make out." Sophronia pushed past the taller girl and into the room. Dimity followed, shutting the door firmly behind them.

Agatha and Sidheag's chamber was much the same in structure and layout as Sophronia and Dimity's. Which is to say it was small, with two beds, two wardrobes, and a vanity with a wash basin, and not much else. It did not, however, have Dimity's touch. Dimity's touch in their sleeping chamber involved draping brightly colored silk scarves on all the surfaces and pinning sparkly glass brooches to them. Sophronia didn't mind, although she did think it made the place look a little like an opera singer's boudoir.

Dimity approached the bed where Agatha lay facedown in a hunch, head buried in her pillow. "I'm sorry, Agatha, I shouldn't have said that."

Agatha didn't move.

Sophronia came over and said, "Couldn't you let us help you, just a little bit? I mean, we are *trying* with Sidheag."

Sidheag snorted.

"Well, we *are*. She helps us with boy-type stuff, and we coach her in how to be a girl."

Sidheag snorted again.

Sophronia gave her a look. "Well, we *do*. You're simply bad at it!"

Dimity patted Agatha on the back. "We could do it with you, too."

Agatha sniffed and rolled over. Her face was, as Mademoiselle Geraldine had pointed out, very blotchy indeed. "But what can I exchange?" she asked shakily.

Sophronia and Dimity grappled for a reply.

Finally Sophronia said, "You're good at sums and calculating household management. I heard Sister Mattie compliment you the other day. And we could all use help being more mild-mannered. You are particularly good at *that*."

Dimity came in to assist. "Yes, I talk too much, and Sophronia is overly bold."

"How kind of you to say, Dimity." Sophronia raised her eyebrows.

"And of course Sidheag is perfectly hopeless," added Dimity.

"Yes, thank you, Dimity."

"Well, it's true!" Dimity was truculent.

Agatha started to chuckle damply. "There you go, talking too much again, right, Dimity?"

"See, that's the spirit!" said Sophronia.

KEEPING PROPER RECORDS AND
HOW TO STEAL THEM

S o their little private study parties of three became four. If Agatha observed Sophronia and Sidheag's occasional jaunts to the boiler room, there was one thing Agatha was really very good at, and that was holding her tongue. Their private club didn't help modify Monique's behavior, however. Later that week, a rumor sprouted up that Dimity had stepped out with Lord Dingleproops, alone and unchaperoned.

Dimity was absolutely crestfallen. "I never! I'm a good girl, much to Mummy's disappointment. We always stayed in company. Besides, I don't think he likes me in that way."

Sophronia began pacing about the room. "Monique started the rumor, I know it. Something is going to have to be done about her."

"I don't think any of us are ready for a full-on covert reputation destruction. Monique has four extra years' training. She may not be a natural intelligencer, but she certainly is a natural pain." Dimity chewed her lip, still upset.

"She's a natural cod-slinger, is what she is." Sidheag had rather taken to Dimity. *Dimity is like that; she wears you down eventually.*

"Sidheag, language!" Dimity gasped, then she turned to Sophronia. "What do you suggest?"

"I don't know yet, but it had better be good. And something where I don't get caught or turned in."

Dimity, who was on Sidheag's bed, flipped over onto her back and stared up at the ceiling. "You mean to say, where *we* won't get caught."

"We?"

"I'm going to help you," said Dimity.

"Me, too," insisted Sidheag.

"And me, though I probably won't be much good," said Agatha.

"And there's Bumbersnoot—he'll help," added Dimity.

"Really? What's Bumbersnoot's difficulty with Monique?"

Dimity considered this seriously. "I don't know, but I wager he has one. Oh, she dented him once. Didn't she, Snooty darling?"

Sophronia took a deep breath. "We could go after the prototype. That would show them all. And she wouldn't be able to pass it on to her employer, whoever that is."

Sidheag and Agatha, who hadn't really been involved in her covert investigations thus far, looked as though they were trying hard to understand what she was talking about.

"So what's the plan, then?" asked Sidheag.

"You're not going to like it."

"Why not?"

"It involves a ball."

Sidheag and Agatha paled at the very idea.

"I'm not ready for a ball!" said the taller girl with an uncharacteristic look of panic.

"Oooh, a ball." Dimity clapped her hands.

"Well, there's one the night I return home. It's a good excuse to bring you three to visit. I can't write to ask, of course. But it will be an excellent cover for searching the house and grounds while Frowbritcher and the other mechanicals are distracted."

"But that's the start of winter holidays. How are we to get the prototype into the appropriate hands?" Dimity wanted to know. "Even supposing we do find it."

"That's the other part of the plan. Someone told the school to recruit me. We have to figure out who reported on me to Lady Linette. We find out who that person is, we can give her the prototype."

"I don't suppose you know who that might be, do you?"

Sophronia grinned again. "No, but—"

Dimity said, "I know that look. That's the look she gets right before she goes off exploring."

"But?" prompted Sidheag.

"But we could break into the school records to find out."

"Sophronia, that's a terrible idea!" protested Dimity.

"You're mad," added Sidheag.

Agatha only looked wide-eyed.

"Ah, but I have the trump card."

"You do?"

"Oh, yes. I'm going to borrow an obstructor and some soap."

"I could, but it'll take a long time. I spent years learning how. I'm thinking you need it before the holidays?"

Soap and Sophronia were sitting watching Sidheag take on a small herd of sooties in a rousing game of dice during a break in the late-night shift. The two girls had come for coal and stayed for conversation and, in Sidheag's case, gambling. She really was a lost cause. Sophronia had hoped she might get Soap to teach her his neat trick of getting inside locked doors.

She nodded glumly.

"What do you want to know lock-picking for, anyway?" Soap asked.

"I need to find out about school-affiliated intelligencers in my home area who might have recruited me for Mademoiselle Geraldine's."

"You're wanting to break into the record room?"

"That's about the sum of it."

"Sounds like fun."

"Soap, what if you get caught up top?"

"Now, there, miss, you think every time you come visit us we aren't at risk? It's a good thing there are so many sooties and so many places to hide. And that you bribe all of us with them smallish cakes. Because otherwise someone would have long since put a stop to these little visits of yours."

Sophronia only gave him a look. She didn't like Soap taking too many risks for her.

He grinned at her, sidled over, and bumped her shoulder. "Stop your fretting. I can get away. Plus, how you going to do it without me?"

Sophronia felt a little giddy despite her worry. "Oh, very well! But this is becoming quite the expedition."

It took them a week to plan their raid on the record room. Vieve agreed to lend Sophronia the obstructor with remarkably little fuss. She was involved in some new invention and it was taking up most of her time—even the temptation of a midnight record room break-in could not lure her away. She also told them where the room was located. "'Course I know. Whatcha take me for, an amateur? They keep records of inventions there, too." After that there was a good deal of arguing about who should go and who should stay behind.

Sophronia didn't tell anyone Soap was coming; she only said she had a way of getting inside once they found the place.

Dimity advocated most strongly. "I want to come! I haven't had any exciting excursions yet."

"It'll be either you or Sidheag; we have to keep the numbers down." *And Agatha clearly isn't interested.*

Dimity looked pleadingly at Sidheag, who, not unsurprisingly, shrugged.

Dimity took that as an affirmative and clapped her hands in excitement.

"You may have to tone down your sparkles, you know. The point is *not* to be seen."

Dimity, with great reluctance, removed all her jewelry and put on her darkest gown, a royal blue walking dress.

"Will I do?"

"Admirably."

Soap was waiting as arranged on the deck outside Sister Mattie's empty classroom, lurking among her potted plants. He materialized from darkness behind a tall foxglove. *Good as a poison in large doses or for trouble breathing in small amounts,* Sophronia remembered.

"Good evening, ladies."

"Good evening, Soap. All prepared?" He was looking cleaner than usual, and his clothing almost fit. *He put on his Sunday best for me.* Sophronia was chuffed.

"Of course. You have the obstructor?"

"I do, indeed." Sophronia showed him her wrist.

Dimity remained silent, her mouth a perfect O of amazement as she looked at Soap.

"Dimity, this is Soap. Well, Phineas B. Crow is his proper name."

Soap grinned his perfect grin and doffed his cap at the still-dumbstruck Dimity. "How-d'ye-do, miss?"

"This is Dimity Plumleigh-Teignmott."

Dimity bobbed a curtsy and recovered her voice, fortunately remembering to keep it low. "How do you do, Mr. Soap?"

"Oh, just Soap will do, miss."

Dimity looked up at him, eyes wide. "You know we have a stable lad just like you. You know, in color. Perhaps you know him, name's Jim, he—"

"I'm loath to cut introductions short, but we really must get moving," said Sophronia, mostly to forestall anything further Dimity might come up with.

The three of them turned and proceeded in a measured way toward the teachers' section of the ship. They spent a good deal of time pausing to let the obstructor work its invisible magic, dashing around a frozen mechanical, and then going onward.

Fortunately, the record room was exactly where Vieve said it would be: on the upper floor of the front section of the airship.

Getting there was rather less easy than it might have been. Dimity was no climber, and she kept wobbling around and squeaking about the distance to the ground—far—and the difficulty in bridging gaps—impossible. Eventually they climbed a rickety set of steps that wound in a corkscrew around the outer hull from Professor Lefoux's balcony to a small, cupboardlike door.

Directly above was the forward squeak deck, where Sophronia had stood on her first day and acquired Bumbersnoot. Below were the levels containing the teachers' private quarters; below that, the massive boiler room. The forward section housed everything *important*, and the attic level was one of the only ones Sophronia hadn't visited. Consequently, she was dying of curiosity.

Dimity signaled them to keep their voices down. "Professor Braithwope, remember? He's still awake, and he's only a level or two below us, with vampire-acute hearing."

Wish she'd thought of that when she was squeaking, thought Sophronia.

They continued along in silence. The level was somewhat squashed. Even Sophronia felt cramped, and she was by far the littlest of the three. It was not rigged with gas parasol lighting. They had to feel their way along in the dark.

They found the room, conveniently labeled RECORD LIBRARY— CONTAINING RECORDS OF IMPORT in big gold letters.

There was a soldier mechanical directly outside the door. It spotted them approaching and whirred to life, puffing smoke out from below its headpiece in a huff of alarm. Before Sophronia could even raise the obstructor, the mechanical raised one cannonlike arm and shot at them.

Soap dove down on instinct. Sophronia and Dimity flinched.

They found themselves covered in a net of some spongy, sticky material, like tripe, that was nevertheless very strong. The mechanical advanced toward them, hissing menacingly.

I feel like a partridge wrapped in bacon, thought Sophronia. *Most unpleasant.* Sophronia couldn't raise her arm to point with the obstructor, as the netting held it firm at her side. "Dimity, can you reach your sewing scissors?"

"I can't move," peeped Dimity, and then she made a *puft* noise as some of the sticky netting got into her mouth.

"Soap?" Sophronia tried to look about to see the sootie.

"I'm better off than you are, miss. But it's a mite embarrassing."

Sophronia glanced down. In diving to avoid the blast, Soap had ended up partly shielded by the skirts of her dress. Only one side of his body was trapped to the floor by the netting; the other half was under her petticoats.

The mechanical was upon them, and had apparently been instructed to try to capture any intruder, but was confused to have caught three at once. It was making bewildered whirring noises and rocking side to side on its track as it sifted through its protocols for the correct approach.

"Do you have any sewing scissors?" Sophronia asked Soap.

"No, miss, but I have a knife."

"Can you get to it and try to free up my wrist?"

Soap squirmed, fluffing out petticoats as he wiggled his free arm. Dimity made a muffled squeak of alarm at this indignity to Sophronia's person. Soap managed the task barely, cutting away enough of the strands to allow Sophronia to raise her arm and point it at the mechanical. Unfortunately, the strands were now stuck to his knife.

The soldier mechanical appeared to have reached a decision. It leaned back and brought up its other arm, this one spouting smoke.

"It's going to burn us alive!" gasped Dimity.

Before the mechanical could do anything further, Sophronia hit it with the invisible blast from the obstructor. The mechanical froze, but they still had to extract themselves from the net. Soap continued to hack from below with his knife, using the hem of Sophronia's gown to clean it as he did so. Sophronia managed to access her reticule with her free hand and pulled out her sewing scissors. She cut away at the netting around Dimity until she, too, could get to her scissors.

"This stuff is so sticky. I'm sure it's food by nature. Should we be handling raw foodstuffs? My dress is entirely ruined, and even using it to wipe with isn't very effective." Dimity was not pleased.

Sophronia checked the tackiness of the net between two

fingers. *I wonder if oil might work.* She fished some perfume oil out of her reticule—rose-scented. She cleaned her scissors as best she was able and then coated the blades with the oil. It worked a treat.

"Would you look at that?" Soap was impressed. Sophronia dropped the bottle down to him. He coated his knife, then handed the oil up to Dimity. Things went much faster after that, although they all ended up smelling like roses.

All the while they were working to get free, Sophronia had to pause to blast the mechanical with the obstructor. When the sticky stuff was finally gone, they could not push the huge, heavy soldier mechanical out of the way, for it was somehow locked down.

Soap couldn't manage to pick the lock in the space of one obstructor blast. So Sophronia had to stand before the sentry and disable it with the obstructor every six seconds while Soap worked diligently behind it.

Sophronia worried the obstructor might run out or fade in its effectiveness. Vieve had not explained exactly how it worked, and Sophronia could hardly believe it would continue indefinitely, but it showed no signs of stopping.

Eventually Soap got the door open. Sophronia hit the mechanical with one last blast and they squeezed inside the room before the thing woke up again. They closed the door firmly behind them.

Only to be faced with an entirely new problem.

The record room looked like a small factory or cotton mill—machines and conveyors and rotary belts ran along the walls and filled the corners of the room.

"Look up," hissed Sophronia.

Dimity and Soap did.

Above them dangled the records. They were clipped to conveyers mounted on the ceiling, like an upside-down, dangling version of mechanical tracks. The records themselves looked like nothing so much as laundry hanging from a clothesline. They were far too high up to reach, and there seemed no way to know where any particular record was. There were hundreds there, if not thousands—it was a nightmare.

"There must be some method of search and recall," Sophronia said, looking around desperately.

There were three desks in the room, each with a small leather seat, an oil lamp, and a writing pad. Each also boasted a large brass knob with a lever sticking out of the top. Around the base of the knob, and taking up a good deal of the desk space, was a circular piece of parchment paper with writing on it.

Soap went to one desk, Sophronia to another, and Dimity to the last. Each bent to light the oil lamp and examine the writing on the round parchment.

"Try not to touch anything; we are still all-over sticky," warned Sophronia.

Even as she said it, a quill adhered itself to Dimity's bosom as she leaned in. Dimity didn't notice. She said, "Mine is labeled with locations." She craned her neck to the side to read around the circle. "Cities, counties, a few districts, and even some wards. Here's London. Here's Devonshire."

Sophronia looked at hers. "Mine looks like it's skill sets. Knife, seduction, armored umbrella, flirtation. What's yours, Soap?"

Soap was standing over his desk with his head down, not even looking at the paper.

They didn't have much time. "What's it *say*, Soap?"

Soap looked up, clearly embarrassed. "Sorry, miss, can't tell."

"Goodness me, why not? Is it something horrid and unlady-like?" Soap was proving, often, to be far more conscientious of Sophronia's dignity than Sophronia was.

Soap only shook his head.

Dimity said in a sympathetic tone, "You can't read, can you, Mr. Soap?"

"No, miss. Sorry, miss." His voice was almost a whisper.

Sophronia blinked. *Poor Soap! What a thing to go through life without books.* "Oh, right." She ran over. "It's the alphabet." She pointed, "See, A, B, C, D, and so forth."

Soap only backed slightly away, looking hugely embarrassed. Sophronia bumped up against his side, much in the manner he had done to her in the past, and gave him a little smile. This seemed to only embarrass him further. "Aw, miss."

"What do they mean?" asked Dimity.

Sophronia shrugged. "Only one way to find out."

She grabbed the lever on Soap's desk and pushed it toward A.

All around them, with what seemed to be a tremendous amount of noise, the machinery of the record room came to life. Steam hissed out from pistons and rotary mechanisms as they whirled up, thundering, shaking, and groaning. Above them the records moved on those tracks, shifting from one part of the room to another, parting and regrouping. They whizzed around one another, the parchment flapping and crackling.

Finally a large cluster moved purposefully in Soap and Sophronia's direction, coming to a stop directly above the desk.

"Now what?" wondered Soap.

Sophronia searched around the desk for some other operational mechanism or switch.

"This is when I wish we had Vieve with us," she said, frowning. She returned to the original lever, and after tapping and picking at it, pressed down hard on the round brass nodule at the base.

With a loud clunk, the records above her dropped.

She and Soap both ducked out of the way, narrowly missing being whacked by dangling paperwork as the collection above the desk came flying straight down and stopped, hovering, in a manner undoubtedly convenient to whomever was seated at the desk.

Sophronia unclipped and examined one of the pieces of paper, mindful of any stickiness. She read bits aloud, in deference to Soap, and to the fact that Dimity still stood at her desk some distance away.

"'Comtesse de Andeluquais, Henrietta, née Kipplewit,' it says at the top of the file." Below this was a sketch of a personable young woman, with written vital statistics such as hair color, eye color, social position, and fashion preferences. Then came a string of locations and dates, starting with what Sophronia assumed was a birthplace and ending with what must be the comtesse's current residency in France. Below that was written a list of particular skills, which in Henrietta's case appeared to be "Parasol manipulation, hairstyles for concealment, ballistics, quiet footsteps, fast waltz, and rice pudding."

There were a goodly number of additional papers covered in neat handwriting. Sophronia tried to sum up for her audience. "Reports on various assignments, I believe. Yes, here it says she infiltrated French diplomatic offices. And here is a report on her marriage to the comte." Sophronia looked over at Dimity. "You mean we are going to have to marry whomever the school chooses?"

Dimity was unconcerned. "Within reason. This is a finishing school, after all. That's what all finished girls do—marry well. Besides, how else would we infiltrate positions of power?"

Sophronia postponed any protestations for a later date and turned her attention to the issue at hand. She replaced Henrietta's paperwork and depressed the brass knob of the lever, and the records rose back up to the ceiling.

"Which desk had locations?"

Dimity pointed at hers.

Soap and Sophronia went over.

"We need a location close to my home. That's near Wootton Bassett, Wiltshire." Sophronia began reading the place names. "Aha, Swindon should do it." She grabbed the lever and pulled it.

The records shifted and whisked around, rearranging themselves until a cluster coalesced and came to hover above the desk. This time there was a much smaller number of records—three, to be precise. Sophronia depressed the nodule and the paperwork plummeted down.

They were all ready this time and didn't duck or flinch.

It was a moment's work to read through the names of the three women in Sophronia's area who had also once attended Mademoiselle Geraldine's. Of the three, one was now dead, the second had lived there for only a brief time in 1847, and the third...well, the third was...

"Mrs. Barnaclegoose!" said Sophronia.

"I take it you know her?" asked Dimity.

"Yes, indeed."

"Then we've got what you came for, miss?" said Soap.

Sophronia desperately wanted to read the entire file on her mother's dear old friend and chronic teatime companion. She'd always thought Mrs. Barnaclegoose no more than a meddling busybody with stylish propensities at odds with her ever-increasing waistline. "Please, wait!"

"Now, miss, we'd best move. Them machineries make enough noise to spook a poltergeist, and we got us vampire hearing to worry over. Best get the records back the way they were to start and get out." He seemed very nervous. Sophronia wondered if it was all the paperwork.

"No point in trying to make the break-in invisible."

"No?" Dimity was confused.

"No. The place reeks of rose oil, and there is sticky netting all over the hallway. We are going to have to try to cast the blame on someone else. I'll simply put this lot back up and dial in something random. At least that'll throw them off the trail."

Sophronia depressed the nodule, and they watched as the three Swindon records rose up to the ceiling. Then she dashed over to the final desk and pushed the lever toward the "tea leaf encryption" skill set. A new cluster of papers came over to that desk. Instead of pushing them to ascend, Sophronia left them there. They snuffed out the oil lamps and made their way out of the record room.

They managed to blast and then sneak by the soldier mechanical, which was rocking back and forth in confusion. Something about having trapped an intruder and then suddenly having that intruder be multiples and then vanish had put it into a protocol loop. It was paralyzed by indecision and hadn't sounded the alarm. *Luck*, thought Sophronia. *Is that something an intelligencer should count on?*

They made their way back down through the ship, using the obstructor as needed and separating from Soap at Lady Linette's balcony.

"Thank you kindly for your help," said Sophronia, rather awkwardly formal.

"'Course, miss," said Soap, coming in far too close and tucking a loose bit of Sophronia's hair behind her ear before swinging himself back over the railing and clambering away.

Dimity gave Sophronia a long, suspicious look.

Sophronia pretended not to see and said, "Turn around. I'll get your buttons."

Dimity sputtered, "But we are outside! At night! On a balcony!"

"Yes, but sometimes decency must be sacrificed on the altar of not being found out by teachers because we smell of rose oil and are covered in sticky stuff! Now, please, Dimity."

They helped each other to remove their outer gowns. Dimity threw hers over the edge rather sadly. "I did like that blue gown."

"Let's hope Captain Niall doesn't find them." Sophronia chucked hers after Dimity's without much care. She'd grown to appreciate that she needed to learn to be fashionable, but that didn't mean she had vested any emotional compassion into her existing clothing. "I'll steal us some vinegar from the kitchen in the morning; we can soak our smalls in that. It should get out the smell." She bit her lip, thinking. "And suet, for cleaning our scissors."

Dimity looked faintly unwell at the idea. "So much for smelling like roses."

BREAKING, BURGLING, AND
A PROPER BREAKFAST

Despite the fact that Lady Linette must have discovered it, the infiltration of the record room was not announced at breakfast. No doubt this was to keep Mademoiselle Geraldine in the dark. The headmistress probably didn't even know there *was* a record room. However, there was certainly an aura of doom about the repast that subdued even Monique's machinations.

Nevertheless, Monique managed to corner Sophronia in the hallway later that day on their way to lessons with Lady Linette.

"I understand your sister has a coming-out ball soon. Pity your family can't see to a London Season. Or is there some additional urgency to the matter of your sister's entrée?"

Sophronia curled her lip. "At least Petunia is *getting* a coming-out. I understand you haven't been presented. And you are what, all of eighteen? Such a waste."

"Oh, don't you concern yourself with me. Mama plans a spectacular season as soon as I finish. And she won't have already spent the family fortune on an older sister."

"Why are we talking about this now?"

"Oh, did I forget to mention? I have an invitation."

"What!"

"Yes, indeed. I wrote to Daddy shortly after we first arrived at school. Daddy knows people."

How on earth did she get that message off the ship? Sophronia wondered. *I thought she was prevented. I missed something. What did I miss?*

"How did you . . . ?" she started to ask; then she remembered. Monique's *friend*.

She has a teacher, or something like it, working with her, of course! They must have sent the message for her, from Bunson's. Perhaps I can somehow take advantage of this, follow her. "It's going to be a very interesting event," said Sophronia slyly. "Very interesting indeed."

Monique's face sharpened. "Are you meddling, little girl? I wouldn't meddle in things that don't concern you."

"Isn't that exactly what we are being trained to do?"

Monique stepped in close, and Sophronia felt a prick at her throat. Under cover of full sleeves and bonnet ribbons, the older girl pressed a very sharp metal hair stick into Sophronia's neck. "Accidents will happen."

Sophronia was not to be cowed. She jerked away. "So will discoveries," she hissed before moving swiftly on to Lady Linette's. Monique followed her. She was no longer worried for her family;

Monique wouldn't tell anyone the hiding place. *She wants to retrieve the prototype herself. She wants to stay in control of the operation. That's what I'd want.*

The other girls were already seated. They were looking, Sophronia realized, far better than they had in September. Dimity's curls were more controlled. Preshea's expression was not so sour, and Agatha had a nice piece of lace about her neck. Even Sidheag had improved her posture. Sophronia wondered what changes had been wrought upon her own appearance.

Lady Linette entered a few minutes after Monique, almost late for her own class. She looked harried underneath her copious frills and layers of face paint. "Ladies, it has come to our attention that someone tampered with the record room last night. Have any of you information to impart?"

The girls all looked at one another.

Monique raised her hand. "Sophronia, Dimity, Sidheag, and Agatha have been very subversive lately."

Lady Linette turned blue eyes upon Monique. "Indeed, Miss Pelouse? Have you overheard anything concrete?"

"No, Lady Linette." Monique shifted in her seat.

Lady Linette turned her attention to Sophronia. "Have you ladies been plotting?" Sophronia had no idea why she should be selected as the representative of the group, but supposed it was a fair cop. They did, as a general rule, tend to be her schemes.

She said, "I'm attempting to get them invited to my sister's ball. That's why I keep trying to send a message home."

"Of course you are. But not Miss Buss or Miss Pelouse?"

Sophronia shrugged. "Mumsy won't let me ask *everyone*. I mean to say, what comes next—the entire school?"

Monique looked prim. "I already have an invitation. I don't need Sophronia's help."

Dimity gave Sophronia a very worried look.

Sophronia remained impassive. "Oh, yes? I didn't know you knew my sister."

"Nor did I," interjected Lady Linette. "Considering Miss Pelouse's last sojourn into your abode was under false pretenses, she will have to plan her outfit carefully. And you ladies, do you think you are ready for a ball so soon in your careers?"

Sidheag shrugged. Dimity nodded enthusiastically. Agatha stared at her hands.

Lady Linette sighed audibly. "Nothing to do with the record room, then, ladies?" She directed the full focus of her attention on Sidheag, of all people. "Are you certain you didn't see anything in particular?"

Sidheag looked at Sophronia with a slight air of contrition and shrugged. Sophronia frowned. *What does Sidheag have to feel guilty about?*

"Is anything missing from the record room?" asked Sophronia.

"A quill, but nothing else." Lady Linette redirected the query to become a teaching session. "So what do we believe an infiltrator might have been after, ladies?"

"Information," said Preshea promptly. "It is a record room."

"Exactly, Miss Buss. Very good."

"The culprit has to be someone already on board school

grounds," added Sophronia. "Unless infiltrators can get on and off without the mechanicals noticing."

"Good, Sophronia."

"That's why you are interrogating the students."

"Lady Linette." Dimity straightened up. "Are the records of students kept in that room?"

Lady Linette nodded.

Sophronia, seeing where Dimity might be steering the conversation, said, "So the culprit wanted to see information, change information, or steal information. Which means a vested interest. Older student, perhaps, skilled enough to get in, with something at risk?"

Sophronia stopped herself there, not wanting to push her luck, and carefully didn't look at Monique. Casting blame elsewhere was a classic misdirection tactic, but it had to be practiced with care. Particularly as it was Lady Linette who had explained the technique to her.

"So can Agatha, Sidheag, and Dimity come with me to my sister's ball? Are they socially skilled enough for public exhibition?" Sophronia asked, hoping to change the subject now that she had planted a seed of suspicion.

"If their parents approve. You'll have to wait until we exit the gray. Now, what to teach today? Oh, yes. *Posture.*"

That evening, Monique de Pelouse and a few of the older girls were taken in for questioning by Lady Linette, Professor Lefoux, and Professor Braithwope. A new rumor instantly sprang up that Monique was the one who had broken into the record room, supposedly to doctor her files over failing to finish.

"It's a great rumor," said Dimity proudly when they were safely back in their room, changing for dancing lessons. "Did you stash some of that rose perfume oil in her room?"

Sophronia grinned. "Of course."

"Nice to get a little of our own back." Dimity was busy rinsing out their now vinegar-scented underthings in the washbasin.

"How do you think Monique managed to get invited to my sister's ball?"

Dimity said, "Connections. Your father belongs to some kind of gentlemen's club, doesn't he?"

"Don't all fathers?" Sophronia finished with the bacon grease and the sewing scissors and fed the excess fat to Bumbersnoot, who belched black smoke appreciatively.

"A note from Monique to her darling papa right after we arrived here, and your mother is sending out one extra invitation to one bony blonde."

"No, I mean how'd she get the note off the ship?"

"Oooh, good question. She had help?"

"She had help."

"Who?"

"Now that, Dimity, is a really good question." Sophronia wandered over to assist in wringing out the clothing. Dimity had clearly never even observed a washing day, let alone scrubbed clothing herself; she handled it so tentatively it was as though the fabric might be seized with a spirit of disapproval and administer a wet slap across her face.

"This could turn out to be a good thing," Sophronia said.

"How so? Monique is sure to be better-dressed and have more dances than us."

"She could lead us right to where she hid the prototype."

"We'll have to keep an eye on her the entire ball."

"What an unpleasant thought. Still, there are four of us and only one of her."

"With years' more training."

Sophronia made herself sound confident. "We did pretty well last night."

Dimity nodded. "Although I thought in Lady Linette's class that Sidheag might break."

Sophronia nodded. "I know. It's not like her. What do you think that was about?"

Dimity shook her head.

Sophronia slumped onto her bed. Or, to be more precise, she slumped down into her corset, which didn't allow for very much slumping. Then, after a moment's thought, she stood and left their room, heading for Sidheag and Agatha's.

Sidheag wasn't there, but Agatha let her in.

"Sophronia?"

"Could I have a little look out of your window, please, Agatha?"

"Well, um, if you like."

Sophronia went over to the window. She had to stand on Sidheag's bed to see out of it. It was one of those tiny portholes, like the ones on seafaring steamers.

"Sophronia, what are you doing on my bed?" came a sharp question.

"Good afternoon, Sidheag. Interesting how I can see right over to that outer balcony."

"Is it interesting?"

"A balcony, mind you, that I like to use on occasion to get around. You, too, now that you've joined me on my climbing jaunts."

"Do you?"

"Yes, I do." Sophronia frowned at the tall Scotswoman. "Agatha, would you give us a moment of privacy?"

"You aren't going to argue, are you? That's what Papa always says before he yells at Mama. Please don't argue. We've all been getting along so well."

"Agatha!" said Sidheag sharply.

Agatha let herself out of the room, closing the door softly behind her.

Sophronia said, "I know you're not happy here, Sidheag, but I never would have pegged you for a turncoat."

Sidheag looked uncomfortable. "I thought you'd deny it and there would be an end to the matter."

"I wasn't trained up enough yet to know that denial was the best course of action."

"So you got into trouble. Sorry about that."

"Sorry? That's all I'm allowed?"

"You just did exactly the same thing to Monique. Worse, because she didn't actually do it."

"She deserved it."

"I thought at the time that *you* deserved it. Why should you go climbing out at all hours while the rest of us were trapped in our rooms?"

"I wish you'd admitted it was you earlier. Perhaps Monique isn't as bad as I think."

"Oh, she is."

Sophronia sighed. She wasn't really angry at Sidheag—more concerned about what it said about her new friend's character.

Sidheag's look went from militant and defensive to slightly apologetic. She sat on the other bed, facing Sophronia. Sidheag was no Dimity, to flop and lean affectionately on her shoulder.

"I didn't want you to know it was me. I thought you'd hate me for it."

"What did you do it for, then, Sidheag?"

"I thought it would show them what a bad fit I was for this school. A school like this ought to punish scandalmongers. Instead they acted disappointed and put a note in my record. I did genuinely think you'd deny it, too. Then it would be your word against mine and nothing would come of it. I didna ken I'd grow to like you at all."

"You're not going to make it through, are you, Sidheag? I mean to say, you're tough enough, but—"

"I dinna care enough. I got home to worry over."

"Something's wrong with your pack?"

"Something." Sidheag clearly didn't want to relay the particulars.

"I take it you really don't want to come to my sister's ball?"

Sidheag nodded, perhaps a little too eagerly. "I should go home."

"Um," said a hesitant voice. The door behind them cracked open. Agatha had clearly been listening to the whole conversation. *At a school for espionage training,* thought Sophronia, *life can get very complicated.*

"Yes, Agatha?" she said primly.

"Could I not go, too, then? I mean to say, very kind of you to ask me and all, but I don't know as I'm ready, and if Sidheag isn't attending…" She trailed off hopefully.

"I'm certain you and Dimity can handle matters," Sidheag said, attempting to be positive.

Sophronia wasn't convinced, but it wasn't in her training to object. "Once an invitation has been declined, it does not do to force your request; it's as bad as a jilted lover pressing his suit," Mademoiselle Geraldine had said. So Sophronia left the room with a polite farewell.

"Sidheag and Agatha won't be coming with us to Petunia's ball," she said to Dimity upon returning to their room.

"Oh, why not?"

"They don't feel ready."

"Goodness, imagine passing up the opportunity to dress fancy and dance all night."

"Or, more precisely, dress fancy and follow Monique around all night."

Dimity said, "Just us two, then? This isn't going to be easy."

The end of the year barreled down upon them like flywaymen out of a clear blue sky. One week they were learning the last of handkerchief manipulation for fun and profit and having a special session on the language of fans with an eye toward various holiday parties, and the next week the great propellers of the school had wound up and they were no longer drifting with the mists. They left their safe haven of gray and made haste to Swiffle-on-Exe.

The teachers were jumpy. No sooner had they drifted down

and out of the cloud cover than on the horizon they could see the faint dots of airships tracking them. The school sped toward the town and the relative protection of Bunson and Lacroix's Boys' Polytechnique.

During the intervening two days, messages were dropped, presumably to Captain Niall and thence to the nearest post. Sophronia sent a carefully worded missive warning her family of possible flywaymen and asking them to uninvite Monique, both of which items she was tolerably certain they would ignore. She also informed them she was bringing Dimity with her.

Bunson's let out the same day as Mademoiselle Geraldine's, partly because of the system of shared information and partly for safety, Sophronia supposed. The flywaymen would hardly dare tangle with the defenses of an evil genius school, not to mention assembled parents of high rank and threatening aspect. Mademoiselle Geraldine's Finishing Academy for Young Ladies of Quality floated in low over the town and dropped anchor—which apparently meant lashing several mooring ropes to a copse of trees—a quarter of a mile away from the walls of Bunson's. It was midmorning and thus impossible to use Captain Niall and the glass platform for unloading. Sophronia suspected only very few knew about the rope ladders, which left her curious as to dignified disembarkation. *Will I get to see the stairs?*

She and the other debuts packed what few necessities they needed, knowing full wardrobes and shopping jaunts awaited them at home. They made their way to one of the main decks of the midsection of the ship alongside the other students. The deck soon became crowded with giggling girls, full skirts, and assorted fripperies, not to mention hatboxes, carpetbags, and parcels. Sophronia wormed her way to the front and watched with interest as the school came down so low as to allow a long, automated staircase to drop out from under its mid-deck. She bent herself double and nearly tumbled over the railing in an effort to see how it was managed. Sophronia spotted three sooties cranking it down and waved to them discreetly.

Carriages awaiting receipt of students were assembled on a sweeping brown patch of moor between the two schools. Some contained eager parents, but most were staff awaiting charges. There was also a large coach-and-four intended to take some dozen or so girls to the nearest train station.

Sophronia strained to see her own family crest—a hedgehog on the field of battle—on the side of a carriage. It was nowhere in sight, even with binoculars. Vieve had lent the binoculars to her on a semipermanent basis, a consolation prize from the young scamp upon taking back her obstructor. "To be sure," the girl had said, "I need it far more than you, stuck on this ship all on my lonesome for the next two weeks. Here, take these instead."

"Miss Temminnick, remove yourself from that indelicate position!" Lady Linette's voice resounded from the other side of the milling throng.

Sophronia shied back from the rail. With a puff of steam and a clang of machinery, that very rail folded away, leaving the students faced with a long, rather grand, staircase-meets-ladder contraption.

It was a precarious descent for the girls, particularly the debuts, having to navigate a bobbing and shifting staircase with proper poise and carpetbags, but they managed it without upset—even Agatha.

Only when she was safely on the ground and milling through the flamboyance of the waiting conveyances did Sophronia spot their transport.

"Over here, Miss Sophronia!" Her old chum Roger the stable lad stood and waved at her from the farm's pony and cart. It was terribly embarrassing; they would be traveling some fifty miles by cart. What if it rained?

Dimity, however, being a dear, sweet thing, said nothing disparaging. She declared in a shaky voice that it would be exhilarating to travel so far with an open top.

"You're Miss Dimity?" asked Roger. "I'm to collect a Miss Pelouse as well. She here?"

"Oh, must we? Couldn't you forget to, Roger, please?" asked Sophronia hopefully.

"More than my job's worth, miss. Herself gave explicit instructions."

At this juncture, Monique came up behind them and had histrionics. "Your mother sent us *that*? Guests at a ball, and we must travel all day in that!"

"You invited yourself, Monique. You might have ordered your own transport. I suspect our carriage was needed for more important guests arriving from town at the station."

Monique sputtered and, after much fuss, allowed Roger to haul her into the cart, only to sit with her back ostentatiously presented to all.

Sophronia looked back up at the school through her binoculars. She could just make out, peeking out a bottom hatch of the forward section, two small faces, one black and the other that of a grubby child, accompanied by madly waving arms—Soap and Vieve seeing her off in their own inimitable way. Well aware that they probably could not distinguish her in the crowd, she nevertheless waved gamely back.

Sophronia looked beyond the ship. She was certain the specks were closer, and equally confident they represented flywaymen.

"Ready, miss?"

"By all means, Roger."

Dimity yelled, "Oh, wait, I forgot! Pillover. Can we bring him? I suspect Mama might have forgotten he needs a lift. She can be very absentminded when she's being evil."

Sophronia shrugged. "He's small. All right with you, Roger?"

Roger was game. "The missus said to make certain to collect all of you, not that I couldn't arrive with extras."

Dimity scanned the crowd for her brother. "Oh, where is the furuncle?"

"Look for a crowd of Pistons," suggested Sophronia.

"Oh, Pillover isn't a member. He's not dashing enough."

"Did I say I thought he might be? There!" Sophronia pointed to one side, where a group of boys stood with indolent posture and dark attitude. They were all dressed in browns and blacks, their hair was slicked back with too much pomade, and there were evening top hats on their heads—even though they were not yet presented and it was not yet teatime.

"Who do they think they are?" wondered Sophronia.

"Pistons, of course," replied Dimity.

Each boy wore a brass-colored ribbon about his hat and had

a gear affixed to his waistcoat. One or two had some kind of decorative protective eyewear perched atop the brim as well. They all wore riding boots, although not a single saddle horse was to be found.

Sophronia said, in tones of mild shock, "Some of them look like they are wearing face paint."

"Kohl, about the eyes," explained Dimity.

"Roger, head toward those boys over there, would you, please?"

"The pansies, miss?" said Roger.

"I wouldn't let them hear you say that if I were you."

Roger guided the pony toward the group in question with an ill-disguised look of contempt.

Pillover was, indeed, at their center. He was sitting atop a small trunk, shrouded in his oversized oil coat and battered bowler, reading a grubby book while the boys around him heckled him as though he were an emu at the zoo.

Their behavior, however, altered drastically the moment a cart full of girls drew up alongside.

"Lord Dingleproops?" said Dimity in a very snooty tone of voice. "What are you doing to my brother?"

A lanky young man with ginger hair and a less than aggressive chin doffed his hat at Dimity and said, with a cheeky smile, "Simply having a bit of fun, Miss Plumleigh-Teignmott."

His eyes scanned the cart, arrested briefly by Sophronia—who looked at him directly, without flinching, in a most unladylike manner—and then moved on to Monique. Monique, in the style of all older girls when faced with younger boys, pretended the entire crowd of Pistons did not exist. Her attention remained fixed on the road ahead, a pose that emphasized her fine features and the slenderness of her neck.

Sophronia remembered what Pillover had said about them. *Nasty chaps.* One or two of them were, unfortunately, good-looking. She exchanged glances with a dark-haired, pale-faced boy with sullen lips and a petulant expression. He met her gaze and then looked away, restless, like a wild creature. Sophronia thought he was beautiful. His almost gawky quality reminded her of Captain Niall. Was he what the scandal papers might call *werewolf bait*? She said nothing to any of them. They had not been introduced. Instead she smiled her prettiest smile at Pillover.

What Sophronia did not know, and had yet to learn to control, was that her smile was rather more powerful than most. The face she saw in the mirror each morning was passingly pretty, if not terribly thrilling, but when she smiled with the full force of her personality behind it, she came over vibrant and striking. It was one of the reasons Monique disliked her so.

Pillover responded to the smile by closing his book and grinning back. His own dour expression, so obviously a mask for worry, briefly dissipated.

"Coming to the ball, Mr. Plumleigh-Teignmott?"

"Ball? If you insist." Pillover slid off his trunk, and Roger jumped down to help him load it into the cart.

"Ball?" said one of the Pistons with interest. "We like balls."

Dimity gave them her best, most haughty look. "Yes, but are you certain they like you?"

"What's that supposed to mean?" Sophronia whispered to her.

Pillover joined them, as confident in his new situation as if he had always expected to set off with his sister and two other girls in a farm cart.

"I don't know," replied Dimity as they drove away. "It sounded good at the time."

Pillover pretended interest in his book until they were some ten minutes into the journey. "Where are we going?"

"My house," replied Sophronia promptly.

"All righty, then."

The trip began pleasantly enough. For the first few hours, Sophronia and Dimity chatted idly about what they might wear and how they might wear it. Pillover rolled his eyes and tried to behave in as dignified a manner as possible under the circumstances of girlish prattle and open-air transport. Monique ignored them. Roger paid attention to the road.

Sophronia thought she spotted a carriage following them, a high flyer. But it stayed well back and might have simply been utilizing the same byways.

The pleasantness was marred only by Bumbersnoot. Sophronia had tucked her mechanical pet, after some debate, into a hatbox for transport. She'd given him a small lump of coal for a travel snack and strict instructions not to stain the interior with smoke, or to singe it, or to catch it on fire. He did, as it turned out, all of these things, but that is not what disturbed the drive.

Sophronia was not aware that anything was amiss until she looked up in the midst of an entertaining debate with Dimity over the relative merits of pearls versus diamonds for a ball to find that Monique's blue eyes were fixed in horror upon the luggage pile. Sophronia's eyes followed the older girl's gaze, coming to rest on her paisley hatbox, which was vibrating rather more than any of the other luggage.

Sophronia put the hatbox next to her on the bench and put a hand firmly atop it.

Bumbersnoot, as it turned out, might have been trying to tell her something, for moments later, out from behind the hedgerows, they caught sight of an approaching airdinghy.

"Oh, goodness, look," whispered Sophronia. "Flywaymen!"

Dimity let out a gasp.

Pillover closed his book with a snap. "What is it *now*?" Upon following their pointed fingers, he added, "Here we go again," in tones of the deeply put-upon.

However, the flywaymen only kept pace with them for a long time, apparently content to watch from several yards away to determine whether they were worth approaching. Sophronia suspected the pony and cart of throwing them off. As a rule, such a contraption wasn't worth attacking, given the general quality of the merchandise within. Unless, of course, they had determined that Monique was the one worth following in order to regain the prototype.

Roger, slumped and staring at the road before them, finally noticed they had company. He pulled the pony up.

"Don't do that," said Sophronia.

"Miss?"

"If they are going to leave us alone for now, then there is no point in delaying our travel. They will come at us if they want something. Otherwise, keep driving. I think we may have additional followers, as well." She gestured at the carriage behind them.

"If you say so, miss." Roger gave her a look that said he thought she had changed a good deal while she was away at school, and *not* for the better.

Sophronia turned back to Dimity and Pillover. "What kind of defenses do we have this time?"

Dimity canvassed her options. "Handkerchiefs, fans, two parasols, assorted hatboxes, hats, gloves, and jewelry—although I'd rather not use that."

"Much better equipped than before."

Dimity grinned. "And better able to make use of what we have."

Pillover looked resigned. Then he reached inside the pocket of his greatcoat and produced the Depraved Lens of Crispy Magnification. "Still got this."

Dimity glanced at Sophronia expectantly. "So what's the plan?"

Sophronia looked through her binoculars at the airdinghy. "Three of them. Four of us. Five, if you count Monique. Unless the carriage following us is also flywaymen."

"More likely Pistons," said Pillover in a resigned tone of voice. "You told them about the ball. They like to go to events uninvited, put gin in the punch, and steal all the spoons. Stylish shenanigans like that."

"Charming," said Sophronia.

"Not Lord Dingleproops," protested Dimity.

Pillover turned a disgusted look on his sister.

Monique had wrapped herself in a velvet shawl and was staring at the surrounding countryside, ignoring them, the Pistons, and the flywaymen. It seemed she was secure in her own scheme, confident in Sophronia's ability to handle the situation, or simply uninterested.

Sophronia continued planning out loud. "Roger really has to keep his attention on the road. Too bad we haven't any good projectiles."

"They've not actually done anything against us yet. Remember what Lady Linette says; never engage first unless absolutely necessary," protested Dimity.

"I should say they started it by attacking us last time," said Sophronia. "Not to mention the two times they threatened the school." Monique probably figured they were following her with no intention of engaging. An open confrontation had yielded up nothing substantial the first time around, after all. Sophronia, however, had no intention of letting either them or Monique dally along without interference.

The flywaymen continued to track them for another hour, giving Sophronia and Dimity ample opportunity to discuss defensive maneuvers, until a break in the hedgerows allowed the airdinghy a mooring point with easy access to the road. Evidently having decided that the cart was indeed worth their attention, now that they had spent the better part of the afternoon alongside it, the flywaymen lowered their airdinghy, lashed it to a tree, and leapt out to stand before them.

LESSON 17

Conducting Oneself
Properly at a Ball

The flywaymen approached with ready smiles and half-cocked pistols, in the manner of gentlemen highwaymen since the dawn of time, or at least the Middle Ages. They seemed, as before, interested mainly in dismembering luggage. This time, however, the girls would have none of it. As soon as the two flywaymen were close enough, Sophronia gave the signal, and she, Dimity, and Pillover threw hatboxes at them.

In the same instant, Roger whipped the poor pony into a trot and charged directly at the two surprised flywaymen, who jumped aside. Before they had a chance to turn around, Roger had the cart alongside their airdinghy. Sophronia and Dimity committed themselves in grand leaps out of the cart and into the gondola forthwith.

The flywaymen, no doubt planning a quick escape, had lashed their transport loosely to a small tree. Sophronia pulled the tail end of the rope. The airdinghy bobbed upward. Abandoning the notion of attacking the cart in favor of rescuing their own conveyance, the flywaymen dashed over, leapt upward, and attempted to grab on.

It was all to no avail. Perhaps as the result of carrying two girls and not two fully grown men, or perhaps by design, the airdinghy rapidly attained considerable height. Sophronia and Dimity peeked over the edge and down at their erstwhile pursuers, grinning. The flywaymen shot at them with their pistols. Sophronia and Dimity dove back into the basket, giggling.

Only then did they realize they had no idea how to steer the thing.

"Oh, dear, we might have used Pillover with all his book learning." Sophronia looked in confusion at the many cords dangling down from the four corner balloons, not to mention the sail lines in the middle and the levers for the propeller below.

"We might, but my brother hardly troubles himself with practical matters like balloons; he is such a philosopher. Embarrassing for everyone." Dimity plucked at one of the cords.

They decided to start tugging on things and see what happened. Pulling on one rope made the airdinghy spin one way, and another caused it to bob alarmingly. One spiderweb linking system opened vents in all four of the balloons at the same time, at which they all began to collapse. Sophronia quickly let that rope go, and they stopped sinking.

They spent a half hour or so lurching about. The airdinghy bobbed up, down, and around in circles while Roger, Pillover, Monique, and the pony trundled merrily along the road, followed at a respectable distance by the Pistons. The flywaymen jumped around and shouted for a bit before leaving the road, stumbling and running through gorse and farmland, tracking the airdinghy over the countryside, and making the acquaintance of far too many hedgerows, and hopefully a thistle or two.

Finally, through some kind of fluke, Sophronia and Dimity managed to trap a wind with the sail and set a stately pace after the pony and cart, catching it up in a little less than an hour. At that point, Dimity dropped the mooring rope, which, after several botched efforts, Pillover managed to tie to the cart. Thus attached, they made good time, coasting happily all the way through Wootton Bassett and out the other side onto the Temminnick estates. They made quite a spectacle of themselves through the town, which was already in a tizzy over the upcoming ball. The pony, being of the long-suffering variety, hardly seemed to register that he was tugging a somewhat levitated cart.

Mrs. Temminnick looked up from a consultation with the gardener over which flowers to cut for the ball. She caught sight of Sophronia and Dimity disembarking, gracelessly, from the edge of the gondola into the cart. Airdinghies were not made for copious skirts. Her expression was that of a woman with multiple children who was no longer surprised by anything they did, up to and including arriving home from finishing school in an airdinghy.

"Have you learned nothing at that academy of yours?" she asked, marching over. "What have you brought with you? An air balloon? Gracious, Sophronia, what next?"

"Mumsy, may I keep it? *Please?*" Sophronia jumped from the cart to the ground, swayed elegantly up to her mother, and executed a perfect curtsy. "Balloons always lighten up an event, don't you feel? We could host small trips over the vegetable patch."

"Oh, Sophronia, really! And who will operate it? This is intended to be a dignified celebration, not a carnival!" Mrs. Temminnick was distracted by the need to direct the greengrocer's boy with his hamper to the staff entrance. "Frowbritcher will tell you what to do," she explained to the lad. The baker's boy, the cheesemonger's boy, and the fruiterer's boy were met with equal exasperation and stern guidance.

By the time Mrs. Temminnick returned her attention to her youngest daughter, Sophronia had chivvied Roger off, with pony, cart, *and* balloon. "It'll be all right in the stable for now."

Roger expressed his feeling that the size of the stable and the size of the airdinghy might be mutually exclusive.

"Put it in the barn if you must," was Sophronia's answer.

"Oh, goodness, child, how will it fit?" Mrs. Temminnick's hands fluttered.

"Roger will manage." Sophronia had to speak over the delighted cries of her two younger brothers, who had arrived on the scene and were far more excited about the balloon's arrival than Sophronia's return. "Mumsy, please make them stop touching it! They might hurt it."

"Now, dear, don't fuss."

Sophronia hoped Roger could hold the course and that her brothers wouldn't do any major damage. "Mumsy, I should very much like you to know my friends."

Mrs. Temminnick paused in her frantic organizing, remembered her manners, and said, "Oh, dear me, yes."

"This is Dimity Plumleigh-Teignmott and her brother, Pill-over. That is Monique de Pelouse. I understand she is here at your behest, not mine."

"Oh, *Miss Pelouse*, of course! Your father and my husband have some business dealings, I understand. You are most welcome. Sophronia, if you wouldn't mind showing Miss Pelouse where she might freshen up? And, of course, I'm confident your little friends are delightful."

Monique curtsied, keeping her bonnet low and her face well-shaded. It seemed to do the trick, for Sophronia's mother did not recognize her from her guise as headmistress. Mrs. Temminnick only smiled wanly, and then scurried off.

Sophronia jogged quickly after her. "Mumsy, did you get my warning?"

"Warning? What warning, dear? Oh, your odd little note? Yes, but dear, flywaymen are only a myth."

"Oh, Mumsy! Of course they aren't. Where do you think I got the airdinghy?"

"Well, dear, you know...somewhere." Mrs. Temminnick waved an airy hand in the air and consulted her list of pending deliveries. "Now, where is that confectioner's boy? I ordered three dozen sugared violets and two bags of candied citron, and they are absolutely vital to the success of this evening."

"But Mumsy, I think it might be even worse than that. There might be Picklemen involved."

Mrs. Temminnick let out a little gasp that was half laugh, half shock. "Now, Sophronia, why trouble your pretty head about such things? You let your father handle that. I'm quite certain none of them would dignify our paltry little country ball. Now, dear, really, I must get back to it. You run along with your little friends and get fancy."

Sophronia was not surprised by this dismissal. Frustrated, but not surprised. She would simply have to manage everything herself. She whirled and trotted back to where the others waited, Pillover and Dimity bracketing Monique with all the embarrassed menace of two small but dedicated poodles. Grabbing the hatbox that contained Bumbersnoot and corralling one of the footmen to help with the rest of the luggage, Sophronia led the way up to the top-floor nursery, a room that she knew from experience had no escape route. Nevertheless, she set Pillover to guard the hallway while all three girls together, despite Monique's protests, washed and changed for the ball.

Sophronia was in a quandary over the matter of her attire. In the few months she'd been gone, she'd outgrown much of her previous finery—what little there was of it. She was finding herself not necessarily more interested in a proper ball gown so much as understanding the usefulness inherent in fitting in to a social event—particularly if there were prototypes on the loose. Leaving Monique under the Plumleigh-Teignmotts' watch, she went to find her sisters.

She located Petunia, her older sisters having not yet arrived.

Petunia was in heaven. If heaven were to be defined as a pink tulle ball gown resplendent with bows and frills, along with giggling bosom companions. She was not pleased to see her troublesome youngest sister.

"Sophronia, you're back?"

"Mumsy said I might be."

Petunia looked her over critically. "You don't seem *finished*."

Sophronia produced one of her newly acquired curtsies. "I assure you, I have many of the necessary requirements." Looking up, she said with no hint of mockery, "You look lovely, Petunia." In truth, her sister looked rather like a strawberry meringue, but Sophronia was determined to apply her education as much as possible. Petunia was merely a test subject.

Petunia and her dear friends, all alike in ringlets and ribbons, tried not to be impressed.

"Well, in that case, nice to have you home again."

"Petunia, Mumsy neglected to realize I was still growing. May I borrow a dress?"

Petunia was not so hard-hearted a sister as all that. "Of course you may. One of mine from last season should do you well enough. You might have to stuff your corset. Now, wait a moment, let me look at you...perhaps not. You *have* grown!"

Petunia rifled through her wardrobe, emerging with a blue dress, wide of skirt and flimsy of material, with a great deal of white lace trim.

"Thank you very much, Petunia!" Sophronia dashed off, leaving Petunia a little bemused by the changes wrought in her sister, until she was once again distracted by the excitement of her ball and the importance of applying only the barest hint of tint to her cheeks.

Sophronia returned to the nursery. Monique stewed in a corner, wearing an elegant gown of pale gold, and Dimity was explaining the relative merits of accessories to her uninterested brother.

"Oh, what a beautiful gown," exclaimed Dimity, who was rather fond of a big fluff of skirts. Her own gown for the evening was of a royal purple—a color entirely unsuitable to a girl of her age—not to mention the great swathe of pearls about her neck.

Monique said, as if she could not help herself, "It's last season!"

Sophronia nodded. "I know, but it's the best I could do. Mumsy forgot to order me one. Truth be told, I don't think she expected me to actually put in an appearance. This will do."

"Imagine going to one's first ball in a borrowed dress from *last season!*" Monique shook her head at the travesty of the very idea.

Sophronia climbed into the dress, the sting of its outdated status somewhat mitigated by the fact that it fit her beautifully. Dimity buttoned up the back. After due consideration, Sophronia decided Bumbersnoot would be more of a help than a hindrance and picked him up.

"You can't carry a mechanimal as an accessory!" hissed Dimity.

Which gave Sophronia an idea. She wrapped Bumbersnoot's sausagelike body in a velvet scarf and tied it with a lace tuck so only his little head, feet, and tick-tock tail were peeking out. She wrapped each foot in lace and tied them with a bow. She then attached another length of lace to his neck and his tail, turning him into a dog-shaped reticule with a brass head.

"Oh, marvelous! That looks so outrageously modish it's practically Italian!" said Dimity.

Sophronia slung Bumbersnoot over one shoulder and instructed him not to squirm, belch steam, or deposit any ash for the next three hours. Bumbersnoot wagged his tail very slowly, as if he understood the gravity of the situation.

The girls and Pillover, who had produced from somewhere a suit that actually fit, stuck close to Monique. They ate a light meal in the front parlor, out of the way of preparations, and sat drinking tea while the sun set and the guests began to arrive. No one was inclined to go anywhere until Monique did. And Monique would not join any party until it was well under way. Nothing was worse than being made available too early at a ball! Finally, she stood, and with a rustle, so did Dimity, Sophronia, and Pillover.

Pillover, although a good deal shorter than she, nevertheless offered his arm gallantly to Sophronia, who took it solemnly. He escorted her in first with all the dignity of an undertaker. Then came Monique de Pelouse, followed by Dimity. Dimity had her eyes narrowed and was clearly struggling to focus on Monique. She was about to enter a ballroom certain to contain much in the way of distracting fashion and other tempting sparkly bits.

Pillover and Sophronia were not announced. Monique was, and all eyes turned to her in interest as she glided in. No one was disappointed—she looked a peach. She quite outshone poor Petunia. Gentlemen descended in pursuit of her dance card, and Petunia's eyes filled with tears. Dimity skirted in after, also unannounced, and joined her brother and Sophronia. The three lurked about the fringes of the group of male sycophants now surrounding their nemesis.

When Monique danced, they danced with one another. They were well aware it was indecorous to dance with one's brother—or one's friend's brother, for that matter—at a ball. Dimity blushed furiously and dragged her feet. But Sophronia fell into her new training easily and found it no hardship to sacrifice dignity to the thrill of the hunt. When Monique sipped punch, Sophronia sipped punch and mimed inane conversation with Dimity. Dimity got distracted by jewelry. Pillover found his way to the nibbles far too often. Sophronia thought only of Monique and her admirers, quite unaware of those few young men who tentatively approached her and Dimity. Dimity was vivacious in her cheerful, roundly pleasing way—all bright smiles and colors. Sophronia's mousiness had somehow been tinted by finishing school with an air of mystery and quiet confidence. She was also carrying the most remarkable dog-shaped reticule, which some said was certain to become the very height of fashion next summer.

One young man, a ginger-haired lordling with an unrepresentative chin, turned away without much disappointment when it became clear Dimity was more focused on the pretty blonde girl than she ever would be on him. Another, a dark-haired, pale-faced boy with a petulant expression, spent a good deal of time courting the edges of Sophronia's notice, trying to look as though he didn't care that her attention was focused elsewhere.

Sophronia did notice him eventually, while still keeping Monique firmly fixed in her peripheral vision. "Dimity, I believe Pillover is correct. My sister's party has indeed been invaded by Pistons. I've seen two so far."

"Oh, dear me, is Lord Dingleproops among them?"

Sophronia gestured with her head at the table of comestibles. At the same time, the dark-haired boy slipped up to Sophronia's side and grabbed her hand.

"Dance?"

Sophronia was entirely startled both by the overtness of the approach and the sudden appearance of the boy so close to her. She inadvertently allowed herself to be drawn into a quadrille with a young man, a *Piston*, to whom she had not been introduced! So many breaches in etiquette all at once! Sophronia was shocked at herself. That said, it was a testament to Mademoiselle Geraldine's training that she executed the quadrille steps perfectly without any thought at all—half her attention on her sullen partner, and the other half on Monique.

Then, suddenly, her focus was diverted by a hullabaloo. Pillover seemed to be trying to stop Lord Dingleproops from pouring a flask of some liquid into the punch bowl. Her dance partner saw Sophronia looking and made to direct her attention back to the quadrille. Sophronia narrowed her eyes at him and left the set. He probably didn't deserve such a cut direct, but something was afoot.

In the same instant, Monique made a break for it.

"'Ware!" Sophronia hissed, grabbing Dimity's arm. She was about to follow when another observation froze her in her tracks for a split second. Lurking in the shadows behind the scuffle was an older gentleman, perfectly dressed in evening garb, wearing a stovepipe hat with a green ribbon tied about it.

Their eyes met. Sophronia flinched and turned quickly to Dimity. "You're going to need to stay here. Keep an eye on that man, there. See him?"

Dimity gasped. "The Pickleman?"

"Yes. Monique is mine."

"Right!" Dimity nodded once and threw back her shoulders, edging toward the fracas at the punch bowl for cover.

Sophronia took off after Monique, who had slipped gracefully away from her crowd of admirers on the arm of an impressive gentleman and out into the back garden. Sophronia followed the couple as quietly as possible, at a distance, taking a lesser-used gardener's path between two rows of rhododendrons. The skirts of her wide dress brushed softly against the bushes, but her footsteps were silent. She walked carefully, toe to heel, in her kid dancing slippers, just as Lady Linette had instructed. The dirt path was far quieter than the dry straw on which they had been forced to practice.

Monique and her escort made their way along the brick walk and through a copse of trees to a birdbath at the center of a wisteria-covered gazebo surrounded by huge lilac bushes. It was the sort of birdbath that cranked into motion, spinning a tiny wheel that raised and lowered a little flock of automated birds for when the real ones were otherwise occupied. It was motionless at the moment.

"Very well, Miss Pelouse. Westminster received your message. You have the merchandise?" said the gentleman after a moment of standing in silence.

Westminster? Is Monique working for parliament? Sophronia inched in closer, using the lilacs for cover and tucking her copious blue skirts in about her in an effort to remain invisible.

The gentleman was a remarkably good-looking chap—well-dressed, well-coiffed, and well-suited. Sophronia's mind instantly went to her lessons with Professor Braithwope. Did she detect the vampire touch? Was he dapper enough? There were no hives near her house, not so far as her parents had ever said, and he didn't appear to have fangs. She assessed his attire again. *Simply a very well-dressed government representative, or a drone?*

Looking furtively around, Monique pulled her gloves off, then tipped the brass birdbath over with her boot and reached inside the hollow of the pedestal to remove a brown paper parcel. It was about the size of her fist, very innocuous-looking, and tied with string.

She popped it into her reticule and straightened, brushing her hands together before pulling her gloves back on. With a self-satisfied smile she turned, removed the reticule from its waist hook, and held it up, dangling, just outside of the gentleman's reach.

"My payment, if you would be so kind?"

The dandy held up a small purse. "As agreed, minus a fee for the inconvenience of several months' delay."

Monique's lip curled. "How much of a fee?"

"Now, there, Miss Pelouse, a lady never discusses money outright."

Monique, still holding the reticule with the prototype, began backing away.

A gentleman in a top hat wound with green ribbon emerged from the shadows before she could go very far. "Good evening, Miss Pelouse. I believe you have something that belongs to me?"

Monique whirled to face this new threat. "I believe not."

"Ah, better to say that I believe you have something I *want*." The Pickleman tipped his hat at the dandy. "Westminster is here? I should have guessed."

The man tilted his head back. "Your grace." In the same movement he pulled out a small gun, which he pointed in turn from Monique to the Pickleman. "Give it to me, Miss Pelouse. Now."

Sophronia watched, wide-eyed. Her attention was focused on the prototype, which now dangled from Monique's hand. *The key is to try to sneak it away while the others are distracted and get it back into the safety of the crowded ballroom. Clearly no one wants a public scene—not the Pickleman, not Monique, and not the man from Westminster.*

The Pickleman raised a whistle to his lips and blew it sharply. At Sophronia's waist, Bumbersnoot the reticule woke up and began thrashing about, hissing steam, his little legs churning and catching in the skirt of her gown. As he was suspended from a lace strap, he could go nowhere, but he did make an awful noise and a terrible fuss.

Luckily, he wasn't the only one. Something much bigger and much louder was causing even more of a racket. A hissing, clanking, crashing sound commenced as some large mechanical object made its way through the shrubs, destroying Mrs. Temminnick's garden. It broke through the lilacs behind the Pickleman, careening into one side of the gazebo.

It was a huge mechanimal, shaped like a bulldog and as tall as man. It belched smoke out its ears; its four stubby legs were as big as birch trees; its mouth was a wide-open cavern of flame. Unlike Bumbersnoot, this mechanimal was not made to transport, only to destroy.

The Pickleman held a small object in one hand that he was threatening to throw at Monique. She now faced the mechanimal on one side and the dandy with the gun on the other.

Assuming her nemesis was well distracted, Sophronia edged her way around through the lilacs to get behind the girl. Bumbersnoot quieted once the noise from the whistle faded. Suddenly, the lilac bush in front of Sophronia rustled all on its own. She only just managed to swallow down a shriek of surprise.

Dimity popped up.

"Where's Pillover?" Sophronia whispered, the noise of the massive mechanimal providing some cover.

"Dealing with Pistons. He said he would tie them up right and tidy as a cravat." Dimity did not sound optimistic. "Oh, my, what's that?"

"Monique, an angry Pickleman, a dandy from the government, I think, and a very big mechanimal."

She could see Dimity pale, even though it was nighttime. "I thought they weren't supposed to build them big. And it's not on tracks. Is that legal?"

"I'm thinking very little of any of this is legal." Sophronia considered their options. "We need a distraction. Could you and Pillover get the Pistons to come outside, cause a kerfuffle? It seems a particular speciality of theirs."

Dimity wrinkled her nose. "Must we? I hate kerfuffles."

"Best solution I've got on short notice. And please bring me one of those pies we saw the cheesemonger deliver this morning. You remember the ones, wrapped in brown paper? I know Mumsy didn't allow all of them out for the party. She loves cheese pies and would have kept some in reserve."

"If you think it best." Without further argument, Dimity crept back to the house.

Sophronia turned back to the conversation before her.

"Instead, I offer you...your life," the Pickleman was saying melodramatically to Monique.

Monique was not impressed, even trapped as she was between a gun and a mechanimal. "Throw in an engagement to your oldest son and we have a bargain."

The dandy did not like that Monique was negotiating with the Pickleman. "Now, now, Miss Pelouse! We had an agreement." He pulled back the hammer of his pistol.

The Pickleman laughed. "Not that you wouldn't make an admirable wife to the boy—appropriately cunning, and well-trained, I'm sure, but no." He rolled the object in his hand threateningly. Sophronia suspected it was like Professor Braithwope's crossbow—whomever he threw it at, the mechanimal would attack.

"Come back here, you little worm!" There came a sharp yell and a series of yodels and cries. Pillover, flask in hand, came bumbling through the garden on chubby, rapidly churning legs and stumbled directly into the middle of the lilac dell that housed the Pickleman, Monique, the dandy, and the mechanimal.

Dimity reappeared at Sophronia's elbow, panting, and handed her a cheese pie wrapped in brown paper.

"Thank you," said Sophronia politely.

Dashing after Pillover came Lord Dingleproops, the dark-haired boy who'd danced the quadrille with Sophronia, and two other Pistons, all looking annoyed, yet thrilled by the chase. Lord Dingleproops grabbed Pillover and began pelting him about the chops. Pillover instantly dropped to the ground in the middle of the gazebo and curled into a ball around the flask, like a grub. The dandy swiveled his gun around to point it at them instead of Monique. The Pickleman looked like he wanted to turn the mechanimal loose on the boys.

Sophronia said, "On my mark, you get the flask from Pillover. Try to pour it onto that mechanimal. I'm going after the prototype."

Dimity let out a little huff of anxiety, but nodded.

Sophronia kilted up her skirts. "Mark!"

Dimity dove for her brother, swirling out from the bushes with a trilling war cry. She went in and down, startling the attacking Pistons with the fluffy presence of a *female*.

Sophronia rushed Monique. "Oh, Monique, you poor thing, are these men behaving ungentlemanly toward you? Should you be out in the garden unchaperoned with all this roughhousing? Let me help you back inside. You're missing the better part of the ball."

Sophronia pretended to trip as she rounded the tussling boys. She lurched to one side, knocking the gun from the surprised dandy's grasp. "Oh, dear, pardon me, sir. Whoop—oh!" In the same movement she spun, simulating a continued stumble—Lady Linette would have been proud.

She blundered against Monique. With one hand she reached out and tore down the front of the older girl's dress, popping the decorative buttons and making certain to expose plenty of undergarments. "It is a certain truth," Mademoiselle Geraldine had said, gesturing at her own heaving cleavage illustratively, "that a lady's attention dwells overmuch upon the state, condition, and sanctity of her own assets."

Monique shrieked, clapping both hands to her exposed corset, and dropped her reticule.

Sophronia continued to the ground, rolling both her upper body and the reticule underneath Monique's full skirts. Under cover of those copious petticoats, she slipped the prototype out of the reticule. In almost the same movement, she replaced it with the wrapped cheese pie Dimity had handed her only moments before.

Monique kicked at her viciously, but Sophronia was already rolling away, her borrowed ball gown mitigating the force of the blow. She emerged in time to see Dimity wrest the flask free from Pillover and the Pistons and pour its contents over the head of the massive mechanimal bulldog.

Monique bent and retrieved her reticule triumphantly and turned to run, no doubt thinking to take advantage of the chaos. The Pickleman, not as distracted as the others, hurled his target blob at her fleeing form. The mechanimal roared to life and charged Monique. Acceleration required the creature to send new power to his limbs from the internal boiler. All it took was one excess spark for Sophronia's plan to work. The contents of the flask were, as she had guessed, alcoholic, and thus highly flammable.

The mechanimal caught fire; so, too, did one of Mrs. Temminnick's lilac bushes, part of the gazebo, and the hem of Monique's gown as the creature blundered after her. Monique dropped to the path and rolled around to put out the flames, at the same time stripping off what remained of her overdress. The target must have adhered to that, for now that she had squirmed out of her gold gown, the mechanimal began savaging it to smithereens with sharp, superheated teeth. The dandy and the Pickleman came running up.

The Pistons were partly distracted by this short but excitingly fiery chase, and partly distracted by a new threat in the form of a small but enraged Dimity. Dimity, bless her heart, was reciting one of Mademoiselle Geraldine's longest lectures on proper behavior at a dance, finger shaking in autocratic fury, Lord Dingleproops notwithstanding.

Still seated on the ground, Sophronia fed Bumbersnoot the prototype parcel, trusting that it was not actually combustible, but figuring it was better destroyed than in the wrong hands, regardless. Bumbersnoot immolated the paper and the string and swallowed the contents whole. He emitted a puff of steam and donned a contemplative look. There was crystalline clanking inside his metal belly cavity. Fortunately, there was still so much noise that no one heard it.

Sophronia stood, adjusting her Bumbersnoot reticule slightly. No one noticed her. The Pistons were shouting and tussling with Pillover, who in turn was squealing loudly while Dimity yelled at them all to get away because the gazebo really was going up in flames and could come tumbling down on them at any moment. A little ways off, Monique lay in the path, half undressed and screaming as the stomping, flaming mechanimal moved ever closer to her. The great beast had one foot placed firmly on her petticoats, effectively immobilizing her. The Pickleman was slapping at his mechanimal with his overcoat to put it out. The dandy was standing over Monique, waving his gun around and instructing her to hand over the prototype, which Monique thought was still in her reticule, which she was clutching firmly to her breast.

"Good dogs," said Sophronia softly to both mechanimals.

Getting the prototype to safety was of paramount importance. The dandy or the Pickleman could get hold of Monique's reticule at any moment and discover it contained no prototype valve at all, but a cheese pie.

From among the tussling Pistons, the young man with the pale face paused indolently and looked over at Sophronia. He tossed a lock of dark hair out of one eye with a casual sway of his head. One corner of his mouth twisted up into a heart-breakingly sweet smile. *Rake in training*, decided Sophronia.

She shook her head at him once and then took off toward the house at a dead run. "Dimity, Pillover, scatter!" she yelled as she did so, using Soap's favorite term.

Dimity and Pillover understood the instruction. Pillover managed to extract himself with a quick twist, and Dimity left off her yelled lecture. Sophronia could hear them panting behind her.

She attained the relative safety of the crowded dance floor feeling as though she had been through a small war. No one noticed her entrance at all. Dimity and Pillover followed shortly after. The Pistons did not. They had taken Dimity's lecture to heart, or were still cavorting with the burning gazebo, or had realized they had stumbled upon something more dire than their normal uninvited antics and escaped to their carriage.

Sophronia, Dimity, and Pillover looked as if they had been rolling about on the ground in their fine dress—which they had. A quick smoothing of one another's hair, repairs to smudged faces with handkerchiefs, and brushing off of dirt, and they were mostly respectable. Sophronia was merely once more the Sophronia of *before* finishing school—scruffy youngest daughter, a mild embarrassment. Her appearance resulted in nothing more than a few disparaging glances from some of the older matrons present.

That was partly because Petunia, belle of the ball, was having hysterics in one corner of the room. Apparently, someone had done something to discolor her punch. Once a cheerful pink, it was now swamp-grass green. Mrs. Temminnick was ordering up barley water and lemonade, which Petunia felt were summer beverages and thus embarrassingly out of season. Why could they not have mulled wine?

Dimity, Sophronia, and Pillover snuck through the crowd, looking for Mrs. Barnaclegoose. Well, Sophronia looked; the other two, who had never met that good lady, were busy saying, "Is that her? Is that her?" in a slightly annoying way.

Petunia's hysterics were just winding down when Monique de Pelouse came dashing into the ballroom. Her appearance caused more of a stir than Sophronia's had. All attention drifted off of Petunia and the problematic punch to this new exhibition.

Miss Pelouse was *decidedly* indecent—her fine gold dress was entirely gone, and she stood in a towering rage, wearing nothing but singed and torn undergarments.

Behind her Sophronia swore she could see the dandy and the Pickleman skulking in the garden shadows. If they had the right kind of mind, they would suspect any one of the Pistons of absconding with the prototype. That is, if they believed it had been stolen from Monique and she wasn't still hiding it about her person.

Monique, however, had a pretty good idea of who would have pinched the prototype. Her hair was wild, her eyes were flashing, and her tattered underskirts floated around her. She looked like a glorious avenging goddess from some ancient erotic myth. She marched through the room, in a vicious temper, and straight into a halfhearted waltz.

Sophronia pretended not to notice her. The crowd parted. *Simply behave as though nothing is out of the ordinary*, she told herself. *I do this every day, hide extremely desirable inventions in my fake reticule.*

Monique stood, arms akimbo, some six or seven paces away from Sophronia, and letting forth a scream of unadulterated anger, she hurled a cheese pie at Sophronia's head.

Petunia Temminnick's coming-out ball was pronounced a resounding success by all in attendance. There had been highly intoxicating punch, a variety of dances, good music, and intermission entertainment. No one knew why the beautiful Miss Pelouse had stripped, rolled about in the garden, and then chucked a cheese pie at the youngest Temminnick girl before being taken away in floods of tears, but it was surely the highlight of a most enjoyable evening.

Sophronia, covered in pie, was removed from the room by her mother, only to deflect Mrs. Temminnick's embarrassed clucking with a very odd request.

"Mumsy," she said, "it is imperative that I speak with Mrs. Barnaclegoose *immediately*. I have been looking for her all evening. Is she not in attendance?"

Mrs. Temminnick was not having a pleasant night. Her eldest daughter was overset, the beverages were in chaos, and this was all capped off with indecency and the inexplicable flinging of pies. She was in no mood to give consequence to Sophronia's irrational desires.

"Oh, really, Sophronia, must you be so difficult?"

"I'm afraid I must. She is here, isn't she?"

Mrs. Temminnick waved her hand about arbitrarily. "I believe she retreated to the front parlor. If only I could do the same. Go on, if you must." She looked wistful for a moment. Then she drifted away to find Frowbritcher so he could deal with the cheese pie remnants.

Sophronia made her way to the parlor and was delighted to find Mrs. Barnaclegoose alone, sipping tea and watching the arrivals and departures out the front window. She looked up as Sophronia entered.

"Miss Sophronia? What has happened to you? You are covered in cheese and onions. Have you learned nothing at finishing school?"

"I have learned a great deal, as a matter of course."

"Clearly not."

"And some of it was about you."

"Pardon me, young lady!"

"We don't have time for avoidance with niceties, Mrs. Barnaclegoose. Although I do remember the lesson. Any moment now Monique will have *noticed* I'm gone. Or the Pickleman. Or the man from Westminster. We must keep *your* disguise intact."

She sidled up to the portly woman. This evening Mrs. Barnaclegoose wore a tambour net gown of midnight black embroidered with pink roses along the various ruffles of the skirt and a quantity of pink fringe about the neck and sleeves. It was the kind of gown to be favored by a young and not very pious widow half Mrs. Barnaclegoose's age. *She disguises herself with the ridiculous*, realized Sophronia. *Nice tactic.*

Mrs. Barnaclegoose looked at Sophronia as though she were wearing Scottish tartan while dancing an Irish jig.

Sophronia handed her the Bumbersnoot reticule. "Take this mechanimal, please. I have just fed him the you-know-what that everyone wants. He should, um, emit it shortly. It would behoove you to be well away from these premises when that happens. Then you must give it to either Lady Linette or the necessary authorities. I trust your discretion. Be careful; simply gobs of flywaymen, a Pickleman, and possibly the government or the vampires are all after it."

Mrs. Barnaclegoose's eyes narrowed. "I have no idea, young miss, what you are on about."

"No, I suppose you might not. Nevertheless, this is a matter of finishing in the *other* way."

"Ah." Mrs. Barnaclegoose gave Sophronia a once-over. "I take it the cheese is the result of your procurement of this object?"

"Exactly so."

"So you *are* learning something." The woman was beginning to look less affronted and more pleased with herself.

"Oh, Mrs. Barnaclegoose, I am learning many things. Thank you for recommending me to the academy."

"Ah, good, well. I thought you would be an admirable fit." Mrs. Barnaclegoose looked like she might actually be blushing with pleasure.

"You are very wise, Mrs. Barnaclegoose." *How have I never noticed she only required praise to find me acceptable?* wondered Sophronia, not quite realizing that this, too, was a mark of her new education. Many was the lady whose belief in another's sound judgment was based solely upon that other judging *her* favorably.

The older woman actually smiled at her.

Sophronia smiled the smile Lady Linette called "winning" and nodded to the reticule, which Mrs. Barnaclegoose had now taken and tucked under the edge of her copious skirts.

"My dear girl, I have it all entirely under control."

Sophronia curtsied.

Mrs. Barnaclegoose approved the maneuver. "Such an excellent education."

Sophronia curtsied again and then hurriedly made her way from the room, dashing upstairs to change her dress. It was as good an excuse as any to be absent from the ball for a short length of time.

She confiscated another one of her sister's dresses, figuring Petunia's evening was ruined regardless, and did it up as best as she was able without a maid, finally throwing on a shawl to cover the missed buttons at the back. It was a sage-green confection with fuchsia trim, most ill-suited to her complexion, but it would have to do.

The remainder of the evening was rather anticlimactic. Neither Pickleman, government dandy, nor Pistons returned. Sophronia hoped she had set things up so that the two men would chase after the Pistons, and the Pistons, being wild young men out for a night of tomfoolery, would lead them on a merry chase. Mrs. Barnaclegoose made her excuses at a respectably early hour for a respectable lady, and no one—not even Dimity, who was looking—noticed that she had a mechanical sausage dog for a handbag. Petunia danced the last of the ball away with a succession of appropriate young men. Pillover danced with Sophronia and Dimity with gravitas, if not skill, although he was a head shorter at the very least. The lemonade was pronounced superior to the punch, and the cheese pie was not at all missed.

Monique de Pelouse spent the rest of the event in the best guest bedroom and insisted on a carriage being called for her in the wee hours of the morning. In the interest of his business concerns, a very worried Mr. Temminnick lent her his personal conveyance to catch the morning express train to London.

Upon discovering the burned-down gazebo and crushed lilac bushes, Mrs. Temminnick declared categorically that her youngest daughter must be responsible and thus still needed the benefits of finishing school and was not at all ready to return home. She noticed that Sophronia had emerged a politer, more mannered, and stylish young lady, but she had also emerged covered in cheese pie. Clearly Mademoiselle Geraldine's still had work to do, and as they were willing to keep

Sophronia on, she was most certainly willing to be parted from her youngest daughter.

Sophronia pretended to be most upset at the idea of continued exile, although she was secretly delighted. She packed with far greater care this time around, including her riding crop, three steel lug bolts, and a small dissection knife among the hand-me-down dresses her mother insisted on including and Dimity insisted they could easily "make over." Sophronia considered the airdinghy; there was no way to keep it at school, although she supposed the sooties might find one. Instead, she and Dimity deflated the balloons, lowered the sail, and convinced the builders to incorporate the remaining gondola and mast as a decorative element on the roof of the new gazebo. It disappeared seamlessly there, hidden in plain sight.

Dimity and Pillover stayed the length of the winter holidays. There were so many Temminnick children that Sophronia privately suspected her mother of not noticing the extras. Mrs. Temminnick was occupied with preparing Petunia for a London Season, her little country ball having garnered enough attention to warrant a mention in the *Morning Post*. It came as a relief to pack her youngest daughter and associated compatriots back to what she could only surmise was a respectable finishing school that would hopefully rid Sophronia of her many manifest flaws.

Little did she know.

Sophronia returned to Mademoiselle Geraldine's to find the prototype safely ensconced at Bunson's and already under reproduction, a commendation in her school record for unwarranted but well-executed fancy-dress operation maneuvers, and

Bumbersnoot waiting quietly in the sitting room with a note pinned to his buttocks.

"Next time," read the note, "please use a more genteel method of object transfer. There is ash all down my evening dress. Yours, etc. Mrs. B."

Sophronia patted her mechanimal on his head. "Nicely done, Bumbersnoot."

Bumbersnoot belched a puff of steam in satisfaction and wagged his mechanical tail—tick-tock, tick-tock.

The End

THESE LADIES PUT THE POISE IN POISON.

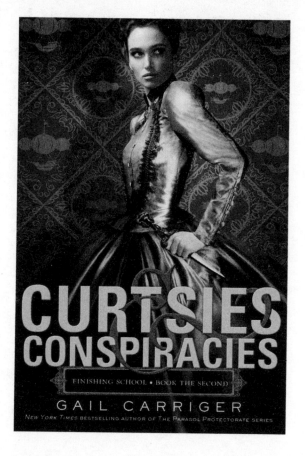

Class is back in session for the enchanting students of Mademoiselle Geraldine's Finishing Academy for Young Ladies of Quality in *Curtsies & Conspiracies*, the second book in Gail Carriger's Finishing School series. Turn the page for a sneak peek!

Available November 2013
however books are sold.

"iss Temminnick. Miss Plumleigh-Teignmott. With me, please, ladies."

Sophronia glanced up from her household sums. She was glad of the distraction. She was convinced she was miscalculating the purchase of the three most deadly flower arrangements. *Does one need four fully grown foxgloves for decorating a dinner table for six guests? Or is it six foxgloves to kill four fully grown guests?*

Unfortunately, what Sophronia saw when she looked up did not fill her with confidence. Lady Linette stood at the front of the class wearing an austere expression that clashed with her copious yellow curls and a bonnet covered with drooping silk lilacs. She was wearing a good deal of face paint and a purple-and-jade plaid dress of immense proportions. It was neither her expression nor her location at the front of the class that made Sophronia nervous. It was the fact that she was present in *this* class, for this was Sister Mathilde Herschel-Teape's lesson on domestic accounting. Sophronia and her age-group were to go to Lady Linette *after* tea, for drawing room music and subversive petits fours.

"This decade, Miss Temminnick!"

Dimity was already standing next to Lady Linette. Sophronia's friend gestured her forward with a hand hidden to one side of her skirt. Ordinarily, it was Dimity daydreaming and Sophronia having to chivy *her* along.

Sophronia leapt to her feet. "Apologies, Lady Linette. I was so very absorbed. Foxglove quantities can be most illuminating."

"Very good, Miss Temminnick. An excuse couched in terms of academic interest. Nevertheless, we must be away."

For most of Sophronia's six-month sojourn at Mademoiselle Geraldine's Finishing Academy for Young Ladies of Quality, lessons had *never* been interrupted. Not even when flywaymen attacked. Young ladies of quality stayed *in* class in times of strife. Certainly no student had been removed from one teacher's purview by another teacher. That was quite rude!

Then over the last month, starting with the dratted Monique, every one of Sophronia's fellows had systematically been taken away by Lady Linette in just such a manner. They returned traumatized and silent. All Sophronia's skills, many of them learned at Mademoiselle Geraldine's, had been put to figuring this out. To no avail. Even her particular friends, Sidheag and Agatha, wouldn't explain what had happened when Lady Linette absconded with them.

Sister Mattie was unperturbed by the interruption, sitting placidly in her mock-religious attire behind a wide desk surrounded by potted plants and bottles of deadly poison (or tea concentrate, one never knew which). Sister Mattie was a bit of a mystery; her preference for a simulated nun's habit—wide-skirted and to the current fashion, with a wimple partly config-ured like a bonnet—remained unexplained. The girls saw her as a nice sort of mystery and one of the more benign teachers, so they mostly respected her eccentric choice of dress.

Sophronia's fellow students were looking on with wide eyes. Sidheag and Agatha tensed sympathetically. Monique and Preshea sat with arms crossed and ill-contained delight on their faces.

Sophronia wended her way through the plush chairs and rolltop writing desks to the front, where she curtsied before Lady Linette. It was a perfectly executed curtsy, not too deep, with a slight tilt to her head but not enough to seem obsequious.

Sister Mattie said kindly, "I shouldn't worry, Miss Temmin-nick. I'm certain you'll do very well."

"Follow me, please, ladies," snapped Lady Linette.

"Good luck!" Agatha said quietly. Agatha rarely spoke, so it had to be something serious.

Sophronia sidled up next to Dimity. The hallway was hardly big enough to accommodate two ladies in full day gowns side by side. Their multiple skirts smushed together. Neither minded the wrinkles as they linked arms for comfort. Mademoiselle Geraldine's Finishing Academy was housed in a massive airship that looked like three dirigibles crammed together. Its corridors twisted and turned in a noodlelike manner. Sometimes the passageways led up stairs or out onto balconies. Most of the time, they simply got darker, lit by gas lamps that looked like upside-down parasols. Whatever attire the corridors had been designed to accommodate, proper lady's dress was not one of them.

Lady Linette led them toward the upper squeak decks. These open-air decks sat under the massive balloons that kept the academy afloat and adrift over Dartmoor. It was an odd place to be headed at this time of day. Dimity's hand on Sophronia's arm tightened.

The two girls swung to flatten themselves against the wall, like a hinged gate, so a maid mechanical could roll past. Its face was a mosaic of gears instead of the metal masks worn by most menials. It had a white pinafore over its conical body and gave the impression of busy superciliousness.

If the students had been alone, the maid would have whistled the alarm upon encountering them, but Dimity and Sophronia were in the company of Lady Linette. All the models, from buttlinger to footmech to clangermaid, had protocols that instructed them to ignore students in the company of teachers. Most of the hallways were laid down with a single track upon which the school's many servants trundled, performing the myriad of menial tasks needed to keep a ladies' seminary running smoothly. Sophronia had once seen a footmech model carrying a whole stack of doilies, some of them quite deadly, from Sister Mattie to Professor Lefoux. In her parents' country estate, such an important task would never have been entrusted to a mechanical, but here steam-powered staff far outnumbered human.

Sophronia had thought, after six months, that she had most of the school mapped. But as they walked from the midship student section, which housed classrooms and sleeping quarters, to the rear recreation area, they entered a place she'd never seen before. While the massive dining hall and exercise facilities above the warehouse and propeller engine areas were familiar to her, Sophronia and Dimity were being taken farther up.

"I didn't know there were rooms *above* the dining hall," said Sophronia to Lady Linette.

Lady Linette was not going to give in to Sophronia's hunt for information. She ignored the comment and quickened her pace.

Sophronia and Dimity bounced in order to keep up—they had not yet had lessons on rapid walking in full skirts, though both of them were admirable gliders at a more leisurely pace.

This section of the ship smelled of old candle wax, chalk powder, and pickled onions. The mechanical track was not oiled properly and there was dust in the corner grippers. The walls were hung with paintings of disapproving elderly females and framed feats of crochet.

Finally, Lady Linette stopped in front of a door. The sign read ASSESSMENT CHAMBER ONE: ENTER AT RISK. It reminded Sophronia a little of the record room. She didn't say anything about that, though. The record room infiltrators of several months ago had never been caught. Sophronia wanted to keep it that way.

Underneath the sign someone had scrawled in white paint NO MUFFINS FOR YOU! Underneath that, it said NOR GALOSHES, NEITHER, in what Sophronia knew was not proper grammar.

"Miss Temminnick." Lady Linette gestured. "If you would?"

Sophronia stepped into the room alone. Lady Linette closed the door behind her.

Sophronia's attention was entirely taken by the huge mechanical thingamabob in front of her. It looked very like the difference engine she had seen last summer when her family visited the Crystal Palace. This one, however, was not being used for sums. It was rigged and draped with objects—fabric hung at the back, paintings dangled, and a few pots and pans drooped uncertainly to one side.

Sophronia frowned. *Didn't Vieve once describe something like this to me? What did she call it? Oh, yes, an oddgob machine.*

Next to the oddgob, positioned to operate a crank, was a mechanical designed to accompany the apparatus.

Sophronia faced both, hands crossed lightly at her waist, a position that Lady Linette encouraged her girls to assume whenever at a loss for action. "The crossed hands denote modesty and religious devotion. The placement draws attention to the narrowness of one's waist. Bow your head slightly and you can still observe through the lashes, which is becoming. This exposes the back of the neck, an indication of vulnerability." Sophronia's shoulders tended to hunch, a habit Mademoiselle Geraldine was trying desperately to break. "We can't have you tensing up like an orangutan!" she chided. "Do orangutans tense?" Dimity had whispered. Dimity, of course, crossed her hands divinely.

Sophronia worked to relax her shoulders.

Neither the machine nor the mechanical seemed to care, for nothing happened even when her posture was perfect.

Sophronia said, "Good afternoon. I believe you are waiting for me?"

With a puff of steam, the mechanical whirred to life. "Six-month. Review. Debut upmark," it said, clicking as a metal tape fed through its voice box.

Not knowing what else to do, Sophronia said, "Yes?"

"Begin," ordered the mechanical, and with that, it reached out one clawlike appendage and began to crank the oddgob.

An oil painting flipped over from the top of the engine and dropped down, dangling from conveyer chains. It depicted a girl in a blue dinner dress, decades out of style, that embarrassing nightgown look. The subject was pretty, with cornflowers in her hair, enjoying an evening gathering.

The mechanical continued cranking, and the painting was jerked away. A hatch opened, and a full tea service on a silver tray rolled forth.

"Serve," ordered the mechanical.

Sophronia stepped forward, feeling silly. The service was for four. The tea in the pot was cold. She hesitated. Ordinarily, she would have dumped the contents into the receptacle and sent it back with sharp words to the cook. *Do I act as I would in real life? Or am I to pretend to serve the tea regardless?*

The mechanical was still whirring, indicating that she had only a set amount of time to decide.

Sophronia served. She did as etiquette demanded, pouring her own cup first and then the others. With no one to ask if they wanted sugar or if they would prefer lemon, she only checked to ascertain both were provided. The sugar pot was half full. There were four slices of dry lemon. Like the tea, they had been sitting for some time. She opened the top of the pot and checked the leaf. Top quality. As was the tea set—Wedgwood blue, or a very good imitation. She sniffed the pot, the milk, and the cups. They all smelled as they should, although one of the cups might have boasted a slight lavender odor. There was a plate of three petits fours dusted with sugar. Sophronia poked each gently on the side with a glove-covered fingertip. She was unsurprised to find that one of them was fake, no doubt from Mademoiselle Geraldine's personal collection. The headmistress had a mad passion for fake pastries. The other two appeared to be real. They both smelled of bitter almond. Sophronia raised up her Depraved Lens of Crispy Magnification, a present on her fifteenth birthday from Dimity's brother, Pillover. It was essentially a high-powered monocle on a stick, but useful enough to keep at all times hanging from a chatelaine at her waist. The sugar on the top of one of the cakes looked odd.

The tray was whisked away.

Next, a string of dangling hair ribbons paraded before her, pinned like wet hose to a stretch of twine. Sophronia's dress today was a pale-yellow-and-blue ruffled monstrosity her mother insisted would *do*, even though it had been worn three seasons already, by three older sisters. Sophronia's absence from the Temminnick household was combined with an absence from Temminnick expenses. She hadn't had a new gown in ages. One of the ribbons was cream and blue in a similar shade to her outfit, so Sophronia unclipped it. Because her hair was covered— as it should be—by a respectable bonnet, she tied the ribbon about her neck in the complex knot of a Bunson's boy. Bunson and Lacroix's Boys' Polytechnique was an evil genius training academy, sort of a sibling school to Mademoiselle Geraldine's. If one thought of those siblings as hostile and estranged.

The ribbons were taken away, and the oddgob machine presented Sophronia with a new selection: a letter opener, a pair of ornate lady's sewing scissors, a large fan, a crumpet, two handkerchiefs, and some white kid gloves. Sophronia felt she was on firmer ground at last. These were tools of great and fateful weight when applied properly. She chose the scissors and one of the handkerchiefs. The other options were removed.

Next came a slate upon which had been written the phrase SEND HELP IMMEDIATELY. In front of it, on a wooden board, lay a piece of parchment with ink and quill, an embroidery hoop with needle and thread, and a bag of raspberry fizzy sweets. Sophronia chose the sweets, cracked one open with the aid of her scissors, and dumped out the fizz. She used the needle from the embroidery to prick her finger, smeared the blood on the inside of the broken sweet, and popped it back inside the little sack. Then she cut off a bit of the ribbon tied about her neck and used that to secure the bag.

The remaining items disappeared into the oddgob, and the mechanical stopped cranking.

Sophronia stepped back and let out a sigh.

Her stomach rumbled, informing her that a good deal of time had passed. She had been given longer to contemplate each test than she realized. A bang sounded at the door. When she opened it, a maid mechanical sat there, bearing a tray of food. Sophronia took it gratefully, and the maid trundled off without ceremony. Sophronia closed the door with her foot and, in the absence of chairs, balanced the tray precariously on one section of the oddgob.

She assessed the food. Nothing smelled of almonds. Nevertheless, she avoided the leg of mutton in glistening currant jelly sauce and the Bakewell pudding and ate only the plain boiled potatoes and broccoli. Better to assume everything was still a test until Lady Linette returned to tell her otherwise. Sad, because she loved Bakewell. When nothing else happened, Sophronia put the tray down and examined the oddgob while it was not waggling things autocratically in front of her.

It was a fascinating apparatus. She wondered if Vieve knew of its existence at the school. Genevieve Lefoux was a dear friend, a mercurial ten-year-old with a propensity for dressing like a boy and a habit of inventing gadgetry. If Vieve didn't know of the oddgob, she would want to, and she was certain to ask all sorts of questions. Sophronia took mental notes in anticipation of conversations to come. When tired of that, she used the scissors to extract a small part from the machine. It was a crystalline valve, faceted, and awfully familiar in shape and style. It looked like a smaller version of the prototype Monique had tried to steal last year. This valve appeared to have been only propped in, so Sophronia was certain that removing it would make no difference to the function of the oddgob. When they'd first discovered the prototype valve last year, Vieve had prattled on about point-to-point transmissions. A revelatory breakthrough indeed, since the telegraph machine had recently proved a dismal failure. If this was a new version of that same prototype, Vieve would want to see it.

The door behind Sophronia creaked open, and she hastily

stashed the mini-prototype up her sleeve, where the pagoda style allowed for secret pockets.

"Miss Temminnick, have you finished?" Lady Linette asked.

"Isn't everyone finished at the same time? The oddgob cycle seems to be prescribed," replied Sophronia.

"Now, now, manners."

Sophronia curtsied apologetically, although she did feel as if she had been abandoned for longer than necessary.

"I had to assess Miss Plumleigh-Teignmott first. Technically, she was admitted ahead of you. If you'll recall, you went for tea with Mademoiselle Geraldine before you were formally allowed into the school."

Sophronia recalled it quite vividly, as a matter of fact. All those fake cakes.

"Now for your report." Lady Linette removed something round and mechanical from her reticule and shook it violently. Was she mad?

Nothing happened.

"They said it was working. Oh, bother." Frustrated, Lady Linette marched over to the oddgob and jerked a few cranks and switches on the underside of the mechanical's carapace. In response, the mechanical turned a smaller, hidden crank at the back, well out of human reach. On the far end of the oddgob, a massive roller ratcheted down, dipped into a pan of ink, and rolled across a series of letters. These then beat down in a sequential blur onto a taut piece of parchment. A large pink blotter rocked back and forth across the finished text.

Sophronia was impressed. She hadn't noticed that the oddgob contained a printing press.

Something rattled in the machine and then whined.

"Stop that," said Lady Linette to the oddgob, shaking the mysterious object in her hand at it again.

Oh, dear, perhaps the mini-prototype was vital, thought Sophronia.

The oddgob whined louder and began to shake.

"Stop cranking," Lady Linette instructed the mechanical, shaking the object harder. "Miss Temminnick, I think we had better make haste." The teacher gestured for Sophronia to precede her from the room.

Too late, however, for the oddgob exploded with a terrific bang. Hair ribbons fluttered up into the air, the tea service shattered, the fake tea cake bounced like a rubber ball, and ink squirted out from the printing press.

Sophronia and Lady Linette flattened themselves on the floor, heedless of crushed dresses and flipped petticoats.

"My goodness," said Lady Linette into the resulting silence. "What did you do?" She stood and walked to the oddgob, now tilted to one side as if it had a limp.

"Me? Nothing at all!" insisted Sophronia, sitting up.

Lady Linette tutted as she brushed ink spatter off her well-powdered cheek with a handkerchief. "Where's the new valve gone?"

"What valve?" Sophronia blinked wide, confused eyes at her.

Lady Linette gave her a long look. "Probably rolled free during the explosion. I told Professor Lefoux it wasn't tight enough in the cradle. And I said it wouldn't work properly regardless." Sophronia didn't say anything. "I wish we could have tested it

on a less valuable machine. Never mind, we've got your results."
Lady Linette waved the oddgob's printed paper.

Sophronia stood and innocently offered her teacher the additional handkerchief she'd acquired during the test. Lady Linette took it absently, then paused, pondering. She did not apply it to the remains of the ink on her face, instead handing it back with a little smile.

"Oh, very good, Miss Temminnick. Very good indeed!" She examined the printed sheet. Closely.

"Let us begin your review. The painting, time period?"

"Eighteen fourteen, by attire," said Sophronia. "Give or take a year. Evening party."

"Dress color?"

"Blue on the central subject, green and cream on those in the background."

"Bonnet style and decoration?"

Trick question! "None of the ladies were wearing hats. The subject had cornflowers in her hair. As I said, it was an evening party."

Lady Linette arched an eyebrow over her spectacles. "And have you any additional thoughts?"

Sophronia straightened. "A great many."

"About the painting, Miss Temminnick. Don't be coy."

Sophronia forbore mentioning that Lady Linette had said only yesterday that there was always time for coyness in young ladies of quality. "The painting was well executed, but the artist was probably poor."

Lady Linette looked nonplussed. "Why do you say that?"

"No expensive pigments, like red and gold, were used. Either that, or the painter feared toxicity. He did not sign it. There were approximately twelve people in the image." Sophronia paused delicately for effect. "And one cat. The wallpaper was striped, and the garden through the window had a Roman feel."

Lady Linette nodded, dislodging her spectacles. She reseated them on her nose with a sniff of annoyance. Lady Linette always dressed younger than she was. Spectacles, under such circumstances, might be considered a fate worse than knitwear.

"Moving on to the tea service, Miss Temminnick. The tea was cold. Why did you still serve it?"

Sophronia nibbled her lip. It was another habit her teachers were trying to eliminate. "If you must draw attention to the lips, a small lick is superior. It is too academic to nibble" was Lady Linette's customary admonishment. "It's all very well to be an intellectual, but one shouldn't let others see. That's embarrassing" was Mademoiselle Geraldine's opinion.

Sophronia stopped nibbling. "I did consider dumping it entirely, but I thought the oddgob indicated I was to be evaluated on the *act* of serving. Had there been other people present, I would have sent it back."

"Milk first, the lower-class way?"

"But necessary if the cups were lined with an acid-based poison. The milk would curdle or discolor. Also, one of the cups smelled of lavender."

Lady Linette said, unguardedly, "It did?"

"Yes. I don't know of any poisons with that smell, but it might be used to cover over another scent or, of course, it might have been your cup, Lady Linette."

"My cup?"

"You *always* smell of lavender."

"The tea cakes?"

"One was fake. Of the other two, both smelled of bitter almond—one because it was an almond cake, I believe. The other was powdered in cyanide." Sophronia had been saddened by the cyanide lesson with Sister Mattie. For the rest of her life—unless she learned to bake—almond cake was right out. There was no surefire way to guarantee lack of cyanide in any almond-smelling confection.

"Moving on to the ribbons."

Sophronia explained, "I selected the one that matched my outfit and tied it in a Bunson's knot."

"There's a piece missing."

Sophronia grinned. "I must beg your patience in that matter, my lady."

Her teacher was taken aback but continued. "Why the Bunson's knot?"

Sophronia parroted a recent article she'd translated from the Parisian fashion papers. Vieve, of all people, had given it to her. Vieve might dress like a newspaper boy, but she took an interest in current styles, particularly hats. This article had delighted the young girl. "It has a pleasing military feel. I read recently that the juxtaposition and power of masculine elements can inspire confidence in the wearer, and the accompanying aura of authority is never a bad thing," Sophronia paraphrased.

Lady Linette looked impressed. This was not part of any lesson. "And *do* you feel more confident and authoritative, Miss Temminnick?"

Sophronia touched the ribbon. "Actually, I do."

Lady Linette nodded. "It would be a good style for you to pursue. I suggest you encourage your mother to have at least one new dress made up with military detailing." She gave Sophronia a pitying look.

Sophronia blushed. She and Dimity did their best to make over her dresses. But her older ones had such a narrow silhouette, and with skirts getting progressively wider, there wasn't much they could do. It was impossible to add volume to a dress. And this was a finishing school—everyone *noticed* such things. Still, if Lady Linette thought more masculine fashions might suit her, perhaps gold tassels and epaulets were in order. Dimity would be over the moon.

Lady Linette interrupted her reverie. "You chose the sewing scissors and one of the handkerchiefs from the next test. Why?"

"We have not completed knife training with Captain Niall, so I wasn't confident in the letter opener, but I know I can work scissors to my advantage, and it is always good to have an extra handkerchief."

"Why not the fan or the gloves?"

"White kid is impractical for a lady of covert activities. We have not had any fan training yet."

"The crumpet?"

"Oh, no, I'm not worthy."

"Lastly, we had you send a coded message. Give it to me."

Sophronia presented her with the bag of sweets tied with the bit of ribbon.

Lady Linette nodded her approval. "Ribbon used to indicate character of the sender. Nice touch, Miss Temminnick. You made use of the scissors from the previous selection." She opened the bag and poured out the contents, including the one carefully broken sweet with the blood inside.

Lady Linette sniffed it and examined the stain. "Show me your hand."

Sophronia removed one glove to display the finger she had pricked.

"You would have had to set up the code ahead of time. Nevertheless, an innovative method of getting a message across, and virtually untraceable, particularly as your recipient can eat the sweet." Lady Linette looked down once more at the printed paper, then produced a stick of graphite and made some notes at the bottom.

Sophronia could feel her shoulders tensing and fought to keep them down. *Were my choices correct? Do they want the expected route, or is it better if I did something out of the ordinary? Will they send me down?* Sophronia was in ever-greater fear that her sojourn at Mademoiselle Geraldine's might come to a premature end. Only half a year ago she had resisted finishing school with every fiber of her being, until she realized Mademoiselle Geraldine's offered no ordinary education. Now she dreaded the possibility of returning home to her former life.

Lady Linette said, "Everyone's results are given together. You will receive your final marks in front of your peers."

Sophronia's heart sank. This explained the pale faces of the other girls—anticipated trauma. Agatha, in particular, hated public exposure.

"However, my initial assessment is that your capacities are suited to our institution. You are overly independent. I suggest focused study in social congregation and deportment. Groups, Miss Temminnick, are your weakness. Generally speaking, most *lone* intelligencers are men, not women. We ladies must learn to manipulate society."

Sophronia could feel herself flushing. It was a fair assessment, but she did not like criticism. She knew she was good. Better than many of the other girls of her age-group. True, Sidheag could beat her in physical combat, Dimity and Preshea were more ladylike, and Monique was better at social graces, but Sophronia was the best at espionage. Nevertheless, she held her tongue and stared at her hands, forcing herself not to clasp them tightly. Lady Linette had only said that *most* lone intelligencers were male. Perhaps once in a while there was room for a female.

"Thank you, Miss Temminnick. You are dismissed."

Sophronia bobbed a curtsy. It was just shy of being too high and too brief and thus rude. But before Lady Linette could comment, Sophronia swept from the room in a manner so grand that no teacher at Mademoiselle Geraldine's would critique the action.

THE PARASOL PROTECTORATE

BY GAIL CARRIGER

A COMEDY OF MANNERS SET IN VICTORIAN LONDON FULL OF WEREWOLVES, VAMPIRES, DIRIGIBLES, AND TEA-DRINKING.

Alexia Tarabotti is laboring under a great many social tribulations. First, she has no soul. Second, she's a spinster whose father is both Italian and dead. Third, she was rudely attacked by a vampire, breaking all standards of social etiquette.

Where to go from there? From bad to worse apparently, for Alexia accidentally kills the vampire—and then the appalling Lord Maccon (loud, messy, gorgeous, and werewolf) is sent by Queen Victoria to investigate.

With unexpected vampires appearing and expected vampires disappearing, everyone seems to believe Alexia is responsible. Can she figure out what is actually happening to London's high society? Will her soulless ability to negate supernatural powers prove useful or just plain embarrassing? Finally, who is the real enemy, and do they have treacle tart?

"WICKEDLY FUNNY." —Angie Fox, *New York Times* Bestselling Author

"*SOULLESS* HAS ALL THE DELICATE CHARM OF A VICTORIAN PARASOL, AND ALL THE WICKED FORCE OF A VICTORIAN PARASOL SECRETLY WEIGHTED WITH BRASS SHOT AND EXPERTLY WIELDED. RAVISHING."
—Lev Grossman, *New York Times* bestselling author of *The Magicians*

"CARRIGER DEBUTS BRILLIANTLY WITH A BLEND OF VICTORIAN ROMANCE, SCREWBALL COMEDY OF MANNERS AND ALTERNATE HISTORY. . . . THIS INTOXICATINGLY WITTY PARODY WILL APPEAL TO A WIDE CROSS-SECTION OF ROMANCE, FANTASY AND STEAMPUNK FANS." —*Publishers Weekly* (Starred Review)